The
Eternal
Return
of
Clara
Hart

The Eternal Return of Clara Hart

LOUISE FINCH

Little Island

Books create waves

THE ETERNAL RETURN OF CLARA HART

First published in 2022 by
Little Island Books
7 Kenilworth Park
Dublin 6w
Ireland

First published in the USA by Little Island Books in 2023

A British Library Cataloguing in Publication record for this book is
available from the British Library.

Print ISBN: 978-1-915071-02-6

Cover title lettering by Holly Pereira
Cover design and typesetting by Niall McCormack
Proofread by Emma Dunne
Printed in the UK by CPI

Little Island has received funding to support this book from the
Arts Council of Ireland

10 9 8 7 6 5 4 3 2 1

For someone so much braver
than anyone should ever have to be

There's a body at my feet again.

The sky is pierced with stars and there's glass littering the ground. Cold, damp air and leaves on the verge. Blood on the road, grit in her skin. My breath scratches my throat. My knuckles plug my mouth and I bite.

What's wrong with this day? Death's strung through it like barbed wire – the one from a year ago, and this one now. Five is too many times to watch the same girl die.

There's a body at my feet and her eyes are closed, but not for long. A few more hours to go before she wakes up and we do this all over again.

I'm sorry.

I crouch. Smooth her hair. Lean in.

Wake up, Clara. We're in this together, you and me.

THE FIRST TIME

1.1

This day's a thief.

People call it Mum's 'anniversary'. But nah, that doesn't sound right to me. Not for a day like this. A date that's been lurking on the calendar, stealing happiness day by day and preparing for the sucker punch. I've kept my head low – don't look directly at it – but every morning wondered, is it here yet? Today?

How typical that when today finally arrives, this question isn't the first on my mind at all. It's this:

Did some prick just hit my car?

Bloody hell, this day's fulfilled its destiny within seconds. Exceeded expectations. Of course, I don't believe in destiny. Irony, though? Cheers, Universe, but really, you shouldn't have.

I flick away eye-crust and yawn. Waking up in my car is a new low; my neck complains from a night against the door, my joints snap, tie's too tight and mouth's thick and grungy as dishwater. There's a slice of school car park in the rear-view mirror. Ah, yeah, here, I remember. Tucked in the corner where the teachers won't notice. Apparently neither did this idiot.

The car that hit me pulls into the next space over, some battered red Micra – another rare student driver, though I don't recognise the wheels. I fall out my door, tuck in my rumpled shirt and stride down the side of the offending vehicle. I jam my body in the driver's open door before they've got more than a leg out.

'Oi,' I say.

I clock her, Clara Hart. Black hair, pointy nose studded and ears to match, but a pristine uniform. Her lips are pulled together in her usual disapproval under narrowed eyes. No wonder she hit me – probably couldn't see past her own inflated sense of superiority.

'You've just hit my bloody car.'

'Happy Friday to you too, Spence. You know you're late for form room?' Clara tries to squeeze by.

I grab her arm and pull. 'Look here.'

'Excuse me.' She rips her arm free and shoots me a dirty glance, but follows me round the back of my classic MG. I jab a finger towards the shining silver rear and then stop. After hundreds of hours in a garage with that car, I know every inch better than the hands I worked on it with. And the bumper's flawless. It's damn perfect.

I say, 'Bumper's scuffed.'

'Sorry, where?'

'Right. There.' Even to my own ears I sound unconvincing.

Clara squints, hands to hips. 'There's nothing. What would you like me to do about literally nothing? You want my insurance details?'

4

Her dark eyebrows are raised ready for combat. I slide my eyes over her dinged-up Micra. Slick my tongue over my teeth and feel the warm creep of embarrassment up my chest. Aren't I the asshole?

I say, 'Surprised anyone would insure yours.'

She holds up two fingers and folds the first one down. 'Firstly, I didn't even hit your car, look at it! Secondly, not everyone has a minted mummy and daddy to buy their cars.'

'Don't say?' But my heart winces. Shows what she knows. Hardly minted. No mum.

'Can I go now?' Her second finger's still pointed as if she's forgotten it's there. 'Some of us actually have standards to uphold.'

'You what?'

'Did you sleep in a ditch?' Her nose wrinkles.

'You learn to drive in one?'

Jesus, *drive in a ditch*? I ignore my own shit comeback and pop my boot to grab my bag. Can't stomach the sight of Clara's self-satisfied face. Sure, I might be hanging this morning, but at least I'm not smacking other people's cars. That's what I should've said.

Clara hauls her stuff from her car and stamps off, bag bumping her hip and black sketchbook wedged under one arm. She's an over-stretched exclamation point, dark hair, navy uniform and black stompy shoes interrupted by the pastiest legs you've ever seen.

I'm gearing up to shout something witty and cutting after her when she throws 'Take a shower!' back over her shoulder. Her ankle rolls over and she stumbles, nearly falls. She doesn't turn to see me creasing with laughter. Instant karma's a bitch, Clara.

I trail her at a decent distance to make sure I don't catch up. Wouldn't bother with form room at all 'cept I know Anthony'd be pissed off having to stick it out alone. He's sent a message asking where I am too and I reckon maybe he's remembered the day, which is pretty touching.

I gurn apologetically at Mr Barnes as I slide into a chair. Anthony claps a hand on my shoulder and looks me over, frown deepening. Maybe I do stink. Hard to judge now I've entered Anthony's Hugo Boss cloud.

'Did you have a blow-out with your dad again?' he says.

I shake my head, eyes on the desk. 'Can't fight if you don't talk.'

Can't talk if you don't stay home. And I reckon Anthony's about to acknowledge the day, but then he says, 'Good, mate, good. Did you finish that philosophy essay?'

'Sure.' That memory's somewhere in last night's blur. Started the essay two beers down, but I could write unconscious and churn out something passable. Anyway, it doesn't count for anything much. Few weeks till study leave and exams and then none of this will matter. Besides, I'll proof it. Quality control and all that.

Anthony folds a paper plane and crashes it against my head. 'Not just a pretty face, eh?'

'Not even.'

Around us students are slumped to their desks, revision-sapped and Friday-feeling, waiting to tumble into the weekend. Clara's a few rows over scribbling in a notebook. I stare, willing her to turn and be embarrassed all over again that she almost crunched my bumper, but she keeps her head down.

The bell goes. I stand with the crowd, but Mr Barnes catches me with, 'James Spencer? A word.' He shuts the door on a tangle of students waiting to take their seats for first period and we're alone.

Barnes shuffles on the corner of his desk until he gets uncomfortable enough to blurt out what's on his mind. His eyes go over my crumpled shirt, my wonky tie, my hair that hasn't seen a shower in days. Here it comes:

'Is everything OK, James?'

'Fine, yeah.'

'You were late again this morning.'

Yeah, obviously. He's an all-right guy, Mr Barnes. Thin up to the ceiling and bald. Dressed in brown today with a lime-green tie to quirk up the look; his blazer makes my eyes itch. Don't want to be rude, he gets enough of that, but Clara was late too and is she getting this third degree?

'Fine,' I repeat.

'Your work is suffering too.'

'Right, yeah.'

A pause. Maybe Barnes watches the top of my head.

'You know you can come to me, or any of the teachers, if you need to talk? OK?'

There it is. Wondered when he'd get to the point. Barnes wants what they all want, only my deepest, darkest. Scrape out my feelings for him to examine then tell me they're not as important as an A-star in my exams. No thanks.

'Can I go?'

'I'll see you in philosophy. Try not to be late.' Barnes folds his hands, presses his lips tight. Picture of concern. I know why, of course. They don't want me crying, self-medicating or turning vandal on their watch. Don't want another student statistic going off the rails; at least, not before achieving decent exam results to slap on their school record. Barnes is nice, like I said, but it's better to remember none of them properly knows me. Don't fall into that trap. I'm another kid on the conveyor belt. A job to leave at the end of the day.

I waste the first half of free period at the gym block getting showered. Body spray takes the edge off what's lingering on yesterday's shirt. Still looks slept in, but once the blazer's on you couldn't tell. Gum sorts my teeth. Two paracetamol tackle my clanging brain.

By the time I re-join my friends I'm halfway human.

Anthony and Worm are in the cafeteria where we fritter away free periods. The two of them look like dinner – an expensive slab of steak next to a piss-poor serving of skinny fries on the grey table. There's a perpetual smell of overcooked veggies in the caf, but it's better than the common room which is all a bit, well, common.

Anthony has his feet on a chair and a grin on his face. Worm's wearing a pout. I've missed something juicy, but can't summon the interest. The caf's nearly empty. Just occasional traffic for the vending machine. This is why Anthony, in par-ticular, likes this place. He's an avid bird-spotter.

'Give us a smile, Mia,' he shouts to the girl making her way across the room. As I slump into a chair, Anthony turns to me and Worm and adds, 'I know what would cheer her up.'

'Chocolate?' I say as Mia feeds coins to the vending machine. She chances a glance over her shoulder, and I swing her a sympathetic smile. It's embarrassing the way Anthony carries on. He goes to say something, but I scramble away from the table, checking my pockets for change and passing Mia as, snack secured, she heads back out.

Anthony shouts, 'Party tonight. Bring your sister.'

Mia doesn't look, doesn't stop.

I fumble a fifty-pence piece at the vending machine for a Mars and return to the table where Anthony says, 'Mia's three and a half stars – wouldn't buy again, but does the job.'

This still. Like I've got brain power to waste on rating Mia. Anthony pokes me with his foot and, since he's forced me to put a number on it, I say, 'Nah, dunno about that. Three max.'

Anthony says, 'You would, given the chance.'

'Nah.'

His smile dips. 'You'll meet me at seven?'

Oh. Yeah. I put my hands to my belly to hold in the grumbles, chew the inside of my cheek. I make a non-committal sound in Anthony's direction. Should've said something weeks ago when the party date was first set. Somehow I'd hoped Anthony'd just twig, spontaneously remember it was Mum's anniversary and rearrange. But I guess he's forgotten – she's not his mum after all – and now here's me, bottom of this deep hole staring up. I say, 'Might –'

'Gonna go easy tonight, Ant,' Worm says, beating me to the punch.

'Yeah, right,' I snort.

Worm'll go easy when he's dead.

Anthony's parties are legendary. Since year ten when his parents first left him home alone they've evolved from soft, beginner's anarchy – games of shit-faced sardines, twenty kids

9

piling into the under-stairs cupboard – to the reputation-breaking carnage of the latest iterations.

Everyone remembers a Mansbridge party, or, at least, the first seventy-five per cent of one. Last time Worm ended up bare-ass naked pissing in the hot tub at 9 p.m. He's not over it. I wouldn't be either if the girls at school still called me 'red rocket.' Not that it's worse than 'Worm', but the rumour is his junk's more canine than man.

Worm looks queasy on those memories.

'Know what? Reckon I'll not make it tonight,' I say, tone packed with apology.

'What?' Anthony gently boots me in the ribs. 'Don't be like that. You can't deprive us of your company just because you had too much fun on your own last night. Come on, strap some balls on.' The judgement in his eyes makes my neck hot.

'Reckon I should lay off a bit.'

'No way. Hair of the dog et cetera.'

'Yeah, but –'

'And we're nearly done with all this bullshit.' He waves a hand at the wipe-clean landscape. 'The last party before proper revision and exams kick off. I know you want to celebrate that, mate.'

I peel my lips from my teeth. No point in pushing the issue and earning a friendship deep-freeze for as long as suits Anthony. He can be petty that way and I can't hack this day alone.

Maybe he'd leave it if I said why I can't go. But there are dead parent rules: don't bring it up more than you strictly have to; death's a hell of a downer. My trauma is far less interesting to other people than it is to me. Besides, aside from the party, my other option is an evening in with Dad, skirting the subject. Pretending the anniversary isn't today. Pretending she'll be back from work in a tick. Nah, if I have to pretend, better to do it around people who don't know the truth.

'Anyway,' Anthony says with a sideways glance. 'What kind of friend would you be if you didn't help celebrate me and Bee parting ways?'

There it is, the ace card, the break-up. Anthony's got me.

He's right. Can't ditch a mate who's just been dumped. Not even if it's only his pride that's stinging. Not even if I've a raging hangover. Not even if I'm the last person who should be commiserating.

'So you're coming?' Anthony says.

I glance at Worm, who's fiddling with his tie.

'Spence, use your words, mate,' Anthony says and then, distracted, 'Oh hello, look at this.'

'Christ.'

It's her again, the idiot who did my car, strutting across the cafeteria as though she can't see us, like we're not even here.

'What?' Anthony says, catching my expression. 'She is fine. Didn't you used to be into her, Spence?'

'No,' I say too fast.

'I'd smash the life outta that,' Worm agrees. 'She always gone here?'

'God bless puberty,' Anthony says. 'Amazing, isn't it? One minute they're sad little freaks, all black lipstick and chub, and the next, all the fat in their body's been sucked into their boobs and bum.' He makes a thick slurping sound and grabs his chest.

'Yeah, that's how it works,' I say. 'Fuck science, right?'

'Four stars. Looks the real deal from a distance. Would recommend to a friend.'

'No stars. Arrived damaged,' I grumble, mind on my car and its emotional scars.

'I'm going to invite her.'

'Go on, Ant,' Worm chuckles.

I say, 'Nah, just –'

'Hey. Party tonight at mine?'

Clara stops. Pauses, unwrapped Bounty hoisted to her mouth – shit taste in snacks added to her offences – and says, 'Yeah, no thanks.'

'Come on,' Anthony says. 'You're guaranteed to have fun or your money back. Come to one party, get another free. Special introductory offer. I'll give you the guided tour personally.'

Clara checks out the floor. Probably feels awkward even talking to Anthony.

He's not wrong. Maybe, once upon a time, I might've been interested for five minutes. We're a small year group. Small town. Limited pool of girls. And Clara's not hideous, though the nose stud and tunnels through her multi-pierced ears smack of effort. If Anthony pushed me I'd give her three and a half stars now – points deducted for driving and personality. Clara's one of those who don't participate. The sort standing self-consciously apart from the crowd, as though *she's* the one rejecting *us*. Someone none of us will recognise in five years when we dig out the year photo. Not fun. Not memorable. Not anything.

People like Clara twitch my nostrils; figuring themselves so above the rest of us who're all trying our best to get by. Parties, sports teams and ill-advised behaviour is all part of the collective uniform she refuses to wear. She's always been that

12

way, always, ever since I can remember. Depending on your perspective her attitude could be intriguing or infuriating, and I know where I stand.

Clara jerks her head up and, inexplicably, it's me she addresses, not Anthony. 'No thanks. I've heard about your parties and I've got better things to do with my night than watch someone take a dump on a table or get myself an STD.'

She takes a bite of coconut nastiness and saunters off, head too high.

'If you change your mind,' Anthony shouts after her. Under his breath he adds, 'Pfft. STD. She wishes.'

I begin to laugh, but pain jolts up my spine, an echo of the phantom impact that woke me, and I lurch forward just in time to hear Anthony say again, 'Pfft. STD. She wishes.'

This time I don't laugh, because what the hell? Some proper insistent kind of *déjà vu* there, the kind that gets you in the kidneys.

Just this day finding strange new ways to kick me when I'm down.

1.2

I scramble through my school day – free period, philosophy, lunch, history, free – and make it out the other side. At home I stand outside my front door, key in hand, eyes on the climbing rose by the window, trying to remember the name of it. Weird how plants have names. Weird how plants outlive us. Give myself a shake and go inside.

The house is quiet as ashes. I sling my bag to the corner of the hall and shut the lounge door. I don't need to see our big built-in bookshelves that used to be crammed with spine-cracked charity-shop paperbacks, now peppered with dust and a handful of Dad's old Stephen Kings. Kitchen's not much better; we've a small flip calendar still stuck at the end of last year and the clock above the door set perpetually at one fifteen; batteries dead. This place is like an unconvincing film set.

I wish I could set the clock hands going, speed it up, be done with today and on to tomorrow. Instead it's the usual drill: microwave pings, toaster pops and I pull up a seat with my spaghetti hoops on toast and a Coke with a tiny tot of vodka from the bottle in my school bag. Afterwards I wash and dry up to remove all evidence of the meal.

By half five I'm starfished across my bedroom carpet, usual perfect order disrupted by day-to-day detritus, books, laptop, Nietzsche revision notes as if studying him once wasn't enough of a mind-fuck. 'Black Hole Sun' is moaning from my speakers. I'm staring into space when footsteps slump up the hall and – here we go again, always the same – there's a pause before the knock. I slam my laptop on three beaming faces.

Dad's head appears. Behind his glasses his deep-brown eyes are smudged, his forehead pinched. He hesitates.

'What's up?'

He rubs the side of his nose. 'How was, er … how was your day?'

I shrug. 'Yours?'

'Oh, you know. Manageable. Bit of a hard one to be honest, James …' Dad says. 'Did you want dinner? I'll –'

'Nah, ate at a friend's.'

'Good.'

'Yeah.'

I stare at the carpet. *Bit of a hard one.* Jesus. *Manageable.* My throat clogs.

'Anthony's last night, wasn't it?'

'Uh, yeah,' I lie. Last night I needed space. Last night I was alone, avoiding Dad. Last night I filled up on beers until I diluted all thoughts of him or Mum or this place or anything at all. Last night I parked up in the dingiest corner of the school car park because I couldn't think of anywhere else to go that wouldn't be polluted by him or her or this awful bloody day I didn't want to see arrive. Would be awkward, but luckily Dad's no clue where I was, his mind not so much absent as emigrated. No forwarding address.

Dad can't sense the lie. Done with his inane questions, he starts to turn, and I picture myself alone in this room again. Imagine it stretching out all night. See, so clearly, a vision of this time last year as I realised the world would never be the same again. Running my mind over every small thing a dead person will never do again, just like Dad's pointless questions: go to a mate's house, eat some dinner, brush her teeth…

'Out later.' I raise my voice so he'll catch it. 'Party at Anthony's.'

'Oh …' His head pops back in. 'Oh.' He frowns. 'Tonight?'

I nod. Wait. Half expect resistance. Half want it, because who'd go to a party on this day? But the door catch clicks into place and that's that.

I flip open my laptop. My desktop background is us – photo of her, me, Dad – all beaming like some cookie-cutter happy family. I can't remember the sound of her laugh.

'Useless, eh?' I mumble.

It's fine, really. Dad doesn't want me mooning about the house reminding him of her tonight. Dad and I do better apart. We live on shaky ground, two dominos teetering on our ends destined for disaster. If we stand too close and one of us goes, we both go.

I cut the music and start an episode of a series I can't concentrate on. The world's ended again and only the sexy people are left. I watch until my brain fizzes away. Another episode auto-plays. Time slips by in thirty-minute chunks until it's time to dress and head to this sodding party.

I shout goodbye and get out before Dad can reply. In the car as I pull away from the kerb, a headache starts. It throbs deep in my bones. Thump, thump, thump, like a ticking clock. Like a countdown.

We party at Anthony's for one reason: his house. It's outside our small market town over by the posh villages, on one of those twisted country lanes cars belt along too fast and where high hedges conceal brick beasts. Big houses, bigger gardens, shiny cars, hobby chickens and horse-sized dogs. They litter the green like our town spat them out. Bougie far as you look.

Anthony's has been my second home since the Mansbridges swished into town seven years ago, escaping the hostility of London. Mr Call-me-Dom Mansbridge got hounded by the press for masterminding some offshore 'wealth management' scheme, squirrelling away the spare millions of quasi-celebrities. Not illegal, but, as Dad tutted over his coffee, 'Not the British spirit.'

Mr M's face sometimes still hits the papers, so the Mansbridges are as close to famous as this town gets. No wonder these parties are massive. The notoriety. The glamour. The absent parents.

On the marble kitchen counter there's booze: cheap stuff and stolen stuff, beer, spirits, cider. Bottles of Prosecco from girls masquerading as classy. Around's a decent smattering of strangers and girls from lower sixth too pretty to engage. I settle in. Drink. Pour. Drink.

While I've got coordination, I grab my guitar from the car and play tunes for the garden crowd. Keep it classic – things even parents could sing along with. The watchers form an audience; some join in.

The crowd's why I learned to play, the reason I begged lessons after packing in violin. Mum said I'd never stick at guitar either, but she misunderstood the draw of being a musician the day she picked violin for me. Doubt I'd please the masses belting out Brahms. I shift into something better, 'One More Cup of Coffee', but no-one knows the words.

'Grief, are you trying to encourage us all to slit our wrists?' Bee asks, collapsing beside me, spirals of strawberry blond flying. 'Don't you know anything else?'

"Given to Fly?" I offer.

'Always so bleak. I mean something a little upbeat, sweets. What have you got for me?' Bee wiggles her eyebrows. There are two beats of intense, weird silence.

I chuckle and run a hand over my hair and say, 'Only dirge. Got to reflect the mood.'

She grabs the guitar, smacks a rhythm on the side of it and sings a line of Arctic Monkeys then stops and pouts.

My stomach goes over a bump. Bee's a bloody lovely human. She's also all symmetry, lengths of leg and eyelash. High-schoolers being the sophisticates we are, her hotness is one of the main reasons people love Bee. And by 'people' I mean everyone, including Anthony until five days ago. Speaking of:

'Not a bit insensitive you're here?'

She scoffs, pushes a handful of curls away while her bangles play percussion. 'God, we're not pretending Anthony is bothered by recent events, are we?'

'Guess he'll bounce back.'

'Precisely his plan, I believe. If he can find a warm body he hasn't already "bounced".'

I shrug.

'Definitely not one of my better decisions,' she says.

For a heart-stopping moment I think she means ditching him, but I follow her eyes over to where Anthony's standing inside the kitchen doors, shoulders quaking, mouth thrown open. He's dressed in pink and turquoise to match whatever bad joke he's telling.

'Yeah,' I say, too emphatically. 'Of all the lads ...'

A smile spreads over Bee's face. 'What other options were available to me, little Spence?'

I make a weird noise in the back of my throat. Bloody Bee knows exactly what options. She kills me with this shit. I snatch my guitar and thumb the strings so they grumble.

Bee produces a cola-flavoured lollipop from hidden pockets. She plugs my mouth with it, rises to her feet, dusts lint from her thighs and extends a hand.

We go inside and I realise I've missed a golden opportunity to talk to Bee alone again, like the miserable bastard I am.

Instead I'm co-opted into pointless drinking games where I spill secrets and liquid. Before the cola lolly in my mouth dissolves, I'm wasted. Drink. Pour. Drink. I dance badly and sling worse punchlines. Drink. The world speeds up. Drink.

Not yet eleven and everything's taken a turn. Outside Mia Turner's slumped on a garden bench artistically lit by golden spotlights. She holds back dark, wavy hair to retch into a flowerpot. On the opposite end, unperturbed by Mia's display, two people lip-wrestle. Then there's Lana practically riding Shaun against the house wall and Felix just inside chugging a funnel; it's slippery underfoot and there's a weedy fug drifting from dark corners.

The lounge has disintegrated into noise and colour and chaos. Bodies slap together, uncoordinated, untidy. Some go up while the others go down. Some wave and others sway. The air's clotted with alcohol and cheap deodorant. The party's heartbeat thumps against the walls and drains my energy. I'm tired of everything now, wishing I could make everyone piss off home. Wondering why I came in the first place.

My vision's all soft edges. My hand's sticky from a misjudged drink. I weave through the denim-walled lounge, trying to locate a friendly face. My shins hit the coffee table and I get lucky.

Worm, half drowned in chestnut leather. He twists his head away as I capsize in the sofa beside him.

'Right, Worm. Went easy?' There's an indistinct grunt from the cushions. 'Not going to spew on the couch?'

Another grunt.

'Want water?'

He turns his face to me, features twisted. 'All I want, you knob, is to be left alone to die.'

'Right.'

'Like a defeated tiger on the Serengeti.'

'Tigers don't live on the Serengeti, bud.'

I pick his glasses up and perch them on his face. He starts to moan, mumbling something about David Attenborough, while his thin fingers squeeze his eyes behind the lenses. I give him a pat and recommend he takes a nap like the proud and noble beast he is, though Worm's more wounded meerkat than majestic predator. He rolls back over. I sit on him to get my bearings.

Something catches my eye through a gap. Black hair swishing, a glittering ear. I stand on the sofa, feet straddling Worm's head, to spy over the crowd.

Turns out Clara Hart didn't have anything better to do with her night after all. She's here – there – dancing in the mix. Strappy dress all low in front so you can see her white chest, a flash of black lace.

Clara's dancing the way people tell you they wish they could, all loose limbs and closed eyes, like no-one's watching. Her hands are overhead, her chin rolling under damp hair. She sloshes the contents of her cup on herself and it spatters on the people around her. With closed eyes she can't catch the looks she's getting, the way everyone avoids her. But I see.

I didn't know Clara liked to dance. Didn't know she liked to party.

I put my cup to my lips and drink till it's drained. Anthony pushes through the crowd. He moves in, and Clara turns to him.

Clara catches my eye and points my way. Beckons. But Anthony has his hands on her waist. Everywhere.

STD? She wishes … I chuckle, but it's dry and scratchy. Clara's still looking my way, but screw that.

I head off for another drink.

1.3

Drink located, despatched, replaced. Stumble, slash, zipper.

At the base of the stairs a tacked sheet of paper reads:

DON'T EVEN THINK IT, MOTHER FUCKER

I think it. I wobble past and winch myself up the bannisters. Upstairs is out-of-bounds thanks to the plush cream carpet underfoot and it's a mark of how much everyone loves a Mansbridge party that people respect the sign. Either that, or it's a mark of how little they want kicking out. Ryan learned his lesson the hard way last time, when Anthony unplugged the music and sent him packing. He let Ryan grovel pretty good first. Quite the spectacle.

Either way, no-one's up here. Not one. Not even desperate souls from the bathroom queue. Spotted them on my way here, a conveyor belt of twitchy bladders, girls crossing their legs and going together in batches, as if you piss faster with an audience.

My brain slops up the sides of my skull. I can barely stay upright.

I need a hiding place, somewhere I can shut my eyes without losing an eyebrow or being mutilated by a Sharpie

21

cock. Been there before and dick-face twice, shame on me, right? But when I open Anthony's bedroom door he's there, over near his bed in the dark. I flick the light and he jumps.

'Oh god, mate.' He sighs his relief and turns back to rifle through his drawers. 'I thought you were a rule-breaker.'

Anthony's bedroom looks raided, clothes everywhere, mugs and plates stacked on the surfaces. There's a pile of laundry by my feet. I wobble as I bend to retrieve a sock.

I say, 'Bloody am. I'm a rebel.'

'Bit gone?'

'Ant. Anthony. It's the bloody apologist down there.' I squint at him. He knows what I mean.

'Uh huh,' he says. 'Know what you need?'

He straightens up, flips his hand over revealing, what? Can't focus. Pills or powder or whatever.

I step back. 'Nah. Nah. Not me.'

'Pussy. It'd perk you up. Maybe.'

Anthony flicks through the contents. I probably am a pussy. Probably missing out 'cos teachers scared the bollocks off tiny Spence, aged twelve, telling me I'd be dead after one.

But as I'm about to step forward and agree for once, to hold out my hand for whatever's going, there's a flash of Mum in my mind, disappointment scrawled on her face as I emptied my belly on the doorstep after a failed first experiment with vodka. She'd hate it and I hate that.

Anthony says, 'You put enough waste in your system. Booze'll kill you faster.'

'We're all dying.'

'Yeah, OK.' Anthony shoves his stuff back in his drawers. 'Do you think you're done with the party?'

'Nah.'

'Need a lie down?'

'Please.'

Anthony guides me to his brother's bedroom, tidy and vacant since Eric left for uni five years ago. We only see him online now.

Anthony deposits me on top of the bedsheets. He takes my boots off and I mumble an apology for still wearing them – the carpets, Jesus, am I an animal? The ceiling churns, but when I shut my eyes the blackness accelerates. Open is better.

'Leave my trousers on, pest,' I say, kicking as Anthony touches my jeans.

He holds up his hands. I roll onto my front. Don't know why mates are always so keen to undress you when you're drunk. As if waking up in jeans with creased skin and ball-chafe is worse than waking up with no bloody clothes on.

I wake up some time later. Still in Eric's room. Still clothed, creased skin and ball-chafe and all. Music's thumping, cackles floating up, plenty of chatter, shouts and the splashing of the hot tub.

A door slams somewhere down the hall.

Check my phone: just past midnight, embarrassingly early to have been sent napping. At least this means it's a new day, no longer the anniversary of anything. I hop out of bed, leaving that weight behind. The timer restarted.

My boots are on the floor, slip-ons I can't slip on. I ignore them and stand onto weak legs. Check my phone again as I'm hauling down the hallway. Anthony and Worm have been busy. Selfies in the group chat of them licking girls' cheeks.

That old game. Surprised girls still go for it, but maybe they secretly like it. One's captioned, 'Tastes like chicken.'

There's photos of Clara. She's wrecked. Eyelids low, dress straps escaping, skin filmy with sweat. She was one wrong move away from a nip slip, when? Half an hour ago.

Clara Hart, who knew? Guess she does know how to have fun.

At the top of the stairs I hear a muffled giggle. Anthony's bedroom door's shut, but I'd recognise Worm's dirty laugh anywhere. I fumble the handle and push. The latch grinds, but nothing gives.

'Worm.' I smack the wood. Again and again and then rest my head against it. 'Oi, you skeevy bastard. Best not be smoking in there.'

The clunk of the door unlocking. I get my hand on it and push. It opens, barely, then comes back at me hard.

'The hell?'

'Spence?' Anthony's voice.

'Open the door, dickhead.'

He cracks it. His head and arm appear, elbow against the frame barring entry.

'Do you mind?' he says. 'I'm kind of busy, if you know what I mean.'

'Oh yeah?' This is solid gold bullshit, because I know I heard Worm. Unless Anthony wants privacy with Worm, in which case I give his veneer of aggressive heterosexuality an A-star for effort.

I try to push, to make space. Anthony stumbles. I spot her. Just a glimpse. There on the bed. Too much skin. Parts of her I never thought I'd see.

The door pushes back. Anthony fills the gap. 'Could you give me a minute?'

'Worm's in there?'

'No.'

'Heard him.'

'He's not.'

I stare. 'What …?'

'Spence, mate, you need to fuck –' he pushes the door hard and I stumble into the hallway '– off.'

The catch clicks into place.

I stare at the door, still not sure what I've seen. Not even who. Was that … nah … not Clara Hart.

I go downstairs. Sit on a sofa.

People dance in and out of my vision. No-one stays. No-one asks, because what would they ask?

I get up, pour a drink. Take the drink back to the sofa and sit. I tap the tip of my finger against the cup. Drink a bit more; the mix of alcohol strong and warming.

Wish I could stop my thoughts. Wish I hadn't seen her all splayed out like that; it's wrong. Embarrassing. Didn't even try to cover up. Bloody Clara waking me up, banging my car, falling all over the party. She won't leave me alone. And it *was* her, I'm almost sure. I rub my eye until it's all warm and the world turns to shards.

Can't believe Anthony pulled her. He'll be proper ashamed tomorrow. Don't care how fun she is now, Clara's a hell of a rebound from Bee. Worm I believe. Worm'd go for her, no problem – if he was even in there.

Think of the devil. Worm bounces down on the couch, eyes all over the place. 'Ey ey, Spence! Napped it off?'

I stare at him. 'Clara Hart? Really?'

'Man, she was after somethin'.' His expression's cheerful. Jaunty. Reckon he'd give a wink if the coordination wasn't beyond him. It's the look on him, more than the words, which gets to me.

'Grim.'

Worry pinches at Worm's lips. They slacken and fold over one another, slapping together like raw meat. 'Cheer up. It's a party.'

'Don't say?'

The smile pushes back across his face. I check the ceiling like I might see through to what's happening beyond. Back to Worm. His stupid face, thick glasses.

'Havin' a good time, kid?' he says as he arranges his skins and tobacco.

I shake myself. Come on. This is a party. It's Worm. It's Anthony. And what's my problem? I tut out loud, rattle the disloyal half-formed thoughts from my brain. They're my best mates. I'm a wanker.

'Girls,' I say and my sigh wrings me out. 'Why'd they get so bloody messy?'

'Shit, you've no idea.'

'No,' I agree.

Worm smirks. 'You seen her dancing earlier? Fuckin' gone.'

'Bet she feels like a right dick tomorrow.'

'She felt a dick tonight.' Worm chuckles, low and dirty.

'As if.' I taste vomit. I see her there on the bed.

It's nothing. This day making me paranoid, making everything too big. Need to sort myself out, need to –

'Know what I need?' I say. 'Need you to get me very high. Right the hell now.'

Worm rolls. I watch him, wired and wide-eyed. Wondering how the hell Clara's problems became my problem, thinking how much better I'll feel once I've had a smoke and a drink and she's come back downstairs high-fiving her mates because she's spent thirty minutes with the most popular lad at school.

Else I'll feel better after a smoke, five drinks and sleep. All problems obliterated: hers, mine, the whole world's.

I'm jiggling my elbows on my knees when there's a noise out in the hall. Rumbling and bumps. Bad sounds.

Over the back of the sofa there's a view through the open door. The base of the stairs is framed and so's Clara. She's straight-legged, half on the floor, half on the stairs. I stand. Look back at Worm whose eyes are on his weed.

Clara's dress is lodged round her waist and her underwear's on show, lacy and black.

I wobble, unbalanced, as though it's me and not Clara who's just skimmed downstairs like a stone. I should move in, help her pull her clothes back in place, but it seems wrong to touch her, so I stand uselessly.

I can't take my eyes off her.

'Oh god, Clara.' Bee shoots by and crouches at Clara's side, helping her sit, smoothing her clothes down. I wander over as casually as possible, before realising, as Bee throws me evils, casual is the wrong note to strike.

'She right?' I ask.

'She fell down the stairs.'

'Oh yeah.'

27

'Is your head OK, Clara? Where hurts?' Bee says and Clara stares, eyes like empty windows.

'Drink a bit much?' I throw in and Bee scowls at me. 'Anthony still up there?'

Clara shakes her head.

'Everyone give her some room,' Bee shouts, even though no-one's paying attention.

'Is everything OK down there?' Anthony appears at the top of the stairs, gazing down at us, backlit like some omnipotent being. He takes a couple of steps down.

Other people begin to notice now, drawn in by Bee's shout. They cluster in doorways, poke their heads round corners, move down the hall. They hover, not close enough to be accused of wanting to help, but enough to see what's happening, enough so I catch their half-whispers. 'The absolute state …'

Clara's head snaps up. 'I'm going home.'

'Oh grief, don't be silly, no-one saw,' Bee says. 'It was only a little fall.'

Clara makes it to her feet, lumbers for the front door and wrenches it open.

'Where are you going?' Bee says.

'Home.'

'No, Clara, you can't drive like this, sweetie, you're drunk.'

Clara's eyes dart around, checking all the unoccupied spaces. She wraps her arms around her body so tight it's like she's trying to disappear. 'I'll walk.'

'Wha –?'

'Sorry, I've just got to,' Clara says from the open doorway, facing inward. Wet eyes and a mouth tucked too small. Her arms are white and blotchy, red where she's gripped too hard.

'Tell her she can't.' Bee gestures my way and I answer with a shrug.

Clara starts out across the driveway and Bee follows. I stay in the doorway with Anthony.

'All right, mate?' he says. We watch the girls.

'Clara, where are you going?' Bee shouts.

Clara picks up her pace, staccato over the gravel. She runs and stumbles, jolts and yelps, but doesn't fall. She runs out of the open gate and stops. There's nowhere to go. No footpath, no lights.

Time stretches taut and slows down as it presses against this moment. I see Clara out in the dark and Bee closing in on her. Clara lit up in a flash. Bee screams.

Everything skips ahead. A car's where Clara was standing and Clara's gone. Nothing makes sense. Gravel grinding. Cold gulp of air into my mouth. Fists clenched white. And then I'm at the road and there's splintered glass and broken lights and a naked foot at a wrong angle and I'm not seeing this. Won't see this. But, no, I can't shut my eyes.

1.4

The police station is blue and white, clean colours, but the floor's littered with smudges. The too-bright lighting makes my eyes water. Makes me want to confess something.

One cop is quiet and tall. The short one speaks. The hair under her hat is brown and pulled back so hard it stretches her face. A coffee stink wafts from her mouth when she leans too close, but she's kind, so I can't say she's making me nauseous.

I'm polite. When I answer her questions I stumble over the words.

Clara's in the hospital, they say.

Bee and I waited by the gate. We latticed our fingers together. We shivered off each other, our lips too cold to control over lies like, 'It'll be OK.' Bee's bangles jangled on her wrist and she slipped them off and threw them into the gravel. Anthony'd gone who-knows-where.

The ambulance came, police too. Blue flashing lights bouncing off the house, the trees, the clouds, our faces. They took Clara.

I've lost details between the house and the station. Can't remember seeing Clara out on the road or the questions the police asked. Can't remember the answers Bee gave them. Can't remember this officer's name. These facts have gone missing and so have loads of others the police officer keeps asking me for.

'She ran into the road. It hit her.' This is all that matters. It's the thing I can't stop thinking. Just like –

'Do you know Clara well?'

'From school.'

'Can you explain to me how Clara ended up in the road?'

I shake my head. She writes something down. 'She was walking home,' I say. She writes.

'Do you know if she took anything?'

I shake.

'Drink?'

Nod.

'Drugs?'

Shrug.

'What else did Clara do at the party?'

That last one.

'Huh?'

'Could you describe Clara's activities at the party?' Her expression's soft, but the question's a trap. My heart ticks faster. My mind goes to Clara on Anthony's bed, but no, not that. Clara'd not want them knowing.

I watch my fingernail run over the arm of the chair, feeling the rasp of goosebumped plastic underneath. It's ridiculous I'm still in my socks. My toes clench. Grass and muck stuck in the fabric; I'll have to throw the socks out. Clara had bare feet.

Tiredness comes on sudden. It grabs me, drags me. If I don't sleep I'm worried I'll say strange things. They queue at the edge of my consciousness.

I can't keep the pleading out when I ask, 'Can I go?'

Clara was out of it, that's why she was in the road. She never should've come to the party if she couldn't handle herself. Everyone saw how smashed she was, dancing and falling down the stairs. Running in front of cars. Ruining my day from start to finish.

Clara, there in the road. Today of all damn days.

Before I go, the officer gives me a leaflet that I fold and pocket without reading. She thanks me for my time. I can't meet her eye when she tells me what a great job I've done, how helpful I've been. I've not been helpful.

31

'James. Oh, James,' Dad says when I come out into the waiting area. Don't know who called him, but Dad fits right in among all the worn plastic furniture. The sight of him feels like failure. Him having to come here to get me.

He walks forward like he's going to touch me. I put up a hand and he ricochets off my invisible barrier.

'Thanks for coming.'

'You're …' He shakes his head, brow furrowed as the sentence dies. I wait to find out what I am. Useless. Time-waster. Dad's mouth trembles, I can't think why. He says, 'Of course. Let's get you home.'

'Seen Anthony or Worm?'

'Sorry, just a girl.'

'Clara?' I frown at my own stupid question. Of course not Clara. Clara's in hospital. 'Bee?'

Dad shakes his head sadly. Yeah, he's no clue about my friends. That was Mum's job.

There's a guy in uniform. Familiar. Someone I might've seen at the house. I say, 'Hey, um. Any news? The girl? Clara Hart.'

I guess this guy remembers me too, because he looks at me like I'm scum. Maybe I am. Maybe he knows what I did. But I didn't do anything. And now I'm not even sure how he's looking at me.

He says, 'She died about an hour ago. Dead on arrival.'

I nod. Turn hollow.

On the drive home Dad says, 'You know you can talk to me,' 'What an awful thing to have seen,' 'That poor girl.' He gives me these meaningless soundbites. I wonder if he can't hear

32

himself. I wonder if he doesn't see the parallel. If it doesn't kill every feeling he has inside of him until he's numb with horror at what happened. This happened. Today. All over again.

Fuck.

'I'm fine.' I try to push my lips up. 'Just need sleep.'

'We'll talk in the morning.'

'Maybe.'

Dad chances a shifty glance, whips away when he catches me looking.

My mind is crammed too full. No space for anything. My forehead judders against the metal car and I see me and Dad splintering into pieces and strewn across the road in skin and blood and glass.

No.

We drive in silence. I get into bed. Stare at my dark light-bulb. The metal and glass are gone. Instead there's a phrase I can't get out of my head. When Clara was dancing, the down and up, standing to floor to standing again. What does Anthony call it? Oh yeah. Slut-drop.

THE SECOND TIME
2.1

My car jolts, shaking me awake.

Wait. Car?

Someone hit my fucking car again?

I struggle up. Could swear I fell asleep in my bed. Would swear my whole life on it. But here I am, in my car, surrounded by snack wrappers, cans and papers, exactly the same as yesterday.

Yesterday. The memory catches up on me. Police. Clara. Mum. I rub my face and wish these thoughts gone, but they pound through me like blood. When I bring my hands down a tatty red Micra is manoeuvring into the space beside me, wide, apologetic eyes fixed on mine. A familiar face I don't believe.

'The fuck?'

I scramble out and round the back of the car as she's opening her door. Her. Clara.

'You're here,' I say. And she really is. The relief isn't a wave, it's a bloody tsunami, and I cling to the car door like it's my life raft. This girl is here and not just here, she's perfect. Not a scratch.

She died.

'Why the fuck are you here?'

'My human right to an education? You know you're late for form room?' She attempts to walk past.

'But … you were at Anthony's.'

'Anthony Mansbridge? I think not.'

I run fingers through my hair and catch a sniff of my body. Stale sweat over yesterday's spray.

'It's Saturday.'

'If you like.' Clara widens her eyes.

'You hit my car again.' I grab her by the arm. It's warm, solid. She jerks out of my grip and eyes my silver MG, makes a show of examining it as I try to pull my mind together.

'Hmm, no,' she says.

I'm staring. I know I am. She died. Clara Hart, shonky parker, wrecker of my dreams. She's here. This is some *Black Mirror* shit, some real David Lynch what-the-fuckery.

'Where did you go?' I reach out and grab her wrist again and she's still real. Still warm. I squeeze tight enough to feel her pulse. Real.

'Could you not!' She pulls away, freaked. 'I'll give you my insurance if you really think I hit you. But we need to get going. You should maybe … take a moment. And check a mirror.'

I stare.

She strides towards school. I watch.

'And maybe a shower,' floats back on the breeze. Her ankle turns and her body goes with it, arms shooting out to balance.

35

She carries on without a backward glance. Every movement exactly to the beat.

'Shit.' I sink to the ground. Knees hit the tarmac and pieces of something sharp try to get inside me. 'Shit.' My mind runs away. I take deep breaths of clean air, swallow the acid at the back of my throat.

She's here. She's real. I'm here. I'm real.

What. The. Fuck.

I don't get up from the ground until the distant clatter of the school bell signals the end of form room. I stumble up. Head to gym block, clean up, dry off and put my clothes back on. My hands tremble so I put my face in them and scream, but it doesn't feel better.

Anthony and Worm are in the cafeteria where I imagined them.

'Give us a smile, Mia,' Anthony shouts. 'I know what would cheer her up.' He grins. Worm chuckles. I stare.

Anthony laughs. 'Mia, you know, she's three and a half stars – wouldn't buy again, but does the job.'

'Guys,' I say, breathless. 'I'm … not OK. Think I'm drunk from last night. Or …'

'Tell me something new. From your messages I'm surprised you're even alive,' Anthony says. I nod, grateful for this change to the script, until Mia begins her walk back the way she came.

'Party tonight,' he shouts. 'Bring your sister.'

She doesn't look back.

Anthony turns back. 'You'll meet me at seven, Spence? Worm?'

'Gonna go easy tonight, Ant,' Worm offers.

'I'd love to see that, Worm, really I would.'

I whip back and forth between them, glad my belly's empty.

It's nothing. Every day of our last 365 has been the same. Girls, sports, games, movies, shows, lash; an endless rinse and repeat. Recycled anecdotes broken down and reassembled so many times they're gone gritty brown. It's no wonder I could chime in for the chorus.

It's this fucking day. I dreaded it too hard, for too long, convinced myself it'd be impossible. Then fell asleep getting sloshed in my car and too much beer gave me tie-dye, acid-rinsed sleep-premonitions. Don't drink and dream, isn't that what they say? I should lay off.

The things I imagined, though: a whole mucked-up imaginary day. A girl dying on the road. Jesus, what's wrong with me?

'You 'K?' Worm asks, as he pulls his sleeve down over his hand. This simple question pushes me over.

'Had this dream,' I start, my voice low like a secret, low enough it's near drowned by the tinny ringing in my ears. And then I stop, because if my mind is snapped or I've a brain tumour the size of a turnip making me dream-trip, is that something I'm going to share? I'll sound cracked. The realisation's a dirty bomb.

I gurgle, 'Something messed up's happening.'

'Get yerself a drink,' Worm says.

'Yeah, mate, hair of the dog et cetera,' Anthony agrees.

I unzip my backpack and take out a small glass bottle. Glance about before throwing a hasty swig down my throat where it burns a trail to my blood before a chewing gum chaser. I pack the bottle away and lean back in my chair, stretch my fingers out until the tendons sting.

'Ooh hello, look at this,' Anthony says and I know without seeing. It's her.

'I'd smash the life outta that,' Worm agrees. 'She always gone here?'

'No,' I say. 'Don't invite her.' The noise inside my ear drums rises a notch, turning my vision fuzzy. Not Clara. No.

'Amazing, isn't it?' Anthony muses. 'One minute they're sad little freaks, all black lipstick and chub and the next –'

'Leave her alone,' I say. 'She's a witch.'

'She's what?' Anthony laughs and frowns in one as he turns to shout after Clara. 'Hey. Party tonight at mine? Come on. You are guaranteed to have fun or your money back. Come to one party, get one free. Special introductory offer. I'll –'

I seize Anthony's arm and whisper, 'Don't. I'm serious.'

'What's your problem?' Anthony hisses. He doesn't take his eyes off her.

'She doesn't want your diseases.'

'Hey?'

'No thanks,' Clara says, finally catching up. 'I've heard about your parties, and I've got better things to do with my night than watch someone take a dump on a table or get myself an STD.'

She exits the caf. Anthony holds his hands out and says, 'Are you having a stroke?'

I take it in. Worm's scuffed shoes with the threadbare laces, the zit above Anthony's left eyebrow. Worm's tongue darting out, Anthony's broad face clenched in exasperation. The fist of paper under the table. It's identical. It's yesterday. Every detail the same.

But isn't it always?

Philosophy follows first period. Just like yesterday, or, I guess, today. Just like my weird brain-blip. When I get into class and sit down, I realise Mr Barnes has written 'Nietzsche and the affirmation of life' on the board. Again. I skim the room hopefully, waiting for a classmate to wave a hand and tell Barnes he's got it wrong, we revised this already.

'So, folks,' Barnes says, clapping his hands below a smile set to shrink over the course of the next hour. 'What can you remember about Nietzsche?'

'Gesundheit, Ian!' Jay shouts.

'That's Mr Barnes to you, thank you.'

'Double standards.'

I whack my hand in the air and prepare to speed this lesson along to the subject I suddenly badly want covered.

'Yes, James?'

'Freddy Nietzsche, notoriously confusing philosopher and daddy of eternal return: what if time went round in circles for ever?'

And my eyes go dry in their sockets as I wait for the answer. Because I truly, genuinely need to know.

'Thank you, James. It's nice to know at least one of you can read, although apparently you still lack the ability to accurately summarise. Let's delve into it.'

Barnes strides behind the desk as he natters. 'As James rightly highlights, one of the ideas Nietzsche gave us – among many others – was the concept of eternal return or recurrence: the idea that this universe and our lives recur in an identical form an infinite number of times

'This is not a truth, of course, but a thought experiment. If this were true, would we react with joy or despair? Would

39

we affirm life or not? And if we had to live our lives over and over again, what implications would there be for our moral choices?' Barnes rubs his palms together and grins. He loves it. Bloody loves it.

Eternal return. Infinite repetitions of time. Events taking place again and again. Freddy Nietzsche left some good ideas, though he would've bombed high school philosophy thanks to his inability to write a coherent essay. But there's been plenty to argue over in the hundred years since he died. Eternal return is the most screwed up – imagine if history repeated itself in an identical way for ever and we never escaped and never knew. Hamsters on a universe-sized wheel.

Is this what I'm experiencing? Some kind of looping universe giving me *déjà vu* on steroids? Or psychic insight into other versions of this day? But no, I don't believe in mystical precognition or looping time. I believe in wrongly wired brains and emotional breakdowns, and both those options are looking plausible.

Anthony nudges me and slides a piece of paper over. I unfold it under the desk as my chest shrinks. He's drawn a phone with a jagged speech bubble:

'Are you a victim of Mr B's boring-ass philosophising? Do you need lobotomising? Call free on 0800 F-M-L-I-W-A-N-T-T-O-D-I-E NOW!'

I've seen this before. Exactly this. Another fleeting moment of my dream-version of today, so inconsequential I barely remember until it's shoved under my nose. I'm sure Anthony will see my panic, but he smirks and says, 'Check out Barnes just eating it up.'

Anthony reckons Barnes tries too hard, points it out with a sneer on his face like it's a character flaw. Reckon he thinks the same of me, though I'm scraping by on natural aptitude and the bare minimum.

Barnes whacks the wall in excitement and Anthony whispers. 'I'd like to eternally return to a time before this dullness.'

He's got a point. It's boring, because I've heard it all before. Barnes drones on and on about eternal return, eternally repeating himself until I want to shout for him to stop.

The reason I always liked philosophy, apart from how easy it is when you've a decent head for names and concepts, is how it's all problems with no answers. You can mull over the biggest questions without needing solutions. Never seemed like an issue before, but today it's making my pits prickle.

My chair catches on the carpet as I stand.

Barnes pauses mid-sentence and everyone looks my way. There's Jay and Anthony and Mia and Lana. They're sitting exactly where they sit, wearing the same uniform we wear every day.

'Sit down, twat.' Anthony tugs the back of my blazer.

'Are you all right?' Barnes asks.

I open my mouth to say I'm fine, but nothing comes out. My midsection twists and I'm going to spew. With my hand over my mouth I bolt for the door.

2.2

After school I arrange to meet Anthony to help with the supplies run. The benefits are twofold: 1. Change the day. 2. Avoid Dad. The idea of a do-over with him makes my skin wither.

Bingo Booze is an off-licence located a few blocks from the semi-detached where Dad and I exist. It's between Happy Shopper, the dreariest corner shop on earth, and a barber's some paragon of originality named Sweeney Todd's.

As I pull into the car park Anthony's gleaming black Audi hatchback's waiting. She's called 'Bonnie', and she's a nice car. No soul, though. She arrived shiny and new from a production line last year without Anthony needing to lift a finger. But then, Anthony doesn't work for anything.

Maybe it's not fair to compare, but I sweated my balls off in the garage for weeks the summer before last. Working whenever I could, Mum doing her bits then inspecting my work. Checking my edges and sucking her teeth whenever she caught a blemish.

I didn't love the car then. Hadn't yet passed my test and couldn't fathom how Mum'd talked me into helping her fix up some hunk of 1970s junk. Didn't understand why she'd gone and bought something called an MG Midget. What a treat when I could finally drive it, right? Begging for a lifetime of midget-dick jokes. But the car has a life. History.

Don't know why I'm overthinking the car. Fool.

I kill the engine and hop out.

'Looking suave, mate.' Anthony throws an arm round my shoulders and jams a finger in my ear. I'm relieved to see him.

It's new. The further I get from this morning, the easier it is to brush off last night's nightmare. My dream-today had no Bingo Booze trip, no finger in my ear.

Anthony says, 'I expected you to be wearing a bib after today's display. How's your stomach?'

'Fine. Sorry I vommed on your shirt, though.'

'Hey?' Anthony releases me and claps his belly. He's wearing jeans too, though his are frayed and threadbare in the wrong places – around the hem, at the back of his thigh. A creased salmon-pink shirt hangs open over a turquoise T-shirt emblazoned with a mermaid and the legend *I sleep with the fishes*. Anthony's got a distinctive style I can only describe as: 'The world's tallest toddler. That's what you bloody look like.'

'Ha, screw you. I'm deeply intriguing.' Anthony raises an eyebrow.

'Nah. No-one thinks that.' I'm surprised at how angry I sound, my brain-strain of a day getting to me.

'Everyone thinks it,' he says.

Wish he was wrong. Anthony has one of those broad, symmetrical faces mums go gooey over. Reckon he'll grow into his slick-dick politician name when he ditches the slogan T-shirts and ancient jeans that are a blatant fuck-you to his double-oh-seven-looking dad.

While I'm hardly suave, I'm decent enough in blue-grey button-down, jeans and boots. My hair's that good point between cuts, and skin's been worse. Not been working out lately, but I'm a stretch of elastic, lean in a way my unbalanced diet can't touch.

'Worm late?' I ask.

'As per. That dickhead has zero respect for my time.'

'Maybe if he had wheels.'

'Mate, Worm would already have a bike or a car if he didn't spend all his dollar on weed, lazy shit.'

'Hmm, dunno 'bout that.' The bell above the door drowns me out.

Anthony loads up with an eight-pack, while I grab whatever's on offer. Jane, the mouse who lives behind the counter, is bored as she says, 'ID please.'

I flip out my driving licence. She doesn't read it.

'Spence, I'll get these.' Anthony barges me aside. I pocket my wallet as he slides four twenties across the counter, plus ID. Generosity keeps punctuality company on Anthony's short list of virtues.

'Do you fancy a party later, sweet cheeks?' Anthony says with a barely disguised smirk as he puts out a hand for change.

'Not if this was my last night on earth.' Jane drops the coins on the counter beside Anthony's hand so he has to scrabble to pick them up.

'Suit yourself.'

She dead-eyes us before disappearing behind a fat fantasy paperback.

We're at the door when Anthony says, full volume, 'Imagine, though. Bloody one-star humourless bitch.'

The bell jangles. As the door closes behind us I'm just in time to see Jane flip her middle finger at Anthony's back.

At Anthony's we have time to spare. We get FIFA on and it's reassuringly normal. Same old drinks on the table, same old sweaty palms trying to level the score. I pause the game and shift my formation, trying to find a weak spot in Anthony's defence, him swearing back at me for being a loser, as though he wants it any different.

Despite the palatial proportions of the Mansbridges' place, I'm comfy here. Mainly thanks to the fully stocked fridge and minimal adult supervision. Even when they're in the country, his dad spends all week at the flat in London and his mum's always on a spa day or organising some philanthropic knees-up. They're lucky Anthony and Eric didn't turn feral.

This place has settled my nerves. It's a deviation from all the freaky familiarity that's been dogging me. Everything will be fine as long as the scene keeps changing. New venue, new chat and now, between matches, Anthony reaches over to the coffee table and hands over a postcard I've never seen before. 'Check out this pair of jokers.'

The picture shows stripy colourful wooden boats floating together on a deep turquoise river. Two stick figures sketched in biro shout, WISH YOU WERE HERE!!! Elaborate stamp and scrawled message on the reverse, unintelligible except for the 'Mum & Dad xxx' at the bottom.

'Nice they miss you,' I say.

'Yes, they so genuinely wish I was there. That's why they went in term time, isn't it? When I couldn't go.'

''Cos of work?'

His chin juts. 'It's standard these days, that's my point. Do you think they ever jetted off alone while Eric was here?'

They definitely did. 'How's golden boy?'

'For all I know? Taken and ransomed. You're lucky you don't have siblings.'

My fingers trace the words 'Mum & Dad xxx'. The letters blur.

'What's wrong with you? You're being a fucking weirdo.' Anthony leans back and settles his attention on me.

'Yeah.' I deep-blink and flick the edge of the postcard.

I could tell him, I guess. About the anniversary.

This last year he's been the one checking on me, sitting next to me, tolerating me. The one distracting me with games, movies, gigs, rugby, parties, anything to keep my mind off. He's let me say nothing for hours. Left me alone when necessary. Kept me blinkered forward, tried to help me leave the past where it belongs. For months I've been personality-defective and he's stuck by without complaint. He makes plans and I follow in his slipstream, happy to oblige, which keeps him happy too.

Anthony's had my back from the get-go, since we were scrawny eleven-year-olds with no rugby-team physiques to get us by. No-one who knows Anthony would believe it. He's a good friend. But there are limits on what you can subject a mate to. Limits on the misery you can lay out day after day and expect anyone to keep putting up with you.

I throw the postcard on the table. 'Yeah. Fine.'

'Good, mate, good.' He leans forward, eyes on the screen. 'Then excuse me while I kick your arse.'

Worm wafts in forty-five minutes late, not long before the rest of the party riff-raff are due to show. He shuffles into an armchair and jerks his head at the postcard. 'Where's the parental controls at?'

'Vietnam,' I say. 'Sensitive subject.'

Anthony says, 'I'm not "sensitive", just royally hacked-off I missed a sweet holiday because my mother can't read calendars.'

Worm reaches past for a swig of my beer. 'Fair 'nough.'

'It's what? Past midnight there now, so she'll be lying awake hating Dad while he drunk-snores in her face. They're welcome to all that "quality time" without me.'

'Right.' Worm and I exchange glances.

'To be fair, they're not even necessary to my life at this point,' Anthony grumbles on. 'They could permanently shuffle off and I wouldn't care.'

Oof. My heart bombs. Anthony smacks a ball into the back of my net and turns to gloat.

I chuck my controller to Worm and head to the kitchen, leaning my head into the cavernous American-style fridge until the blood slows to normal. Fuck Anthony and his casual disregard for permanence. Death's no holiday.

The dark marble counter's scattered with crumbs; the sink's stacked with bowls where the cleaner can't keep up with Anthony's carnage. I wipe the side down, wash up and feel better when everything's clean.

Back in the lounge, I set two beers and a Coke on the table. Worm and Anthony play while I stretch out on another coffee-leather sofa. Into my phone I type a name, the first one on my mind.

Clara, it seems, doesn't like to share. We are not friends or followers. I have to make do with a profile pic of her private account, but it's a beauty. Face contorted into a jokey snarl, tongue out. Of all the people to kill off in my dreams, an interesting choice from my subconscious. Perhaps the back of my brain's keeping secrets from the front.

I flip the screen around. 'Why'd you invite her?'

'Why not?' Anthony says. 'The more the messier, mate. Also, let it not be denied, she's fit.'

'Nah.'

'Tasty.' Anthony licks his lips.

'She's bloody bread,' I say. 'Bland.'

Anthony laughs and leans over. 'Clearly the feeling's mutual. Access denied. Here.'

I catch his phone and there's Clara's feed. Exposed. Apparently she doesn't like to hide from everyone. But I knew that already.

'Who followed who first?' I ask.

'Am I the sort of desperate bastard who remembers that?'

When Anthony turns away Worm quickly mouths, 'Him.'

I scroll. Selfies, overdone filters and legs by the pool from last year's summer in Santorini – though Hart's more raw chipolata than hot-dog legs.

'You rate her?'

Anthony snorts. 'I wouldn't say no. If she begged. I mean, if she got down on her knees ... you know?'

Worm laughs. I don't. And then it's over, because Worm asks, 'If you'd got one superpower, what'd it be? I'd do flying.'

I say, 'We did this yesterday.' And Worm's face creases because he doesn't know he's on repeat.

I can't hack this. This day that doesn't change. Don't want to be here at all. So I timeout and get lost in Anthony's phone, scrolling Clara's feed right to the beginning. A silly selfie of her in a blue hoodie. Face angled just-so like all the girls know. If she's at the party tonight, if she dances, if she drinks, if she pulls Anthony like she did. If she tries to run. If she dies. What then?

I turn the screen black. That won't happen. None of it.

2.3

I'm on the grass, my arms wrapped tight around my guitar and I'm cold to my bones. My joints ache where they're longing to flex, but somehow I haven't been able to move a muscle. Not for the longest time. I've downed enough booze to kill my thoughts, but they keep on kicking like some indestructible villain.

The house is rammed. Anthony's sending photos of girls I don't know. His messages flood my phone and one is captioned, 'How old's this one?' My belly's sloshing, I should be having fun, but my mucked-up dream is still giving me the willies. Everything's the same and I'm done with it. Ready for everyone to *déjà* fuck right off.

I wobble up, get into the house and wade through the party, knee-deep in self-pity.

Why am I here? Think, Spence, think. To try again with Bee and hope Anthony doesn't mind? Nah, that's the quickest way to lose an arm. My mission's to keep an eye out, make sure my twisted imagination was bluffing me. Right?

And there, like an answer, is Clara-bloody-Hart. Couldn't avoid her all night, I suppose.

Clara's already sloshed, like everyone is. She dances with Anthony. Her mate Genni's nearby with Jay, but then Jay steers Genni away and it's just Clara and Anthony left.

Her again, him again, me again. All of this again. Except now I'm awake for everything; now I can see what I missed.

Anthony leaves and goes upstairs. Clara sways on her own. I stand up, watch her. But Anthony's back in no time. He pops out of view for a moment and then there's two drinks in his hand and one's for Clara.

I sit back down. Clara giggles and weaves on the makeshift dancefloor, head bowed. She drops low and stays, peep of black lace to the wood floor. Anthony hauls her up. She pushes him playfully and falls backwards into Bee who mouths, 'Desperate much?'

It all happens again, just like it must've before. But that wasn't real and now this isn't either. She's not going to die.

Anthony pulls her from the room. Stoops to pick her back off the floor. She goes with him. All floppy and smiling. They go upstairs.

I stand. Stare out of the lounge doors towards the base of the stairs and wait, jostled by the crowd for I-don't-know-how-long until a pathetic tangle of limbs appears, crawling upward.

'Worm,' I shout. 'Don't go there.'

Worm turns. Eyelids struggling not to touch each other. 'Soaked.'

'Right?' But he's not wrong. Worm's clothes and hair are wet, his glasses fogged with moisture. He smells like clean bathrooms. But Worm's dampness isn't the mystery I want solved. I say, 'Come down. Sit. Smoke.'

'But …'

'Nah, come here.'

As he scoots backwards, I stare up towards Anthony's room. The door's closed.

At the bottom of the stairs is a note:

DANGER! STRICTLY OUT-OF-BOUNDS! CHOKING HAZARDS AHEAD.

That doesn't seem right. And not because of the cartoon dicks illustrating Anthony's warning. Is the sign the same?

'You see Clara Hart?' I whisper, like she's a ghost or something.

Worm giggles. 'Dutch courage and eyes on that Mans-bridge-prize.'

'Look, stay there.' I point at the sofa.

He goes, collapses sideways and curls his knees to his chest.

Worm was upstairs last time. Him and Anthony and Clara all go upstairs, she falls back down, she runs. She dies? But no, none of that's right. I watched and she was dancing, happy, she went upstairs giggling. She won't run, she won't fall. Besides, all of this is some messed up hallucination of my grief-fried imagination.

But the last version of this day carries on churning in my memory. Headlights. Broken glass. A body on the road. Sirens. I can't watch it happen again. I step into the hall, grab my phone and dial. The last thing I say is, 'Come quickly.'

The line fuzzes as the person down the line breathes. There's the tap of computer keys. 'He'll pick you up in five.'

Clara's none of my damn business.

2.4

On some level we all know this ends. Maybe someone first explained when you were seven years old and Mr Whiskers didn't get up in the morning. Maybe parental bribes for visiting that old neighbour with the paper skin abruptly ceased. But you don't really believe it happens, that people die. You don't believe you'll die, that one day, if you're lucky, you'll blink out like a light bulb. Or, if you're unlucky, you'll be torn apart by nature or trauma.

I didn't believe. Wasn't prepared. In my heart I thought death was something that happened to other people. Other people's families and friends. Their parents, not mine.

It happened too soon. That wasn't fair. But maybe it always happens too soon.

Ever since Mum, I've known the truth – everyone I know is walking around with a secret expiry date. Could be fifty years, could be an hour. And this new knowledge drains me, my optimism leaching out, leaving me sore and tired – the emotional equivalent of the flu. My skin hurts, my bones hurt, my heart hurts. I'm exhausted. For a year my mind's been busy expecting. Every out-of-the-blue message or phone call, every car journey Dad takes without me, every international flight the Mansbridges make. I'm anticipating death and disaster from the moment I wake up so I'm never side-swiped again.

But now I reckon I've reverted. I've lost a year and no longer believe bad things are coming. People don't die. If I don't see, it can't happen. Shut my eyes, run away.

It's better this way. I'm a bad omen. A glitch in the day. Maybe I caused it, somehow. But not tonight.

Yellow and red lights sweep by and cars filter past, slowed by the tracking of my vision. My hands are trapped tight between my knees. The rest of me jitters.

'Huh?' I jerk forward to catch words I've already missed.

'Heavy night?' the taxi driver repeats, but he doesn't care as long as my insides stay down.

The taxi drops me off. I pay and stand to watch him manoeuvre. Painful five-point turn in a street choking with parked cars.

In the dark, the house looks unfamiliar. I take my phone out, surprised it's not even 1am. There's a barrage of messages in the group chat, a pointless litter of commentary that shouldn't exist if the idiots sending them were having fun.

A private message pings up. Something new, something I didn't already cook up in my depraved subconscious.

Anthony: Something's happened. Call me

I squat to the cool concrete step, my body heavy and unbalanced. The phone screen so bright it makes everything else recede until it's just me and Anthony. He picks up on the second ring.

'Spence, where are you?'

'Home.'

'Jesus. Come back. You wouldn't believe what's happened. Some girl fell down the stairs. There's police here. I can't even find Worm –'

'It hit her,' I mutter.

'Who? Spence? The stairs, her head. It's … god. Serious.'

No. I prod the red call button. Three attempts before Anthony shuts off. I pocket my phone and claw my way into the house.

Trying to be quiet, I trip up the stairs and miss the top, stamping hard on the landing. In the bathroom, dazzled by the brightness, I smash my fist downward into the sink. Dad greets me in the hall, his face weird without glasses.

He says, 'How did you get home?'

'Taxi.'

'Good. Good party?' A wide yawn rips his face apart.

'Death, awfulness. The usual.'

Dad squints at me. He says, 'Is that … is everything OK?'

I look past him into the dark. 'Fine. Just a joke.'

I stumble across the landing and through to my room, kicking the door shut as I crumple into bed. I lie on my back. The ceiling's blank.

She hit her head? On the stairs? That's not how it goes. Despite all the similarities, the words, the lessons, the party, the dancing, the death, it couldn't have been real and there's an ugly relief to that. She fell. She wasn't hit. It was different. It wasn't my fault. God, I can't wait for Saturday.

THE THIRD TIME
3.1

Under the fluorescent lighting of the police station, I reach across the desk and grab a piece of paper. I start scrawling the address I've known by heart since I was eleven years old. Adrenaline turns my writing to scribbles and I force myself to slow. Block capitals. Be clear.

'You're saying a girl has been hurt?' The officer behind the counter's bored, as though I'm pranking him.

'She's going to die.'

'Someone's dead?'

'*Going* to –'

'Ah, that's very serious. How is she going to die?'

'Accident,' I say, and in the dead air of the police station, no background music to dilute me despite the phantom party tunes still thumping in my eardrums, the word comes out wrong, a thick slush at the centre. Ack-shh-dent. I should've stayed sober tonight. Maybe then they'd understand, but I've been freaking out all day, watching all night, letting events play out and it's the same. All the same. It's real: this day, this trap.

It's real that I'm losing my fucking marbles. Nah, they're all lost already and in their place there's resolve.

It can't happen again. Even if my slurry-filled brain can't understand why the universe would stick me here to deal with this, it has. And I'm not the kind of fool who sits around and does nothing. At least, not a third time.

Clara isn't dying on my watch.

'Please … close the road or something? Or arrest her? Anything.'

'Sir –'

'Look.' I smack my fists on the desk with a metallic clink and my keys dig into my skin. I try again. 'A girl's going to die if you don't fix it.'

Our eyes meet. This guy will be here beyond midnight. He and I are old pals except he's never seen my face before. I know how crazy I look standing here spouting off about the future. The urgency keeps the shame away as I watch this officer figuring out his move. He runs a visual assessment. He lingers on the contents of my fist. Bingo. Now he sees a problem he recognises, now the pieces go together.

The drinks I've had tonight. Few too many.

'How did you get yourself here?' he says.

'I'm eighteen.' I scrape the fist holding my car keys slowly off the desk as though it'll undo the damage. He watches it go.

'Have you been drinking tonight?'

I shake my head. 'I'll stop her then.'

I walk from the station, into the street. I start to run. The clean, cold air burns my throat.

'Hey, wait! Stop!' someone shouts, but my legs keep going.

Only, now I'm outside, there's nowhere to go. If I get back in my car I'll be screwed. They'll follow me, arrest me for something real and then they'll never believe me. I stop and wait. I sink to my knees and they come and they lead me back inside.

'Go to the address.' I smooth the paper and push it forward. 'Bring her in, please.'

'Is this your address? What's your address? Can you give us a number? Someone to call?'

I can't and I don't and my wallet's in the car, so good luck. They put me alone in a room with cream walls carved with graffiti. A hard bed with a plastic mattress and a dull metal toilet.

I rap the door and shout, 'You going to save her?' But they don't come and don't reply.

Much later I'm startled out of my ceiling-meditation by the sound of the door. Footsteps. A man sobbing.

I go to my window to watch the crier being escorted past by another officer. I stick my hand to the opening and shout, 'Oi, I know you.'

They stop and I register his scent. The sour twist of alcohol under sweat. I recognise the desperation in his eyes. It's him. From the first time. I was standing on the road with Bee wrapped around me. He was on the phone, crying just like now.

'Hit her again, didn't you?' I say. He flinches.

'OK, that's enough,' the officer says and they walk on.

'Why didn't you stop her?'

'Quiet down.'

'I told you!'

THE FOURTH TIME
4.1

'Girls are crazy, mate. I mean, take Bee, she doesn't know what she wants.'

Anthony ends with a tuna-littered grin then swallows the mouthful of sandwich he's been working on, a feat of lunchtime multi-tasking I've already witnessed several times before.

I'm in the caf, half paying attention, mind on last night. Tonight. Because here's what's going on: it's identical. Over and over: Clara's drunk, she dances, she pulls Anthony, she falls, she dies. The chain of events kicks-off every time with Clara getting messy at the party and ends with her, well, ended. So I start at the beginning: stop her getting drunk and maybe it'll break the chain. Stop her dying. That has to be the answer.

Someone drops their lunch tray: Jay. Even though he's on the rugby team, Jay's not popular enough or hated enough to earn a proper cheer. There's a spatter of ironic clapping.

This day. This bloody day. I'm glad to be alive and free after going to sleep in a cell. Gutted to wake up again to this instant replay.

At least the paralysing churn of panic has settled. Yesterday was a mess, but there'll be no running around town like a maniac asking people if they know time's looping today, no babbling to the police tonight.

There's no point anyway, I'm the only one who's twigged this is Friday number four. Maybe I'm the only one it's real for. Perhaps everyone else is living in next Monday with an empty, zombie version of Spence, while my mind is stuck here. How would I know?

What I do know is this: the events aren't concrete. I've shifted them – I stopped Worm going upstairs that second time. And if I can change the small things, I can change the big. Focus, Spence, focus. Fourth time's a charm.

Doesn't help that Clara's bloody everywhere. Passes me in the halls; bumps into me at the water fountain; and she's here again now, a table away in the caf with Genni. She's chatting, swinging her hands. Can hear them laughing away the hour. It's distracting, is what it is. Here's me rattling my skull for answers and instead the dead girl keeps pulling my attention. Every time I look at her, all I see is scraped skin and wonky limbs, and I don't want it. Can't handle it.

So this time I'll fix Clara. And then I'll work out how to make Saturday happen. With some effort it'll be easy. Smooth sailing.

'As if you did, Ant,' says Worm. I've missed a bit. Some brag about Lana.

'Damn well did. Jay saw. Just because you've never touched a girl.' Anthony checks around and settles on Jay, who's still scrabbling for the contents of his dropped tray. 'Hey, Jay –'

Worm pipes up, 'At least I never –'

'It's delicate, isn't it?' I say, seeing an opening.

'Hey?' Anthony says.

'Girls. Specially at parties, you have to mind yourself, right?'

There's a confused pause. Anthony exchanges looks with Worm, as though I'm the only tragic virgin at this table. Maybe I am, but I don't care. The only girl I liked has been off with my mate and I've been preoccupied lately, plus it turns out girls don't go for strong silent types. Or maybe that's giving me too much credit. Silent sure, but strong's a reach.

So it's been a while. A year and a half, in fact, before grief stole my personality. Party, of course. Anthony's, of course. Hand in Sophie Cobbett's knickers for five minutes while she wore an expression like she wanted to switch channels and made no good noises. Afterwards she sucked me off, probably to get me to stop touching her, and, after I finished in her mouth, she wiped her lips and said, 'Nice of you to warn me.'

How was I meant to know the etiquette? But I said, 'Sorry, yeah. Next time.'

And even though I meant next time with the next girl, Sophie – expression letting me know how indescribably stupid I was – said, 'Sorry if you got the wrong idea, Spence.'

Spent an anxious weekend afterwards, deleting any message I drafted to her. Then the Monday. Jesus. Sophie whispering and smiling while every single one of her girlfriends swivelled and giggled.

While I've never upset a girl so badly she ends up pasted to the road, I'm pretty sure Sophie thinks I'm a filthy loser. Never known what to say to her since. Never known if she regrets it or hates me or even thinks about it at all. I didn't even tell Anthony and Worm about her. Although that's only half due to the embarrassment; the other reason being it's Sophie's business too.

And, god, I'd rather she didn't tell her mates about my dick.

'Spence, want to dial down the obviousness?'

'What?' I blink, back in the caf as Anthony's wide hand waves back and forth in my field of vision. Behind it Clara, lunch finished, is hunkered down over Genni's hand, painting her nails from a vivid pink bottle. Laughing still. Always laughing.

'I thought you said she was – and Worm correct me if I'm wrong, but I believe this is a direct quote – "rank".' It's true, I did say this in my desperation to stop Anthony issuing his invite. Didn't make a lick of difference.

'And?'

'So stop eye-fucking her, dickhead.' His annoyance loosens and dissolves into a smirk. 'You'll get your chance later. Just stop staring – it's sad.'

'Really wasn't,' I say.

'Is she why you need to understand the finer points of seduction all of a sudden? You're getting back into Clara?'

'What? Nah, of course not.'

Saved by the bell, I scoot away from Anthony and Worm, hoping they don't watch as I flow through the student exodus, following a shiny ponytail. Couldn't hurt to chat, right? It'll be even easier to save her life if she doesn't hate me.

'Clara!' I shout and her head bounces back, but she doesn't stop.

'Spence, great. Come to yell at me about your car again?'

'Yell? Nah.' God, she's sensitive. 'You coming to history?'

'I believe I'm sort of obligated. Because school.'

I fall into step. Her history textbooks are already clutched to her chest. She takes an audible breath and lets it out in a rush of words.

'Your friend's not funny, you know. He's actually a bit of a pig sometimes.' Her chin lifts, expecting me to disagree.

'You what?'

'At the cafeteria earlier? It'd be nice to be able to buy a snack without a side order of harassment.'

'Right, yeah. Good to know,' I say and shrug. Force of habit.

Her eyes narrow. 'He makes you look bad by association.'

'Yeah, got it. Doesn't seem to stop any of you, though, does it? All the girls like … what would you call it? A bad boy?'

'Not all the girls.' But Clara's cheeks catch fire and she can't meet my eyes. *Yeah, right.*

'Look, go easy tonight.' I grab her arm and she stops.

'Excuse me?' Her tone turns hostile. Snatches out of my grasp and I flex my hand in apology.

'At the party. You're not used to all that, so pace yourself, Hart.'

'Did I say I'm going?'

'We both know you are.'

'And if I *did* happen to make it, my behaviour would be none of your business, actually,' she snaps and starts walking again. I let her go. She's got an attitude problem, Clara does.

Angry girl. Explains the purple hair phase. All her edges drawn in black, dress-sense a bit too attention-grabbing. It didn't sit well. It was all too much 'look at me' – so no-one did. It was about the time I stopped looking too.

In a small town, people get pigeonholed. We all remember. I remember. Even though she's gone back to normal, it doesn't help. Can't reverse the damage.

Clara stalks off and I wonder how the hell I'm meant to keep her safe if she can't even tolerate me for five minutes.

4.2

I bail out of school halfway through the day and drive. I head out to the folly and park up on a patch of grass surrounded by trees enormous enough to make me feel small. A reminder of my insignificance despite the fact that the world seems to be literally revolving around me.

Couldn't hack another scoop of school day the exact same flavour as the last three, and this is a good place to escape. I try to doze, make the hours whizz by. After all, time isn't fixed. It plays games when you take your eye off it. I've had good days I've tried to savour zip straight past, and I've had a bad one stick around for ever. I've now got a day on my hands I can't shift. But after Mum, whole weeks disappeared into the abyss.

Haven't been to this place in years. We always called it 'the folly', but who knows where that comes from. A grand title for what's now a bunch of stone half submerged in the ground, given over to moss and grass, critters and litter. In a small town you need spots like this; somewhere to go with your mates when you're old enough for freedom but can't get into pubs. When you're too skint for a café, got no licence to drive to the cinema and live in a dead-end town, a crumbling ruin is the dog's-bloody-bollocks.

We were here every summer. Anthony always brought his swish speakers and some fancy leftovers his mum packed up. Worm'd pick the tunes and we'd all lie under the sun by the decimated tower and wait for something to happen.

Clara came here too. We saw her sometimes. One time especially.

I can play the moment over like a movie, seeing her and Genni walking past our group. Clara's pale legs out under a summer dress. Black hair cut with a fringe, black makeup and this oversized pocket-watch necklace swinging down to her waist like she was Alice in bloody Wonderland. She was smiling. Sparkling. One of the quiet girls, but I reckoned the quiet girls were the proper sort for me. I'm a quiet guy.

'Just do it, you utter puss, or I'll ask her out instead,' Anthony said, kicking me in the shin.

'She wants you,' Worm added, tipping salt and vinegar dregs into his gob.

Then snakes in my belly as I called out, asking her to come over so I could ask if she'd want to go out sometime. I remember the slithering turned heavy, a stomach full of stones, when she turned me down.

'I don't think so,' is what she said.

Of course she didn't think so. Didn't think, because it was unthinkable that she should go out with me. Of course she said no.

Anthony and Worm laughed themselves silly. Took the piss until the end of the summer and right up until I got off with Grace Modi at another party.

We must've been fifteen, but I can still feel the same queasy shame as Clara shot me down. It's not like I still want to go with her. Not interested in Clara and her attitude. Just gutted that my particular superpower is the ability to drum up any awkward memory and relive it, as though it's that day I'm stuck in, not this one. Sweating from years-old embarrassment.

But it's a useful memory all the same. It's a problem Clara thinks I'm such a waste of space. After all, how can you save a girl when you're unthinkable?

At home I skirt around Dad and buy time away from Anthony by making good on my strategic offer to do the booze run alone. Another point scored against this never-ending day. Another change. Take that, Nietzsche.

I mope through fluorescent rows, too sober, but uninspired by the shelves of bottles. It'd be a comfort to sip and swig my way to oblivion and take the edge off my existence tonight, but why bother? The edge always creeps back. And I need to keep my wits about me this time.

Still, at Bingo Booze I grab some beers, then head to the counter.

'Pushing the boat out this evening, I see,' Jane says, grim-faced. 'ID please.'

I slide my licence over.

Jane says, 'So Tweedledum, where's Tweedledirtbag tonight? I can't remember the last time I saw one of you without the other.'

I chuckle, shocked to my core to hear Jane make an identifiable joke. 'His party,' I say, waving a hand at the bottles on the counter.

'Bet that'll be a laugh.'

'Yeah. Fancy it?'

'Thanks. I'd rather deep-fry my fingers.'

'Ha. Fair 'nough.'

Jane beeps everything through. After picking up my notes, she drops my change on the counter.

Then she says, 'He's a bona fide oxygen thief, your friend. The way he comes in here, making his little-boy jokes about me. I do notice.'

A twenty-pence piece won't leave the counter. I use my stubby nails.

'You need to get yourself some better friends,' Jane says.

'Yeah, I've heard.' People hating on your mate's like buses, apparently, but it's easy to think anyone's this and that kind of prick when you only see one side of them. I loop the handles of the grocery bag over my wrist, tuck the beer under my armpit and wave. 'Jane, cheers.'

'Hannah.'

'Eh?'

I double-take. She smiles. The first ever Jane smile on record. It has a transformative effect on her. She's younger than I thought, maybe. Jane and I could be mates, I realise. Except she's not even Jane.

'Jane worked here before. They've never bothered with a new badge.'

She flicks the lying lump of plastic on her chest. Not Jane. Months she's been working here and failed to correct me. Beside her not-name are other pins I never noticed: a tiny rainbow, a Shakespeare quote. A kick of regret hits my ribs for every time we took the piss out of her. She's a Hannah not a Jane, and a whole person, apparently.

She dips back behind her book.

As I leave, I call out with her new name and send Hannah a wave, and she waves back. It puts a grin on me. Call me crazy, but it feels like a good omen.

4.4

I don't know how I got here.

In front of me the table's filled with cups of Jägermeister and beer. They're arranged in two opposing pyramid formations and there's a ping-pong ball in my fist. But instead of kicking off beer pong I'm staring, because Clara and Genni are in the kitchen, aligned perfectly with the doors so I can spy them from my spot at the end of the dining table. The minute Clara makes a move on the booze, I'm poised to intercept.

That girl and alcohol are a bad mix. She doesn't usually party, so she handles it badly, acts out of character. She might fancy Anthony, but I never pegged Hart for going with a guy she barely knows. The problem crops up when booze wrestles judgement out of the ring.

So here's what happens tonight: I keep an eye on her, I keep her sober, I keep her alive. Easy-peasy. Will that also fix time? Perhaps.

Clara dances, still laughing of course, and it's not the typical sexy-drunk dance. It's got proper moves and everything. Can't decide if she's being ironic, but I can't stop watching.

'Come on. Your shot.' A heavy hand lands on my head. 'Oh yes, what have you got your eye on?'

'Nothing.' I shrug Anthony off, but it's too late.

'Clara,' he shouts and she jumps. 'Come on, let's see your skills.' She looks at me then Anthony. Genni pushes her forward with a wide grin.

'Could you not?' I say.

'What? I'm doing you a favour.' Anthony gapes, all fake innocence. 'One more for the girls' team,' he tells Bee.

Clara walks forward, turning midway to gesture at Genni, as though she's under duress. Genni laughs and winks and shoots a look my way. Anthony grins between me and them like he's taking it as a personal compliment. Which, I guess, is probably accurate. By the time Clara's standing beside me, Genni's already gone, aimed straight at Jay's lips, happy to offload Clara now she's served her purpose: advice dispensed, encouragement given. I know the drill.

'You came then?' I say.

'I didn't, did I?' She smiles. Yeah, funny.

'Surprised to see you at a party, that's all.'

She says, 'Oh, sorry. Haven't I drunk away enough of my brain cells to qualify for your idea of "fun"?'

'You know how parties work, yeah? You can't go reciting poetry or get in the lounge and judge the art. No-one wants a lecture on women's rights.'

Her wide eyes blink. Perhaps that was a bit much. 'Well, your loss, Spence. You don't even know what fun is till you've heard one of my party-ready artwork critiques.'

A dimple sinkholes one cheek. Her finger wraps up in a strand of dark hair. To my disgust, I realise I'm smiling back. I remember how "fun" the Clara Hart of yesterday was and get serious again. Here's me egging her on like a twat.

'There's no art,' I tell the drink in my hand, 'just pictures of Anthony's god-awful face.'

She doesn't rush to defend him. Nods as if she hardly cares, then says, 'I think you'll actually be surprised by how fun I can be.' My hand jerks. 'Nearly as surprised as I am to realise you still have any grey matter left.'

'I'm smart enough, Hart. Course you'd never be as impressed with me as you are with yourself.'

'Don't you know everything?' Her eyes spark and she shakes her head, and suddenly I can't remember if it's my turn to speak, if I'm meant to say something clever that won't come to me. Clara was right the first time – I'm bloody brain-dead.

I become aware of the group again. Anthony looking at me and Clara and paying the wrong sort of attention. The table, the ball, the cups. Beer pong, right.

I bite back an irritable sigh, but I'm screwed, aren't I? My glorious plan going tits-up before my eyes. The girl I'm trying to keep sober enrolled in my drinking game.

'So I throw the ball in the cup?' Clara twists hair round her thumb.

The ping-pong ball's pinched between my fingers. Anthony turns his hands out, says, 'Are we doing this?'

The problem is beer pong's a game of chance. There's no way to keep the alcohol out of her that way. I shove the ball in the pocket of my hoodie.

'Nah,' I say. 'Cups up. We're doing Never Have I Ever.'

A mixed response of groans and glee bubbles round the group. Mia tries to run off and Bee says, 'Oh god, don't be such a downer all the time!' And everyone stays put in the end. Good. I've got the ball, I make the rules.

Clara goes for a cup, but I get there first, snatching it up and chugging half. I'm relieved to taste just schnapps and lemonade – the girls' team take it easy. Syrupy air bounces back up my windpipe. I hand back the depleted cup and Clara wipes away my saliva with her dress.

'Sorry,' I say.

The group's Anthony, Bee, Mia, Lana, Shaun and us. This game's gonna be easy for keeping Clara sober, surely. Can't imagine she's done half the same stuff as these other freaks. And they'll be going straight in for all the sex, dares and deviance. Still, I'm lacking inspiration until I settle on Bee's placid face and have a spiteful brainwave.

'Never have I ever dumped Anthony Mansbridge,' I say, raising my cup in Bee's direction.

Bee stares in horrified glee, perfect teeth gleaming. She says, 'A brutally passive-aggressive start even for this game.'

Anthony flips me the finger. Without a trace of humour he says, 'And it's on, you sack of shit.'

Bee drinks and the rest of us watch. Clara's cup stays at her side. So far, so good.

And I'm a genius, in fact, as Clara stays dry and dull as she marvels at everyone else's debauchery through three more rounds of Never Have I Ever, in which I learn she has never:

1. Skinny dipped
2. Flashed her bum at a teacher
3. Taken it up the arse

No surprises there. In fairness, I've only been naked in a pool, but I drink on the teacher question anyway. Because it's funny and because I want a drink. Plus I'm starting to feel a bit swish with success. Maybe it's the burn of Jägermeister down my throat, or maybe it's because I'm smashing this night.

I'm so confident of Clara's soberness when the game loops around to me, I realise I don't even have to try. So there's a question on my mind I'd very much like an answer to and it's worth the risk. I pitch out, 'Never have I ever had a crush on anyone at this table.'

I down a finger of my own drink – my long-standing, tragic devotion to Bee's common knowledge. Anthony sips then waves a hand across the circle.

'Come on, girls, get them up.'

Bee sighs. 'Please all observe the use of past tense? This game should be renamed Once I Might've Sort've.'

That stings, it really does. No current crushes, Bee? No lingering regrets? She catches my eye and rolls hers.

'Mia!' Anthony shouts, with a pointed finger. 'Down that drink, there's no pretending for you.'

Maybe Mia drinks; it doesn't matter. Across from me, Clara takes a tentative sip of her schnapps. She sees me watching and looks away, pink tickling her cheeks.

'Yes, Clara,' Anthony says, 'you dark horse.'

I look away, question answered. Of course she likes him. They always like him. And she goes upstairs with him to-night – what else did I think?

71

I lose my enthusiasm. When the question's right, I drink, empty one, start the next.

'Slow down or that cup will never respect you,' Bee says, and I pointedly take another chug. She sniffs.

At Bee's turn she says, 'Never have I ever given a girl an orgasm,' which gives Anthony the chance to showboat. We all watch his Adam's apple bob as he drinks and Bee stands, hands on hips, saying, 'Who is this mythical woman Anthony has satisfied? Do we know her?'

He finishes his drink and clarifies, 'Women. Many, many women.'

'Any who can actually testify?'

'Don't be bitter because I cut off your supply,' he says.

Across the circle Mia looks nauseated. I give her a grim smile of solidarity.

'No drinks for little Spence?' Bee pokes me with her finger.

'Nah, I'm not … I don't … nah,' I mumble as my cheeks burn. 'But I'm thirsty.'

I down my drink wondering why I couldn't think of a better way to stop Clara drinking and Anthony stretches his hand over his forehead as though he can't believe he's mates with me and all the girls make eyes, as though I'm some adorable, naïve animated character. I'm Nemo. I'm Wall-E. I'm baby bloody Bambi. Screw this night.

The game ends well past its sell-by, when the Never Have I Evers have turned into weirdness like, 'Never have I ever thought about a cartoon character in a sexual way.'

Mia's quit the game. Bailed when it all got gross, and Lana went next. Bee drapes a freckled arm around Clara's shoulders, pulls her close. Red curls next to sleek black shine. Anthony breaks in, gets by Bee's side, slings an arm around her and flicks his phone screen up-front. Bee watches the screen, her smile flattens out. Clara twists away, her face unreadable.

'I'd rather look at something like that in private, thank you very much,' Bee says, with a laugh I don't believe and a shake of her head. 'And maybe choose something a little more girl-friendly.'

'That girl looks pretty friendly to me.' Anthony turns the screen around with a snort of hilarity. I only get an impression. A small woman and a large man, a wet mouth pumping, a ponytail wrapped around a thick fist, a grimace and then it's gone.

'You know porn's not real life?' Clara says with folded arms.

'Oh yes? How would you know?'

'Pathetic.' But as Clara stalks off there's a new colour to her cheeks.

'Real nice,' I tell Anthony in a slurry of Jägermeister and spit. 'You're an asshole, you know?'

Anthony chuckles. 'You're mashed, Spence. Drink some water and take a look at yourself.'

I wipe my lips. Whatever. Maybe Anthony's right, maybe he's wrong. My head is sloshing, but nowhere near as bad as I'm used to. So what if I'm a mess? Bee's tipsy, Mia's looking sick and Lana and Shaun are making a run for a dark corner. But as I slope off to the kitchen I see Bee catching Clara in her clutches, red and dark heads together again. Bee's stumbling and Clara keeps her upright. Because everyone else is getting messy, but Clara? She's near enough sober.

Mission accomplished. Right?

4.5

In the kitchen, for reasons unknown, Clara's ransacking the cupboards and, for reasons unknown, I'm watching. My thoughts are in a tangle. I know I was stopping her from drinking; I know this is my move. In between these two ideas the logic is muddy, but staying with her seems smart. I fill my cup with water, hold it to my roasting skin to enjoy the cool, then sip. There's a thin, lingering taste of beer and other leftovers.

'What're you doing?' I ask. Clara's arranged flour, eggs, sugar and oil on the countertop.

'Mug cake.' She gestures at the ingredients as if it's the most obvious thing in the world. 'I told you.' Oh.

'Why?'

'Well, I'm hungry, my best friend's gone walkabout and you're drunk. All those things would be helped by carbs. So, if you can stop ridiculing me for five minutes, you'll get some cake out of it.'

'Deal.'

She reaches in the bottom cupboard. Her dress slides up her thighs and my gaze won't budge. As she mixes the ingredients she lectures me on mug-cake recipes, but the information breezes through my mind, because I'm too busy regretting how I took the piss before. Seems maybe she took it to heart.

'I was only messing earlier,' I say. 'You're OK, Hart.'

She blinks at me. 'Where's the peanut butter?'

The forty-five seconds it's cooking lasts forty-five years. The rich, sweet smell wets my tongue and I realise staying with Clara was a good choice. For her, me, my stomach. She pulls out two steaming mugs and hands one over with a teaspoon, says, 'Don't eat it yet.' But it's too late. My mouth burns and I spit molten saliva-coated chocolate cake into my fist. Clara doesn't say she told me so.

The Mansbridges have these wide fold-back doors to the garden. We lean against the wall, half in the kitchen, half on the patio. Half cool, half hot, hands warm from the mugs. We've a view over the turquoise pool, all tastefully lit, the vista ruined by reminders of Friday nights past and future. There's the bench where Mia chucks her guts up every night and Genni and Jay paw each other like two filthy puppies. I dredge memories from before this mess, different parties with happy endings. The hot tub where Worm had his famous slash, the patio where I mooned everyone after losing at Jenga.

Clara talks loads. She must be tipsier than I reckoned to be chatting like this, helping me like this. Her face is animated, free hand waving. It's hard to keep track, but I'm able to glean a few more facts to add to my profile.

Firstly, she cannot tell a story.

'Oh, oh,' she'll say, 'I have to tell you.' And she'll tell you. And it'll be about Genni and some kid who used to go here, but also somehow related to some small point I made an hour ago. The story heads off in strange directions and loops back on itself. 'Wait, sorry, sorry,' she'll say, but it'll never get on track.

I learn she's a vegetarian except for that one pig-in-a-blanket at Christmas, how her music taste runs to the eclectic, encompassing suspect genres like 'melancholic covers of popular hits' and 'American whinge-folk'. Despite the utter banality – she has a kid brother and a weekend job in a shoe shop – it's easy to listen.

When I get a moment I break in with, 'There going to be a quiz about you later?'

Clara smiles at the floor, says, 'Maybe. But I don't like your chances.'

'Got your life history down.'

'I don't think so, James Spencer.'

'Ooh, mysterious.'

'Uh huh.' She laughs.

The last of my cake has cooled against the sides of the mug. It's soft, sugary. The peanut butter glues my mouth shut.

'Luckily I know absolutely everything there is to know about you on account of you being one of the St Peter's top-tier.' Clara's chin juts forward, her nose in the air. She adopts a tone of gentle, mocking superiority, as if the information's juicy. It's not. There's nothing juicy about me. I'm a cardboard man.

'Go on,' I dare.

She stands up straighter, lists off facts on her fingers. Voice brisk. 'Well, first off you're a failed rugby boy, always on the field, but poor at the requisite arse-slapping and girl-scoring necessary to be part of the team. You're definitely smarter than you want to seem and probably nicer.'

'Yeah, really pegged me and my top-secret pleasantness,' I say, though I'm pleased. At least, half pleased. Or, well, it's hardly a compliment Clara's noticed I'm girlfriendless. OK, I'm not pleased.

She paces away. 'You play guitar and all the girls love that. And something happened to you last year.'

I try not to react beyond, 'Huh?'

'Yep, you totally checked out and stopped participating in history at all. I guess over-achieving isn't cool?'

76

My neck flushes even hotter. I'll say this for Anthony and Worm, they can keep a secret if there's nothing in it for them, no hilarity to be squeezed from my misfortune. Alternatively, Clara's too many rungs down for the gossip to reach. Somehow, I'm simultaneously glad it hasn't and wish it had.

I clear my throat. 'Maybe I'm just stupid.'

'I really don't think so.'

Another awkward silence. Reason number five hundred why it's best not to get myself into situations like these. I say, 'Know you've got a secret crush on Anthony Mansbridge.' Her mouth pops in protest and I get smug. 'Right. And your choice of mates is shocking.'

'Wow, hold on a minute.' She holds up a hand. 'I won't have that. Genni's a great friend.'

'Mouth the size of China. Couldn't keep it shut to save her life.'

'Oh, you'd be surprised,' Clara tells the floor, but I catch her upturned lips and there's the dimple of course. Can't secret smile if your whole face gets involved. I can't think what else to say. Maybe, I know you make bad choices and wind up dead. I know my mate's going to screw you and dump you. I know how you look crumpled on a road. I let the spoon clatter back in my mug, mouth suddenly full of dust.

'Yeah, Genni's a real mate, good of her to keep you company.' Over on their bench I can't see where Genni ends and Jay begins. 'Weird way to suffocate a man.'

Clara laughs. I'm close enough to see the detail of her face. Close enough to see my silhouette reflected in the light of her eyes, and that the freckle between the edge of her lips and her dimple isn't black or brown, but dark blue. Could stretch out and touch it. I don't. Obviously. Weird thought. My heart drums. I step back and concentrate on scraping out the last wedge of cake.

'I can't wait to get out of this place,' she says with a sigh and the residue of a smile.

'Cheers. Enjoying your company too.'

'Not *this* place.' She waves her hands encompassing everything. 'This school, this town, these people.'

'Uh –'

'*Most* of these people.'

On cue Anthony's laugh blasts through the doors like thunder. He's bent double just inside the dining room, Bee facing him with her hands on her hips, clearly pissed off.

'He's *such* a pig,' Clara says wistfully. 'And god, this party, really? Everyone's all, "Come, you're missing out, this party's going to be *amazing*."' She stretches the last word out, exploding her fingers in mid-air to emphasise the point.

'Yeah? Anyone who reckons it's that good needs uninviting. And shooting.'

'Most people don't even like Anthony – that's what's wild. But it doesn't matter. Everyone's social standing is basically determined by how easy we are to mess with. It just so happens I'm easy pickings and he's not, because he's six foot of muscle and rich enough for, well, all this.' She folds her arms. *Muscle*, my brain repeats for emphasis.

'Why'd you come then? All set not to. All "Nah, no STDs for me." What happened there?'

She groans. 'I always meant to. I promised Genni I would, but then I had a bad morning and Anthony riled me up with all his heckling. I bet I look silly now.'

78

I shrug. She does a bit. 'High school's a mad social experiment. We're all trying to get by. Popularity's not real, not really.'

'Easy for you to say. It's easy to ignore when it doesn't affect you.'

She's right; it seemed unlikely even as I said it.

'Is that why you like him?' I throw a hand Anthony's way. 'He's popular or whatever?'

Clara looks confused, as if I've asked her to explain rucks, mauls and the difference between rugby union and league.

'No, I –'

Someone lets out a loud ironic wolf-whistle. The sound is followed by a flailing, running, naked man. Worm, in fact, who barrels out of the lounge, yelling unintelligibly. Minding how stoned he is, his pace is impressive. His nudity is not.

'Red ROCKEEEEEEET!'

He sprints through the kitchen and over to the edge of the patio. The dash ends with a leap. A splash. And Worm is gone. Lost in a fizz of pool water.

'Can't believe he's trying to reclaim that nickname,' I say.

The bubbles thin. Worm stays under.

Ten seconds. More? As wonky as my mind is, I know this is a bad sign.

'Do something.' Clara twists a fistful of my T-shirt. My arms start orbiting my body, pulling off my hoodie, boots, undoing my jeans.

Bloody Worm. I stumble across the patio and jump in. Sink till my toe stubs on the bottom of the pool and I bounce back up. I break the surface, gasp, dancing on tiptoes to keep my chin above the level. Searching the surface for my mate. If he's drowned, I'll …

But the tangy water blinks away and I'm face-to-face with him.

''Sup, Spence?' says a perfectly fine, grinning Worm.

'You bloody shitbag …'

He has a head start. I lurch into front-crawl, but he's already at the side, hoisting himself up, out and gone, shrieking into the night.

I splash out my frustration. The adrenaline leaves my blood and is replaced by the pool's chill.

'Red rocket?' Clara says from the pool edge. 'Because his anatomy is dog-like? Case in point regarding the existence of social hierarchy – if that was my nickname I would never be invited to parties.'

'Worm's no better.' I wade to the side.

'Nope. And that's absolutely my point.'

The pool edge slips under my arms so I flop and collapse on the tiles. My jeans are immediately leaden and shrunk to fit and the air is even colder than the water.

I clench my teeth and wrap my arms around themselves. Clara scoops up my hoodie from the grey tiles and gingerly spreads it over me, but it's useless.

I need to get dry. I need to change. I need not to leave Clara behind.

'Come with me?' I nod towards the house.

'To watch you take your clothes off?' Her eyebrows shoot up. 'What an offer. But I think that's a solo activity.'

I pull my arms tighter, cross my legs, feeble attempts to conserve body heat. There's no good reason she needs to come with me. At least, none I can share.

She went upstairs with Anthony, though.

She says, 'Go on before you freeze to death. I'll wait here. Or somewhere. You'll find me.' Her eyes widen. 'Or not if you don't want to.'

'You'll be OK?'

'Stone-cold sober, approximately five metres from my best friend, in the house of your best friend? Abductions in such circumstances are rare.'

I don't laugh. Clara starts to look buggy. 'Go!'

I slip off my hoodie and tug it over her head. 'Keep you warm,' I explain. It engulfs her, falling almost to the bottom of her dress. It's not perfect, but it's a hell of a lot more covered than she was. Better safe than sorry. 'Stay here, yeah?'

'You must leave.' She gives me a playful push.

After one last reluctant glance, I go inside.

Thanks to the spotlights, it was lighter outside than in. My eyes adjust to the dimness of the kitchen. Unrecognisable people crowd the doorways.

Clara will be fine. It's two minutes. I pull out my phone from my jeans pocket, but it's wet and black from its dip. I'll bill Worm if we survive the night.

The thermostat clock says 10:25. I stare at it, held by a memory I can't quite grip. Worm on the stairs dripping wet. Worm on the couch complaining about tigers on the Serengeti. This day feels wrong somehow. Out of order in the most literal sense.

People get in my way as I speed for the stairs. Some girl nearly punctures my foot with her heel, then grabs my hand and won't let go. I'm accepting her gushing, repetitive apology when Bee spots me.

'Spence, little Spence.' She snags the back of my sodden jeans and stares down in dismay. 'You're wet.'

I shrug. 'Let go, will you? Dripping on the floor.'

'Caution, wet floor,' she sings. 'You're a health and safety nightmare.'

Bee beams at me, eyelids blinking out of sync. If I were drunker or if I didn't have somewhere else to be, she'd be cute. Bee does a wobbly curtsey and falls over. I catch her and she hangs off my shoulder.

'Dance with me,' she breathes, her hand on my chest, her hair in my face. The smell of her. Floral. The warmth of her. Distracting. All very distracting.

'You don't want to dance?' Bee pouts. 'I bet Anthony does. Tell him sending me a hundred messages a day isn't OK. OK?'

'He doesn't?' I laugh. Fucking Anthony pretending to be casual, but begging when he thinks no-one knows.

'I'm very done with it.' Bee sniffs, then eyes me. 'And you. You've spent all night with Clara Hart, explain yourself.'

'Eh?' Embarrassment and bafflement wrestle for control.

'You should see her art. It's deranged. You don't want her?'

Bee is off with the fairies, but not too far. And apparently she knows Clara. I say, 'Look, Clara's outside. Go watch her, will you? Make sure she doesn't … dunno …. Look, Mia's wasted too – she's out there puking her guts up. Go check on them both. They need you.'

Bee clicks dismissively and tries to manoeuvre my hands into a dancing grip. She says, 'Doesn't she just? Poor Mia.' Bee wrinkles her nose. 'Little Mia living her best fantasy where the whole world revolves around her.'

'Hmm.' I prise Bee off, twist free. Honestly, I'm impressed with my own priorities, because I'd love to stay, have a dance and ask exactly why Bee's pouting about me and Clara.

'Girls look out for each other, right? Go look. Out.' I point and shove her in the direction of the garden before making my escape.

4.6

I open Anthony's door first, but the disaster-zone vibe is off-putting, as though any clothes inside will inevitably be contaminated. Instead, I squish across to Eric's room, clean and uninhabited.

The chest of drawers yields some soft joggers, a T-shirt and jumper. Lucky for me Anthony's older brother is a fellow scrawn. Outside the party sounds turn shrill. Something's happened, but the screeches are good-natured – no-one's run into traffic. I look out the window, but all I see is front. Trees. Gravel. Parked cars. Some lurkers over in the dark doing who-knows-what. Never mind, I'm dressed and down the stairs quick enough. I hang on to the smooth, wide curl of the bannister-end, below a wall of glossy, framed Mansbridges immortalised in tasteful black and white.

From the hallway, the double doors open to the lounge, where the mass of humans is writhing to chirpy pop non-sense.

Someone falls hard against my shoulders and chuffs toxic fumes in my ear.

'Oh shit,' groans a familiar voice. 'Oh, I don't feel good.'

I simultaneously turn and catch, as Mia goes limp. Her skin is flat and lustreless, eyes smudged around the sockets, her mouth stuck open. She looks ready to puke, ready for the bench she winds up on every night.

'Want to sit?' I say as a little encouragement towards her final destination. It must be later than I thought.

'Get off me!' She takes one step and folds in half. There is a strangling sound, a splatter as whatever came out of Mia hits the floor. I jump back, but she just kneels as the puddle spreads.

'Bloody hell, Mia. Jesus.'

She turns up a hopeless face. 'I think I had too much.'

'You think?'

I check down the hallway, locked in indecision for a moment. To leave now or stay and delay? Mia's not my problem, but she's hard to ignore. I split the difference.

It's poor party protocol to elbow girls out of the way and barge into the bathroom soon as it unlocks, but needs must. A girl smacks me on the back of the head as I dodge past. I grab a thick fist of loo paper in one hand and the fluffy white hand towel in the other. I douse the towel in water from the sink and it drips, wetting my belly.

Mia's where I left her.

The towel takes care of her chin and her hands, which tried and failed to catch her stomach contents. I drop the tissue to the floor and mop. The smell is bad, but the crying's worse. Between sorry hiccoughs I catch a few words. 'Sorry, Spence. I shouldn't have come.' That's true enough, so I stay quiet and wipe her down as best I can. Scrub at her dress, but it's a write-off.

'Go get some air, yeah?' I say as Mia struggles to her feet.

I go with her to the kitchen, fill a cup with water and shove it into her hands.

'Here, make sure you drink this. Go sit – that bench looks good, yeah?' I point through the doors and check for Clara. I don't see her outside, but it's cold out there now. More people have come in.

Mia says, 'Why, why did I come? It's always the same and he …' She grabs her face and whatever she mumbles gets caught in her hands.

Typical party fall-out. A dumping, a lover's tiff. Whoever kicked off Mia's downward spiral has a lot to answer for.

'Look, Mia, sorry, I gotta go.'

I leave Mia to wobble towards her bench and head back into the lounge, pushing through the crowd into the corners where lone party-people hide. Clara's not in one, nor the other. Mrs Mansbridge's decorating decisions don't make it easy; it's difficult to check for a black-haired girl in a stylishly dark room, dimly lit and full of shadows. In the middle of the crowd a large square of sofas provides an opportunity to lay low, or Clara could be tucked behind the floor-to-ceiling bookcase that sections off the room.

But even when I've searched every corner, I don't see Clara's distinctive dark head. Not sitting, not standing, not dancing, not anywhere. 'Shit.' I jump on the sofa, kneeing faces and crushing bones. 'Shit.' Check my phone and throw it to the floor when I see it's still blank.

Outside the party is calming down to a soundtrack of sploshing hot-tub inhabitants. People have gone quiet in shit-faced solemnity, but I'm razor sharp. The bench is empty – Mia's gone MIA; girls dropping like flies. You'd not think you could lose a girl in a party, but I, James Spencer, lost two. Striding about looking for five foot three inches of person amongst a hundred-odd.

Mia may not be in her usual spot, but Jay and Genni are busy as usual. Stress robs me of subtlety, as I walk to the far side of the pool and tap Genni's shoulder. Then again, harder when it doesn't break the seal.

'Oi, look, stop that.'

'Yes?' Genni undocks from Jay. Her lips are red and slick, expression anesthetised.

'Where's Clara?'

Genni giggles. 'She got dunked.' She points towards the pool area. 'Just after you abandoned her. She was unimpressed, poor, sad damp rat.'

My body temperature plummets. I grab Genni's shoulder roughly.

'Um, no thanks!' Genni stares aghast at my hand.

'Where'd she go?'

'What the hell?' Jay grumbles.

'She was *soaked*,' Genni says. 'She went *inside*. Christ on a stick, you maniac. Take your hand off.'

'What?' I swivel around as though it might not be true, as though Clara might be here.

'Lord,' says Genni. 'Ask Bee.'

Following Genni's finger I stride to where Bee is giggling with some year-below. 'Clara Hart.' I demand. 'Where is she?'

'She's gone to get dry.' Bee pulls a lollipop from between her lips with a plop. 'Or maybe get wet.'

'Fucking tell me.'

'My god, I'm only joking. You're so serious. She had a little water-based accident, that's all. Anthony gave her a hot-tub baptism. It's fine. He took her upstairs. Hypothermia averted.'

And even though I left Clara safe and sober, there's a sudden heaviness in me. Leaden dread.

I take off. Skid on the polished floor of the kitchen, through to the hall, colliding with walls. When I get to the stairs, I see there's no need to go up.

Clara. She sits on the bottom step, pressed to the wall, folded up, staring at nothing. She's dressed in a knitted top and soft black trousers. Expensive stuff. Too big. Mrs Mansbridge stuff. Clara's hair's wet at the ends, but dry at the roots. One long length hangs a centimetre from her nose. Her lips are pulled together. She looks upset, like she might have fallen again. All – I don't know – stunned.

'Clara?' I hear her breath go in. Her arms tighten and she hunches to her knees. 'Where've you been?'

She peers up, then down. Her bottom lip disappears.

'Sorry, I mean …' I run my hand over the bannister and it gives a low groan. I take my hand off and perch next to Clara. She flinches away. I say, 'You OK? You hurt yourself? You fall?'

'No.' She's still not looking my way, and I fight the urge to take her face and twist it to me.

I try again. 'Look, did you go up with Anthony?'

She blinks slowly.

I say, 'I know you like him. Did he maybe say something?' She presses down smaller. Alarmingly, a tear traces down her face, slipping into the cave of her pinched cheeks. I reach out and put a hand on her shoulder.

'Don't,' she says, trying to dodge and knocking her body into the wall. I snatch my hand away. Press it between my knees instead.

I want to find the right words, to say something to let her know I understand. Rejection is hard. Things hurt more when you don't expect them. Things also hurt more sober. 'You guys mess around?' I say in a low voice. 'Was he a dick about it? Sometimes Anthony's a bit … you know. He doesn't think, he –'

She stands up and walks for the door. I get there first, hand smacking out, back jammed across door and frame. 'No,' I say, proper volume now, my soothing tone turned stern. 'Whatever's upset you, you're not going out there. OK?'

'Whatever …?' She unwinds a hand and swipes viciously at her cheek. 'My car keys … will you get them?'

Relief rushes through me, along with a sense of achievement. Exhilaration, even. The feeling of those last few strides before a try in rugby, knowing the guy behind you hasn't a hope of catching up. Clara's sober enough to drive herself, and I've won. Sober girls don't run into roads.

I agree to get her keys and she promises to stay put. I go upstairs to Anthony's room, open the door and flick the switch.

'Woah, lights!' Anthony throws an arm over his eyes and squints at me. He's on his bed in his jeans and T-shirt, his feet in socks. Somehow I didn't expect him to be clothed. I'm thrown. Doubting my interpretation all over again. Maybe they didn't hook up. Maybe she got hurt when she was thrown in the hot tub.

There's a sour smell in the air. I pause at the end of his bed and say, 'Hey, what happened with Clara?'

His hand still shields his eyes. 'What did she say?'

'Nothing.'

'What do you think happened?'

'She's not happy. She's down there crying.'

'Oh.' He frowns. 'She's probably a bit drunk and emotional, you know girls. I'll make it right. Think she expected roses and chocolates?'

'So you did hook up?'

Anthony gets up. Walks to me. 'What are you doing?'

I shrug. 'She wants to head off.'

In Anthony's en suite Clara's bag is on the floor beside the wet heap of her discarded dress. I root in the sodden bag to find her car keys attached to a pug keyring.

She wasn't drunk; that's not right. So how'd they go from barely talking to Anthony's bedroom in twenty minutes? She needed to change after the hot-tub dunking, sure, but is Anthony that bloody irresistible? Charming bugger. All slick, no substance, and you'd think someone like Clara could see straight through him. I take another look at the dress and feel a jab of irritation. I say, 'Do you even like her?'

Anthony clicks his tongue and wiggles his hand from side to side to indicate it could go either way. I go out onto the landing before I say something we'll both regret.

Three steps down and I rattle the keys at Clara. She looks up. Another step down and she turns away.

'Wait –'

'Hey, why?' Anthony says just behind me.

The front door cracks against the wall. Clara flings herself into the night. I drop the keys and run. She starts running too.

4.7

Last words. That's a thing, right?

Like epitaphs, obituaries and the number of mourners you'll attract, your own last words are something you're curious about. But the last words that really matter aren't yours. The very last ones you put out into the world probably won't be great or special. The words that matter most are the ones you say just before other people die. Those are what you have to live with. The careless 'See you' dropped behind as I ran out the door one afternoon, my pointless words to Clara on the stairs, 'Wait,' and before that, 'Promise?' They were the wrong words. They mattered and they didn't stop her.

Yeah, words matter so much. What you say. How you say it. I'm no good at any of that stuff and I know exactly where I inherited that fault. It's a family trait, like holding silent grudges. Those personality flaws sometimes collide in the worst way.

A year ago in Anthony's living room, my thumbs on fast-forward trying to even the score on FIFA and my phone clattering on the coffee table. Could've been any day. It was any day and I was annoyed to see Dad lighting up my screen. Irritated he'd called me at my mate's house when a message would suffice, but I answered anyway.

'James.' Dad's voice sounded chapped. He cleared his throat and the hesitation grated. Anthony was waiting, controller in hand. 'James you have to come to the hospital. I ... I can't drive, but Jess ... Aunt Jess is coming.'

It didn't make sense. 'Dad?'

'James, I have to say ... have to tell you ... your mum's been in an accident.'

There was a pause. My mind spiralled. I made infinite thoughts and plans in the pause Dad left. The pause left so much room to wonder how I'd get to her, how she was doing, because I needed to go now, to the hospital, to get to her.

'She's not …' he said. I held my breath, heard his rasp. 'James, she's … James, she died.'

Just like that. Those are the words he chose. Best he could do.

After I put the phone down, I sat back in the sofa still holding my controller. And Anthony put a hand on my shoulder, 'Hey, you don't look OK.' He peered into my face, all concern and furrowed brow. I started to speak, but I couldn't. I broke apart then and there. Anthony stayed with me until Aunt Jess came. He's stayed with me since in all the time I haven't been able to put myself back together.

And Dad? He told me on the phone just like that. Should he have waited? Would it have been better or worse if he'd left me believing for another hour that Mum was alive in the world?

Maybe there's no good words for something like that. No good way to do it and no good way to lose someone. Maybe there's no way to make Clara stop.

Tonight, after the gravel, after the road and Clara, after the police car ride and the questions and the waiting room, I get in the car with Dad again. His hand is paused on the wheel. Perhaps it's the memory of his last words, exactly a year ago today, keeping those bags under his eyes.

'That poor girl,' Dad says, shaking his head sadly. 'Her poor parents.'

His face is squeezed with sorrow, as though imagining how he would feel if I were to die. Reckon – though he'd go blue denying – he's imagining how he would feel if I were an actual good son, not the empty mannequin he's been lumbered with lately.

The engine starts and dry heat hits me, but I'm cold to my bones.

'All you want to do as a parent is keep your children safe.' Dad puts the car in gear.

'What about your wife?'

'Pardon?' The ticking of the indicator metres our silence.

'Doesn't matter.' I put my head against the window and stare out and Dad's eyes are on me. Maybe this time he'll push it. We'll have it out. Maybe he can tell me how Mum looked when he saw her after the accident. Whether, like Clara, she had grit in her skin. Was she in pain for long? Did she hear him say goodbye?

It was Dad who packed her stuff away. The books and magazines, photos, clothes, all of it. Sorted it out like garbage. Put it in the loft, barely six months after. Reckon he might've tried to give it away if I hadn't put my foot down. The thought of some other woman in Mum's clothes made me roil and I told him if he bloody dared I'd walk – go live with Gran. That was early days and he hasn't said anything since about 'clearing out'.

Time to time I go up there. Only when Dad's out. I drag down the ladder and sit on the boards. Got to check for damp and moths, make sure her stuff's safe. Dad wouldn't bother, after all.

He tried to get rid of her. Like she was really gone.

Now I'm full up and sick with all the things I can't bring myself to say, carrying them with me like overstuffed sacks of old clothes ready to burst.

'Let's get you home,' Dad says after a while. 'We'll talk about it tomorrow.'

'There might not be tomorrow.'

He nods and tells me he knows the feeling. I smother a gurgle of hysteria and press my temple to the window.

A mad thought takes hold. I could unbuckle my belt. Open the door, slide out into the road and see what happens. If it's me who gets hurt at the end of the day, if it's me who ...

But Dad's staring out the windshield with his eyes all screwed-up tired and I couldn't do that to him. Not even if I'm trembling angry. Not even if the day didn't stick.

Nah, I grit my teeth. There's only one way out. Do better tomorrow.

THE FIFTH TIME
5.1

Today I follow her.

It's not creepy, swear. I'm not sneaking after her in a baseball cap and dark glasses, stealing her pants. But after Clara's shouted at Anthony in the caf, I snoop to see where she goes. It's essential detective work, because I've a mystery to solve and I'm badly equipped.

Last night was all kinds of wrong. Thought Clara being sober would keep her away from Anthony and falling. Thought it'd at least keep her off the road. But I failed. There are blanks I need filled, something I'm missing. And, as Clara herself pointed out yester-today, the things I know about her I could doodle on the back of my hand. Even my year-ten crush wasn't based on any deep connection to who she was as a person, more her shiny hair and pretty face. Time to find out who I'm dealing with.

I catch up with her at the quad. Outside the doors she throws the unfinished half of her nasty chocolate bar in the bin and goes storming across the tarmac. Even from a few metres behind her mood is crystal, written in the jerk of her legs and the flapping of her hands. She waves them, as though continuing the exchange with Anthony in her mind, dreaming up better comebacks and coming out victorious.

Into E Block and up the stairs to the paint-streaked floorboards of the first floor, where the only sign of Clara is a cupboard door creaking open. I walk through a narrow gap into another art room, twin of the first. Easels lined up against the windows, a huge crusty sink full of tubs and jars. No Clara, though. I go back to the cupboard door to peer in and, abraca-bloody-dabra, it's not a cupboard at all; there's another staircase, as if this is some cut-price magic school.

I nudge the door at the top of the steps and it opens to a tiny room crammed with colour-spattered benches and stools. The room's stuffed full of art and junk, but empty of anyone but her. Barely eight feet away, Clara has an apron on and earbuds in. She's perched on a stool, slouched over a desk. Absorbed in arranging her supplies, she pulls out a board with a sheet of paper taped on.

It takes me a while to process what I'm seeing. The way she wipes at her face, the faint sound of sniffing. I'm still locked in silent debate when she gets up, reaches for a jam jar and bounces off her stool.

'Flip me! What are you doing?' She rips her earbuds out.

'Sorry.' Hands up, instantly sweaty. 'Didn't mean to scare you.'

'Well then don't frigging stalk me.' Clara puts her hands over her eyes and breathes out hard.

I take a step forward. 'Are you … crying?'

'Are you blind?'

'Is it …? Can I…?'

'No. I'm OK. I'll be OK, just leave me to it.'

I'm on the verge of turning. Balancing on the edge of this decision. But my other choice happens to be two fools who haven't had a heart-to-heart since their voices broke and suddenly I wouldn't mind talking about something real. Besides, it's not like I don't have time for this. All I have is time.

'Was it Anthony?'

'Pardon?'

'Shouting at you in the caf. He upset you?'

'Wow.' Clara turns, wrist bent and pressed to the corner of her eye. 'Do you think I'd let him get to me like that?'

Trick question. I scan the walls either side of her corner. It's easy to see which artwork is Clara's. Her face stares down from every angle. Charcoal Clara, pencil Clara, painted Clara. They're all fixed my way with accusing stares as if to say, *Four attempts already, Spence, really?* I shuffle back and forth. Flat eyes follow me round the room and that's meant to be a good thing, but it's eerie when there's so many pairs.

In the pictures she's Clara, but she's not. In paint, her nose is piggy and squashed, her eyes smaller, her chin pointy as a witch's. Her skin is mottled red and purple and in every single one an area of dark shading covers patches of her skin like bruises.

'These are good,' I say. 'But you know you don't look like that?'

She releases her hair from her pony and shakes till it falls in a sheet around her face. From behind it she says, 'You're in the minority there.'

'Where?'

She shakes her head more sharply. 'I just think it's a fair likeness, that's all. Don't worry.'

She dusts her hands together and turns back to her paper, paints a line. Pauses. Does another one. In the colour versions of her work the painted bruises covering the many Claras are livid green, purple and grey, feathered like mould. The scene flips and all the portraits are corpses, visions of her tomorrow or the day after. Suddenly they're awful. Gory. I blink and fix my attention back on the real live version.

'Good stuff, though, your art. Reckon you should just try painting yourself pretty,' I say, striving for a lighter tone. But, oh god, I hope she doesn't think I just called her pretty. She raises an eyebrow but doesn't bite.

'That's the project,' she says.

'Pretend you're ugly? Weird project. Teachers are cryptic bastards sometimes, aren't they?' She was meant to laugh, but I realise 'ugly' was the wrong word. Realise I'm making a stew of this. A rash of sweat springs up between my shoulder blades. I say, 'They look bruised.'

'Well spotted.'

'Yeah? What happened to them?'

'Life, Spence.'

'Ah. That's what they're about? The paintings?'

She holds my eyes like she's trying to assess whether I'm telling her a lie, even though all I've done is ask a question. In reality all of her features are small and neat, almost symmetrical, apart from that one errant blue freckle. Her eyes are set far apart, but that's a quirk, not ugliness. No-one likes a perfect face.

'You shouldn't be here,' she says, turning away again. 'And your friend's not funny, you know. He's actually a bit of a pig sometimes.'

I start to move my shoulders and then think better of it.

'Yeah, I know,' I say. 'Sorry about him. And, er, sorry about myself too.' Nerves strangle the words. Sincerity is a new and interesting struggle.

'Why are you even friends with him?'

'He's not all bad, you know. He's been there for me, a good mate,' I say on reflex. And then think about it. 'If you're not a girl, anyway.'

'Oh yes?'

I nod. The thought ticks round. But Anthony had a girlfriend – that means something, doesn't it?

Clara prods her paper, and a new mark appears. She squints at it. 'There for you how?'

'There. Kept me company, put up with me when I was … whatever.'

Clara tucks her hair behind her ear, her expression a bit off.

'What?' I say.

She drops her elbow to her workbench and sighs. 'I'm not sure that putting up with you is exactly the same as being there for you. It doesn't sound … I don't know.'

'Yeah, you don't.'

'Fine. You know better than me. He's a great friend, like you say.' She shakes her head.

What I should ask is why, if she thinks Anthony's such a dick, she hooks up with him over and over again. But I guess the answer is looks, money, intrigue, all getting one over. So instead I say, 'Look, if Anthony's so bad, skip the party, yeah?'

'I thought it was an open invitation?'

'Yeah, but –'

'Sorry, is it only for people you and your friends deem fun enough? Or is there some kind of hotness quota?'

'Nah, course not.'

Clara makes a sharp noise, like breath whistling out too quick and hard. I've offended her again. The paintings glare down at me all judgemental. All, *Come on, Spence, don't be a useless prick.*

I clear my throat. I want to say something nice. Reassuring. Some way to cheer her up. I don't want to say 'pretty' again though. She already knows that. Let's not forget who asked who out and who told who to get fucked.

I say, 'You don't have to put yourself down, you know? You're smart, funny, you're nice.'

Clara lifts her head and all her features go small. 'Great.' She blinks and, to my horror, her eyes fill up again. 'Do you know where smart and nice get you round here? There's a shoddy rate of return on smart and nice at the moment. They're bombing in value against nice boobs and the ability to contour like RuPaul.'

I don't know what to say. Every reassuring thing I can think of feels like saying too much, giving too much away. So I dither. Dither for way too long, hands balling and relaxing until my palms feel unnaturally smooth.

'You don't have to stay here,' she says. 'You can go.'

I can. I do.

The feeling of failure isn't new. It's been clinging on ever since this day started repeating like cheese and onion crisps. Maybe longer. But this is a different flavour of failure – because instead of replaying the moment Clara ran in front of that car, I'm repeating the moment I ran from that art room. And that's a disturbing distraction. These things are not equal. I have to stay focused on keeping her safe, I have to understand the pattern of this day. It's not useful to be worried about irrelevant ideas like whether or not Clara is having a good day. She'll have a better day if she ends it alive.

'Girls are crazy, mate. I mean, take Bee, she doesn't know what she wants.' Anthony's tuna breath hits my nostrils from across the cafeteria table.

I smother the sound of Worm with, 'Why don't people like Clara Hart? Like, not "like" as in want-to-see-her-naked, but why aren't people all right to her? Aren't people all right to each other?'

Anthony and Worm gawp at me like I've pulled a magic rabbit out of my pants.

'Are you having a brain haemorrhage?' says Anthony.

There's the sound of a tray clattering to the floor, a drum solo of falling lunch-goods. It's Jay, the clumsy twat. But something's wrong, ironic clapping replaced with oohs of sympathy.

Jay clambers from the floor, as expected. But there's something else, a bright smear of crimson under where his fist grips his nose.

That's different. That's new. And there shouldn't be anything different and new. Not without my intervention. It should be identical, shouldn't it? There's a pattern. It's all the same. Isn't it? My brain rattles through those previous days, suddenly aware of more differences. Small ones. Bigger ones. Things I didn't think to dwell on.

I get to my feet and point.

'Why is Jay bleeding? He shouldn't bleed.'

Anthony and Worm stare like I'm the crazy one here.

5.2

The noise in my head muffles the party. My thoughts are crawling over last night. Keeping Clara sober didn't work. Nor did putting that hoodie over her nothing-dress. Events played out exactly the same: she went with him, they messed around and the regret set in fast. She went on the road.

Even though I failed, the hypothesis was solid. There's a pattern. Things don't change unless I make them change. Jay's a bloody aberration. And because I'm a guy who learns from mistakes, I'm moving up the chain tonight. I'll stop Clara going with Anthony. No Anthony, no upset, no death.

Small issue: only an hour into trailing him around the party and already his patience is picked clean.

'Where's Worm? Couldn't you go hang off him?' Anthony bobs along either slightly ahead or way behind the beat.

'Smoking, naked, sleeping under a bush?'

'Worm loves bush.' Anthony leaves space for me to laugh, but I don't. 'You know he borrowed fifty quid off me for weed and he's still not paid it back? The doss twat. Always baked and broke, that boy.'

'Sure he's on top. Got extra shifts at the restaurant.' Could point out the money shouldn't matter, but maybe it does. Anthony's generous with his cash. He's got more, but doesn't mean he can slash it up the wall. I'll talk to Worm tomorrow whenever tomorrow turns up. No point in trying to talk sense into people in a day that's somersaulting.

Anthony moves past, grabbing at the nearest girl. I manoeuvre between them. Anthony throws up his hands. 'Spence, what're you doing?'

'Maybe you should hang with your mates tonight.'

'I hang out with you all day, every day. To what do I owe this sudden desire for quality time?'

I shuffle my feet then abandon the move halfway through. No clue how people dance when they've working brains. My mind's sabotaging my limbs.

'Life isn't all about getting someone to touch your dick, ever think that?'

'I've considered it.' Anthony's stony-faced.

'What about Bee?'

'She dumped me. Thanks.'

'Nah, why don't you try again? You were good together.'

He narrows his eyes. 'Is this about Bee? Because she went out with me?'

My breath catches in my throat. 'Nah.'

'I can't help that she liked me.'

'That's not ...' I shrug. True, he couldn't help that. But he could've checked it was OK to go after her. He could've not asked her before I'd even plucked up the courage. Could've waited till I stopped grieving. No matter, that water's not under the bridge – it's a half-mile downstream and full of jagged rocks.

'What then?' Anthony says. I raise my hands in defeat. Anthony puffs out his cheeks and blows a long breath, contemplating whether to allow this token of surrender from his weirdo mate.

'Can't believe Bee's here,' he says when the breath is finished. 'Smacks of desperation. Do you think she wants me back?'

I make a noise like an agreement.

'Yeah right, she's a tease. Hey, look at that.' He jerks his head sideways to indicate the corner where Clara and Genni are bobbing away. I know where she is, of course. She's been on my radar from the minute she arrived, but I didn't realise she'd been on Anthony's.

'I wouldn't if you paid me,' he says, eyes still on the girls. There's a liquid feeling at the front of my face, my eyes and nose watering. I try to stammer out a response, something like, *Don't then, you'll hurt her.* But then he adds, 'Can you believe Jay? Of all the girls, he wants to slide into Rebel Wilson there.'

Genni. Anthony's talking about Genni. I pinch the top of my nose. Thank god.

Genni's short and curvy. She's cute, but all her features are drawn on in crayon. 'She's a three,' I say and stop. I slick my tongue over my bottom lip to rinse away the taste of that number.

'Two and a half: too much packaging. Won't someone please think of the planet?' Anthony nudges me. 'Maybe I should cut down on single-use girls.' He lifts a cup high to empty the dregs of his drink and it goes down the wrong way. He splutters and my lips curl.

'Drink,' he chokes out when he's regained composure.

I head kitchenwards, thinking I'll grab a drink for myself and one for Anthony while I'm at it, so he can appreciate the value in having me perpetually on-hand. But, before I've even really thought, I detour over to the corner where Clara and Genni are whispering ferociously. As I close in, their laughter and chatter dies.

'Spence,' Genni says. 'Look at you, all chic.'

She puts a hand on my shoulder and kind of shoves me to the side, all the better to get a view behind me to where Jay's spanking Ryan to the delight of a crowd of onlookers. Lana's watching and clutches a hand to her mouth in mock disgust, while Shaun tries to steal her attention. It's early, and no-one's drunk-brave enough to make the moves they want. Same goes for Genni here – soon as she sees an opening, she'll ditch Clara for Jay.

'You guys … OK?' I say. Great opener there, Spence.

Genni says, 'We were just saying how no-one ever really talks, so what's even the point of tonight? But, *voilà*, here you are proving Clara wrong.'

'Genni!' Clara says.

'Yeah? Why? Who'd you want to talk to?' I try to catch Clara's eye, but she goes from eyeing Genni to staring at her phone.

'No-one,' Genni says, falsely bright, attention flicking behind me again. 'Hey, Spence, aren't you on the rugby team?'

And there we go, now we're getting to the point.

Here's the thing: what I've learned from attempt number four is I'm a terrible chaperone. Clara still ended up in Anthony's bed and under a car. Shame Genni isn't more motivated to look after Clara. It is, after all, meant to be her job, but instead every night she goes running off after Jay.

Maybe I've been multi-tasking too hard.

'Jay's a wanker,' I say. 'You don't want to go out with that guy.'

Genni frowns. 'Thanks but no thanks for the unsolicited advice.'

'It's not Jay you're after?'

'Oh no, don't get me wrong. One day I'm going to have ten of that man's babies.'

'Ten's a litter,' Clara says, still refusing to acknowledge me.

'Not all at once, obviously.' Genni puts a splayed hand over Clara's face.

There's an obvious joke here, but before I get round to making it, Clara places her hands around her lower belly, measuring out the puppies. 'They won't fit.'

'Vierge Marie! Not all at once.'

'Don't reckon he's up for it,' I say, getting to the business of this conversation before it's entirely overrun by their weirdness. Genni's wearing a baggy jumper and the cross-eyed leopard on it's giving me the heebie-jeebies.

'Actually,' Clara says, 'Jay asked Genni to come tonight.'

'Oh?' Bloody Jay. I scratch the back of my ear awkwardly, then blurt, 'Hey, look, about earlier. Didn't mean to upset you.'

Clara hugs herself. 'You didn't, honestly.'

I rub the side of my nose and wonder how I'm supposed to say anything real with Genni watching it all. Not that she's watching. Her attention's wandering all over the party, stalking Jay, and I wish she'd hurry up and slope off with him so I could chat to Clara alone. But, no, Genni leaving Clara alone is exactly how this night gets ruined. And Genni can't be stopped. She's completely mad for the questionable charms of Jay.

I check my phone. Photo of an already wasted Mia in the rugby group chat.

Anthony: Anyone for sloppy seconds? This one's EXTRA SLOPPY

Ryan: Sloppy or slippery?

Worm: Slip n slide

Anthony: Ha

Jay: You guys are gross. How do you get all the girls while all the poets and artists get friendzoned?

Anthony: Calm down Snowflakespeare

Jesus. But then wires cross and connect. And it occurs to me I don't need to stick to Anthony or stop Genni abandoning Clara after all. There's a simpler solution to this conundrum. I say goodbye, make my excuses and scramble for the kitchen, on a mission now. I know exactly what I need to do.

I pocket my phone, grab some tequila and make a bee-line for my target, ignoring the death threats Genni's expression's issuing from across the room as I wind up next to:

'Jay!' He's squeezed in one corner of the room between a speaker and the wall. When I rock up, I block any escape and he grimaces like I'm a bad smell.

'How's your face?'

His hand goes for his nose. 'It's in one piece. What's up?'

'Uh, not much. Good time?'

'I've had worse.'

And that's the end of the conversation. Jay watches me grope around for a topic. We're close to the speakers and the music scrambles my thoughts. I ought to rip out power cables, cut off the party's blood supply, send everyone packing. But nah, in reality it's me who'd be evicted, plugs reconnected in a snap.

'So we had a good run this year,' Jay says with fuck-off eyes. Wonder how long I've been staring at the speakers.

'Yeah.'

Rugby: the only thing Jay and I have in common. Jay's a mean player on the field and he gets a cut of respect for that, but he's never liked me. Him and Felix and the like, they sort of keep to themselves. Quieter lads. Felix's all right 'cos he's dating that ultra-hench barman at the Green Dragon and gets us a percentage off chips. Jay's got his superiority complex, but he's a sounder sort of dickhead than Ryan, who was more useful back when a convincing fake ID mattered.

I say, 'Would've been better if those smug East Grammar lot hadn't killed that final lineout. Dirty bastards.'

'Next time,' Jay says with an air of finality and makes to move.

I dodge in front of him. My mind scarpers back to Jay's complaints in the group chat. There was vulnerability there. Opportunity. This guy's like me, shit with girls. A single knock will do for him. 'Look, don't go embarrassing yourself over Genni tonight.'

Jay's arm flexes; his eyes drop to the phone in his hand.

'Give it up and have a drink? End-of-season celebration. You, me, Ryan, Felix. Yeah? You're in my friendzone and all, but that's far as you'll ever get, so at least you know where you stand.'

For a moment Jay's all indecision. I may or may not have once called him a wanker to his face on one of my more serious benders. I mean that literally: may have, may not. The recollection's foggy.

'Flattered I even made your friendzone,' he says.

'Don't hold a grudge. I was a mess, you know?'

He cracks an awkward smile. 'Yeah, sorry. Heard about your mum.'

'Nah, don't worry.'

'We lost my uncle in January, you know. Obviously it's not the same, nothing like, but my dad's fairly beat up over it and, you know …'

'Not the place.' I scratch my forehead.

'Yeah,' he says and pauses and I hope to god that's the end of it, but then he chances it again with, 'Just, if you need a chat … It was this time last year wasn't –'

'Look,' I interrupt, because another word from Jay and I'll lose my composure. How the fuck does he remember what time of year it was? 'That's decent of you. But no point, yeah? Now … drink?'

He nods and I steer him through the crowd, pressing down hard on everything Jay's brought up. Now's not the time for the past. Dwelling, self-pity, sympathy: those get me nowhere. There's nothing to be gained by looking back. Only forward.

Jay's easy to keep hold of once I've got him, even with tequila in the other hand. Jay's got table salt under one pit and we couldn't find lemons, but make do with the bitter glances I'm catching from Genni who stays exactly where she belongs beside Clara. Best mate. Chaperone. Cock-blocker.

By the time we and a couple of other rugby boys have emptied a bottle, seems Jay isn't a wanker after all – he's my new best mate. I know everything about him – everything important. He's here, now; he's distracting me and himself.

And Clara and Genni are safe together in their corner.

'You'd have better luck cracking on to Mr Barnes, Spence.' Jay chuckles, catching me staring at Clara. I flip him off.

Jay staggers after me to the kitchen. He shoves his head in the sink and slurps water direct from the tap. A few beads cling to his chin.

'Why's that?' I say.

'Why what?'

'Hart.'

'Ha! Knew it.' Jay laughs and I dead-eye him.

'Nah.' I thumb the label on a bottle until it peels back. 'Not interested.'

'So who? Did I see you talking to Mia earlier?' He points towards the patio doors. 'Tread carefully there. Anthony said she wouldn't leave him alone after they hooked up.'

'Nah, not Mia. Don't like her like that,' I say to cover my confusion as I follow Jay's finger to where Mia's lying outside, recognisable by the shower of curly hair. Mia and Anthony? Never heard that before. And I always hear.

'Mia's fine. She's a friend,' I add, though I'm not sure she'd say the same.

But on second glance, is Mia fine? She's on the bench she usually shares with Genni and Jay, but tonight instead of being propped in the corner she's flat on her back, face to the stars. There's a familiar churning in my stomach.

Jay's starting to rabbit about how he was only joking about Genni and the friendzone because he's not a twat, but I don't have time to stop and tell him he probably is. I leave him behind. Scramble over. Mia's on her back, eyes closed.

She could be peaceful from a distance, but up close the details are wrong. Her mouth's crusty.

'Mia?' I tap her face. 'Mia?' My fingers dig into her jaw. Even in this mean light she's a bad colour. 'Mia?' My voice rises to a pitch I don't recognise.

I take my hands off her and put them around the back of my head. Lean my forehead against the iron slats and let my eyes sink into black, but all I see is the gore of Clara's accidents, brutal as one of Worm's favourite low-budget horrors. Real memories mix with fake. My ears pound. My heart speeds up, my breathing with it. All too, too fast. Slow, Spence. Slow.

Hair between my fingers, pressure against my skull. Count. Breathe. One.

Out. Two.

In. Three.

Right.

I tap Mia's face again, then lift and drag her to the grass. I raise her chin and open her mouth, grateful that panic dulls all senses but my scuttling vision. Wipe the leftovers from around her mouth, take a deep breath.

I'm locked in hesitation when Worm's voice comes, 'Red ROCKEEEEEEET!'

I've a new angle on him as he skitters from the house and covers the ten strides to the pool. Naked. Flailing. Thin flesh bouncing. But Worm doesn't leap, he skids. He twists. He hits the pool edge with a sickening thunk and disappears.

'Worm?'

There are bubbles, a sinking shadow. A vein of something curling through the chlorine as everyone else turns away.

I can't turn. Can't breathe. Because this can't be happening. My windpipe blocks. My eyes extrude, my brain swells.

This is how I die; I'm going to explode from everything I've seen, from the myriad ways this night goes from bad to worse. I push my hands to my temples and the pressure builds.

There's blood in the water.

Later I'm out on the road. There's a body at my feet again.

THE SIXTH TIME

6.1

My car jolts.

I'm awake. Gasping. Drowning. Lungs full of last time. Mia choking back to life, Worm's arm breaking out of its skin and me taking my eye off the ball. Clara in the road again. Fragile bodies cracking everywhere. Last night's party directed by Tarantino. I press my knuckle to my eye.

That didn't go well.

'Hello, Friday. Fuck you,' I mumble to my steering wheel, waiting for the fear to leave. 'Six fucking Fridays.'

Of all the days, of all the years, it had to be this one, didn't it? I creak upright, my neck twinging in a way that's new, as though this day's adding years. My morning wake-up knock feels harder every bloody time. The sky's gone off, turned deep, dark and ugly.

I swing my legs out, go round the car. I fold my arms against the back windscreen and lean my head down to wait for her.

'Holy crap, I'm so sorry.'

'Yeah?' This is different.

'I'll pay for it.'

I step back for a proper review.

'Shit.' No wonder she's sorry. 'Jesus.'

The back of my bumper is no longer smooth. It's a scratched patchwork of silver, white and red streaks where Clara's car and mine have fused. Mangled. And this one perfect memory I shared with Mum, all bent out of shape.

All those hours sweating in the garage. Every wash and painstaking wax ever since made pointless in an instant. All my work. All her work. Wrecked. Bloody wrecked.

I drop to my heels and touch it.

'This car's vintage,' I say. 'It's …'

'I can see,' she says in a quiet voice. 'I'm so sorry.'

I turn. Mind cracked. 'How did this happen?'

'I don't even know. I guess I slipped on the accelerator?'

'No.' I grope for her, but she slips through my fingers. 'Why the hell did you hit me? You don't hit me. There's never damage.'

'I said I'd pay for it, I –'

'Don't want you to pay for it.'

'No?'

'How the fuck did this happen?' My fingers dig into my scalp. The question isn't for Clara, but the universe. Why has it changed? How has it changed? Does my car need to be sacrificed to keep her alive? Things were meant to be getting better, but last night and now this?

'This is absolute bullshit,' I say, smacking the trunk.

'Wow. OK. I said I was sorry.' Clara takes a step back. 'Um, do you know we're both late for form room? Ask me later

113

if you change your mind on the insurance. You know where to find me.'

I don't understand how this morning went downhill so fast. 'Shit, Clara, I'm not –'

'It's all I can offer, and an apology.' She waves her hands in a defeated flap. 'I can't turn back time.'

A laugh bubbles up in my throat and wrangles my mouth into a grimace. Even when she's gone, I can't move. I run my fingers over the fresh angles of my car.

This is …

New.

6.2

'What if some day or night a demon said to you, this life you're living is what you'll have to live over and over again? There'll be nothing new, just eternal repetition, everything exactly the same. Even this moment now.'

Mr Barnes rubs his hands together. 'What would you say? Would the proposition fill you with happiness or horror? That is the question of Nietzsche's eternal recurrence.'

I'm back in philosophy. In the colourless classroom, same old faces, bland light streaming in. Sitting here staring into the realisation that this day isn't identical; it's deteriorating. The thought sears into me, rancid-bright in high definition.

There's something else incessantly itching at my mind. The awareness that I can't recall last night's timeline. The established order's gone walkabout and I can't tell what happens when or whether this happened before that. Am I misremembering or are events dancing around each other? When I got the taxi home, was that the first time? No, the first time was tigers on the Serengeti. But I can't be positive. I stick my hand up.

I say, 'What if the repetitions weren't the same?'

'Repetitions?' Barnes says.

I sigh. People are never on my wavelength these days. 'Look, sir. What if your life was happening over and over? And it's not just repeating, it's getting worse. Your cat gets sick the first time, it dies the second. How'd you make that right?'

Barnes juggles a pen in his hands. 'Nietzsche conceived of an exact repetition. It's the crux of the thought experiment.'

'Yeah, OK.' I slump.

'But nonetheless, perhaps the answer is the same. If you really were stuck in that situation you'd try to live it as best you could. That's what Nietzsche attempted to illustrate, how to strive to live as free from regret as possible. Without a god to judge us – after all, Nietzsche claimed god is dead – without the guidelines of religion we should try to live a good life according to our own standards. Would you be happy with the choices you have made? Would you make them again?'

'No regrets?'

'And the courage to face reality. To make our own way.' His mouth turns to a firm line.

'What about the dead cat? How'd you stop it?'

Mr Barnes turns up the sympathy, as though there's a real cat corpse somewhere. 'A literal recurrence of events would be a cosmological interpretation. It would no longer be a thought experiment about moral choices, but a hypothesis about the workings of the universe and time. According to that reading, events would continue in an identical way, including the cat, I'm afraid.'

'What if it wasn't natural causes? That can't be fate.'

Barnes checks the corner of the room. 'Some things simply can't be prevented. And those things, like nature, death, disaster, would continue to be outside our control. When terrible things happen it's natural to –'

'But if you stopped the cat dying, would that fix it?'

It's my worst fear. The idea that this day will go perfectly to plan: Clara stays safe, Anthony enjoys his party, no-one gets hurt. What if all those things come to pass and the day recurs? What if all these days bleed into one another until this is all I remember. Here. For eternity.

'Fix it?' Barnes echoes. I hold in the crazy. He clears his throat, undocking from my desperate eyes. 'We journeyed quite far from Nietzsche for a moment. And while philosophy is, of course, the study of questions, I would like to bring us back to the point ...'

I crush my jittering fists against the table. Anthony nudges me. 'What's wrong with you?'

Barnes catches me at the end of the lesson. Asks for a word. We wait together, him asking stilted, awkward questions about my weekend plans that I evade until the room empties. He smacks his lips, twiddles a pen and I realise, uh oh.

He says, 'I'm so sorry revisiting eternal recurrence has been tough. When there are upsetting events in our recent past it can be difficult to even contemplate a scenario in which they infinitely recur.'

'You're way off.' I shake my head. 'Honestly,' I add when his eyebrows knit. 'Just interested.'

Mr Barnes nods and prods at his lime-green tie. 'But if you ever need anyone to talk to …'

It's my turn to nod along, as Barnes gives me the standard spiel. Sorry your mum's dead, let's chat some time over a packet of custard creams and a tea; he doles out the whole bit. I don't want it. Don't want to spiral off thinking about why this day, this death and not Mum. Don't want to think about the choices I made last year – whether to hold a grudge or let go, whether to be an easy son and do what she asked me and when, whether to be kind, whether to stop and give her a hug or run out the door without a word. Nah, I am not happy with the choices I've made. Not this year, not last. And I'm tired of reliving it every day, in reality and in my mind, where these thoughts go round and round and round.

I have to stop Barnes, so I blurt out, 'Imagine you *were* in a loop, though. Not an eternal one, not Nietzsche's thing and not your whole life. Just one day. Over and over.'

Mr Barnes gets a far-off look on him as it sinks in. A slight smile, as though when he goes home tonight he's going to remember this moment. He'll pour a beer, put his feet up and tell his girlfriend or boyfriend, flatmate or dog – whoever – he reached a kid today. One of us *engaged*.

I say, 'In that situation how'd you get time moving again? Stop it looping on one day?'

'Sadly that question's outside the realm of philosophy and into science fiction.' I droop, but Barnes continues. 'Luckily I'm a fan. I think really what you'd be after is a key.'

'Key?'

'Typically not a literal key, more of an ethical dilemma.'

'Right. Back to that.'

Barnes nods. 'Or a goal, a kind of personal change.'

'And even if stuff kept getting worse, you'd have to keep trying. Work out what this key is?'

'I believe so.'

Typical. I grunt thanks and make for the door. Could keep arguing, but Barnes's philosophical arguments lead me in circles. And, as circles do, it keeps returning to the same point. You have to keep trying. Even if nothing fixes, it gets worse, it seems incomprehensible and unfair, you knuckle down again. Dig deeper.

If that's not a neon-blinking life lesson I don't know what is. Keep trying. There's nothing else.

So what's the key – stopping Clara dying? That's no ethical dilemma; there's no big tussle over whether that's right or wrong. Death is the ultimate wrong; stopping it's a no-brainer. Maybe there's more good I could do tonight. Stop Mia puking her guts up, keep Worm out of the pool.

Maybe Barnes's wrong and there's no way to influence events, no key at all, but it's all I have. Six versions down, there's no hoping this night will pass on its own. There's only this puzzle to solve.

The key.

Anthony's waiting for me after my chat with Barnes. Good of him, though as we walk together my mind is so full of this day I'm barely keeping track of what Anthony's on about. None of it can cut through the endless replay of last night. Worm's accident. Mia's accident. Clara's accidents. I have seen enough blood and body parts to last a lifetime.

Under my feet the tarmac of the quad turns to the tiles of the concourse, as we turn towards the caf. My belly rumbles, reminding me that man cannot live on food for thought alone. When I tune back into the conversation Anthony is saying, 'I treated that girl so well. Spent the cash, bought her gifts, even that new phone.'

'Who? Bee? Did you?' I jerk my head up, in no mood to massage Anthony's ego.

'Did I what?'

'Actually treat her nice? Does it count if you broke her phone in the first place?'

'What the fuck's your problem today?' Anthony says, but I'm distracted again as we swing through the caf doors just in time to see Jay leave the lunch queue. He has a full tray. Sandwich, apple rolling around, two cans of Coke and a plastic cup teetering on its edge. Above him a light panel full of fly corpses stutters a metallic plinking. In seconds Jay'll be on the floor with a bloody nose.

That's an ethical dilemma there: whether to let Jay fall when I know what's about to happen. Not today. I speed up, a quick jog that jostles my frazzled brain.

I say Jay's name as I whack him on the shoulder to steady him. But it's not enough warning. He jumps. Whips around and the tray slips. As he stretches to catch it his balance is lost. The action plays out in slow-mo. The tray comes up, he lurches forward and his foot goes from under him. Jay's face slams the steel edge of a dining table just as I reach for him again. My teeth come together. Jay hits the floor.

I hunker down next to him and put a hand out.

'Dub't', says Jay, cradling his mangled face. Blood drips onto his lips and chin.

'Pinch the top.'

He winces. 'Uck boo. Ib's bwokem.'

True, Jay's nose has a new jaunty twist. A lunch attendant rustles onto the scene, pulling him to his feet and pressing a wedge of serviettes to his gushing nostrils as she leads him away.

I cross the caf in a daze. Halfway down my index finger, in the joint, there's a smear of red. I wipe it on my trousers, but it's already started to dry and it leaves a thin brown outline.

When I collide with our lunch table, Anthony takes a seat and says, 'What did Jay ever do to you?' Which doesn't make sense, but none of this does.

The rest of the day passes in hyper-detail. I catalogue differences, perceived or genuine. Did Ryan always get that question wrong in history? Did Bee always tell me that rumour about Lana and Shaun? Or are these further evidence of wrongness? People turning on each other, people getting stupider. What else is new?

What's the key?

6.3

I finally Googled how to stop someone dying. I'm not proud it's come to this.

Anyway, I've been let down. Even the all-knowing Internet, source of crackpot advice on every topic under the sun, didn't have answers. It threw up pages dedicated to grief and bereavement, which are no solution at all. I'm not grieving Clara until I see Saturday.

I've learned other facts, like the speed a car must be travelling for the odds to stop being in your favour when it hits, and how the forty zone around Anthony's doesn't leave Clara with a chance in hell.

Here's the best and worst thing I learned: 1500 people die every day on this small, busy rock I call home. A statistic so staggering it knocked my breath out. Imagine. All those tragedies unfolding, sending ripples of grief through tens to hundreds of people each time. How can we bear it? How do we all keep functioning? And then it happens the next day and the next, sometimes without warning, always too soon.

No wonder Clara can't survive the night; the real surprise is any of us do.

These are the grim facts I've been mulling over while Anthony and Worm thrash out their frustrations on FIFA. Digesting information and trying to come up with a solution. The key, like Barnes said. There's an answer here somewhere, for someone smarter than me.

I have the clues. I just need to see it through. I need a sharp mind. I need to wake up. I need to focus.

I need to find Mia, I think, as the party thickens and bubbles. Need to test my theory and save her from the bench. Through speakers someone sings about wishing to be numb. Can't blame them. I step outside, hit by air that's colder than before. The people out here stand closer together; the more sober ones keep their coats on. The tight-knit groups make their faces harder to separate from the shadows, harder to recognise. It turns friends and classmates into strangers.

Mia and Bee are leaning against each other over at the corner of the house, both pairs of eyes wandering the crowd like they don't want to look at each other. Maybe they've had a bust-up – Mia's got this sad look on, a bit tired and out of it – but as I head for them, Bee puts her arms out to loop mine, dragging me close.

'Oh my god, little Spence, come warm me up. I was just saying what a nightmare Ms Hargrove was in history. Wasn't she totally victimising me? I swear she hates anyone who reminds her she was ever anything but a shrivelled old spinster.'

'Right.'

Mia pulls a face. Bee's account's inaccurate. It was, in fact, mercifully drama-free. Everyone survived. Dunno what more Bee wants given the psychopathic tendencies of time.

With a feline stretch Bee says, 'Of course, Mercury's in retrograde and it's totally screwing me. Oh god, did I tell you guys I threw my thong at Miss Dunning after netball?'

There's a distracting mental image. I cover my fluster by saying, 'Right, yeah, Mercury gives a shit about your pants.'

'I'll have you know a lot of smart people believe in –'

'Mia, where's your sister?' I say, tired of Bee's woo-woo bullshit. Mercury has nothing on my eternal Friday. And despite Anthony's morning invitation, Mia's sister never turns up. Maybe if she did Mia's night wouldn't end in a mess.

'I'd never bring her.' Mia takes a long swig of her drink.

'How do you know Mia's sister?' Bee asks.

'Don't. It's an in-joke.' But Mia shakes her head.

'Spence, lovely, did you bring your guitar?' Bee pushes her hand into her strawberry curls and her bangles jitter, but I'm distracted by the sight of Mia taking another gulp, then another. If anything, I've put her on fast-forward to fate.

When Mia makes for the kitchen, I untangle from Bee to supervise and can't believe my luck: two more targets at the makeshift bar.

Clara's pouring next to Genni, who's flapping her hands about with an expression like she's ready to murder. Ominously, it gets darker the closer we get. Her hands go to her hips and the sequin leopard on her jumper stretches out in a matching frown.

'Right?' Behind Genni, Clara grimaces a warning.

'Don't even start, you mentalist,' Genni says, pushing past with hands raised high.

'Wha–?'

'She's really the last person you should be talking to today,' Clara tells me.

'Why?'

But Clara is already following Genni into the lounge, spilling in her haste.

Mia takes their place, pouring a tumbler of cheap wine. I take it from her, but she grabs a replacement.

'What's her problem?' I grumble.

Mia reaches over to top my cup with lemonade. 'What's yours? Don't go around shoving people over and maybe people will feel more warm and fuzzy towards you.'

Mia's matter-of-fact; no sign of panic. It shows a disturbing lack of judgement, because, if Mia believes I shoved Jay and broke his nose, she shouldn't be hanging with me. When I point this out, Mia says, 'Just try it.' And glares.

'Nah, your nose is fine as is. Wait. Who's saying I pushed him?'

'Everyone.' She gestures at the nearest group, the swinging of her arm making her wobble precariously, and I glare at these strangers from the year below as though they're personally spreading fake news, here and now.

'Bloody didn't. What about that bastard Jay?'

Mia sips her wine. Fills me in. Jay's saying I pushed him too. And he's not at the party because his nose's broken. No wonder Genni's raging. I lean against the kitchen counter, cool marble pressing through the light fabric of Anthony's brother's T-shirt. Tonight's outfit is a new low – Mansbridge brother hand-me-downs from the get-go – price of evading Dad. I swill Mia's news around my skull, then give her my version of events, less the time travel.

'It's Genni who's bothered, not me,' she says when I'm done and throws back some more wine.

I snatch Mia's cup from her hand and say, 'Stop that. I like you better sober, OK?'

'Bullshit.' She gives a single sharp bark of laughter. I sling Mia's drink down the sink, which earns me an emphatic and totally fair, 'Fuck you, Spence!' Mia's kind of feisty for a girl who goes running head-down through the caf every morning. But maybe it's the cheap wine with the fighting spirit.

Job number two of the night is Worm, who I track down out in the garden getting higher than a helium balloon and puffing smoke rings. I give him a lecture on the negatives of public nudity. 'No girl dates a flasher' and 'Reckon dicks aren't that alluring'. Sensible chat.

Worm listens, but when I'm done, all he says is, 'All them stars might be dead already.'

I'm halfway across the lawn when he dashes past, pulling his T-shirt over his head, bare feet winking with every stride.

Brilliant work.

Still, that's Mia done, Worm attempted. Two down, one to go. Next is Clara Hart.

I catch sight of my face in the living-room mirror. Mismatched eyes with deep scores underneath, worn out skin. It's my dad's face, like these days are passing in dog years, making me old before my time.

Someone ricochets off me and bounces back into the room. It's not yet ten. People are too far gone for this time of night. Everything is speeding up.

My vision zeroes in on Anthony. He dangles a girl off each arm. They orbit his massive body, twirling in his gravity. Genni, Clara. Two feels safer than one, and as I get closer I can tell that Clara's the exception to the rule tonight – the only one not going downhill. With Jay absent, her friend's by her side, and she's bright-eyed and steady.

Still, she's not defending herself against the hands that creep over her waist or Anthony pressed up against her back with an expression I can't bear.

I go over, grip Anthony's arm. 'Oi, come here.'

'What? No, I'm busy.'

'Mia's puking.' On another night it'd be true. I supplement the shout with a mime so he'll understand this complex concept over the beat of the music.

'Where?'

'Garden.'

'Then why do I care?'

'Sweet baby Baudelaire, it's the St Peter's Nose-Basher,' Genni says, arms folded and getting in my way. 'You know Jay had to go to the hospital? You've a hell of a nerve.'

'Didn't touch him,' I say. But Anthony is grabbing Genni and she is giving me evils and Clara won't meet my eye.

I take a quick nip of the drink in my hand. Anthony's broad swaying back obscures my view. 'Don't know where Worm is, do you? Oi, Anthony.' I lever his shoulder. He swings around, puts a hand on me. He pushes. Not hard, but I move.

'Come on. Leave it, Spence. The girls don't want you.'

'Clara?'

'Mate. Leave.'

Clara says, 'Sorry.' I can only see the shape of the word.

'Know he only wants to screw you and ditch you?' I say.

Clara flinches, but Anthony pulls her tighter against him.

Genni seethes. 'Asshole.'

Anthony stretches round to plant a kiss on Clara's hair. She dimples and it's the last thing I can take.

'Fine,' I shout. 'Fine. Don't come bloody crying to me when you're dead.' That's when the song ends and the last word clangs in the quiet.

6.4

Anthony learned to party from his parents. Sure, Dom and Olivia Mansbridge's shindigs typically involved fewer minced teenagers spewing in the bushes and more charity auctions, but there's bad behaviour all the same.

My mum and dad only ever went to one. I think they felt obligated, thanks to my friendship with Anthony. A make-nice thing even though my parents' idea of a good time involved a pub quiz, not canapes. Anthony and I hid upstairs while the parents got messy, creeping down to nick the good snacks and an occasional glass of bubbly.

I remember pretending to snooze in the back seat on the way home while Mum and Dad rowed. Mum was hacked off because Mr Mansbridge had been inappropriate and Dad had done bugger all. Dad was annoyed because, well, I dunno why. If I had to guess I'd say he was annoyed precisely because he'd done bugger all. But he couldn't shout at himself about it, so he sniped at her all the journey home and she cut him down.

'I'm not the first wife to say it,' Mum had said.

'We won't go again,' Dad said.

'And that's the solution, is it?'

Dad was banished to the couch for that gallant display. Found him there in the morning looking sheepish.

Later I filled Anthony in over a coffee-shop debrief in town. Picked my marshmallows out of the whipped cream and casually mentioned that his dad had cracked onto my mum and caused a family rift.

'Must've been a misunderstanding or something,' I offered, then licked my spoon.

Bee was queuing at the counter with Mia, the two of them giggling. I'd have bet a tenner they were cracking up over the rudely formed croissant I'd clocked on the way in. Bee wore her hair even longer then and the swish of it was distracting.

My timeline now is split into before and after Mum. But then my eras were defined by crushes. After Clara was Grace and by year eleven it was Bee. Always Bee.

'Sounds like wishful thinking to me.' Anthony leaned back and rubbed a spot on the table.

'Eh? Nah, don't reckon.'

'Dad's a charismatic guy. Bit of a flirt, but she shouldn't flatter herself. Maybe she's just trying to make your dad jealous.'

It didn't ring true. Not the way she'd been going on about it in the car. Anyway, Dad had seen. I popped another marshmallow and let my eyes wander to Bee again as she and Mia took a booth just over from us.

'She's not exactly hot,' Anthony said. 'No offence intended. She's fine, she's just a mum, isn't she? I wouldn't bang her.'

'*My* mum, you bloody pervert.'

Anthony made a face. Sipped his latte.

'Never mind.' I shrugged. Bee and Mia exploded with laughter and I swear Bee glanced my way. 'Think she's looking,' I said to Anthony.

He checked over his shoulder. 'You know what they say about red heads?'

'Hot tempered?'

'Recessive genes.' Anthony laughed at my confused face. 'Shit, I'm joking. I don't know why you bother. Bee's …' He shook his head.

'She's five stars,' I said. And I didn't mean it like that, not like she was a number or a thing. I meant she was five-out-of-five. Perfect.

'No way. Four stars,' Anthony said firmly and catching on quick. 'Like that jumper Mum got me from London.

Would've been better in grey. If Bee lost the ginger she'd get another half.'

Bee was any other girl to Anthony. For the last ten months I've tried not to think about how Anthony went out with my five-out-of-five. It didn't seem like the sort of thing a mate should dwell on. A petty thing to grumble over after years of friendship.

Now I'm wondering if I should have thought longer and harder. Now I'm thinking he should get the fuck away from Clara.

I perch on a sofa, high up with my feet on the seat so I can get a good view. I've my drink in one hand and the other gripping smooth leather. Not moving except to top myself up time and again. Eyes on them. Her and him.

I'll be damned if I'm letting Clara out of my sight another goddamn time, no matter how little she and Genni want me around. Even if I have to see Anthony's hands on the small of her back – it makes my insides clench, but it's not a crime. His hands run over her the way mine run frets on the guitar, fingers always moving, clutching her close. Clara grabs Genni and reels her in, smiling, all her attention on her friend. She avoids my gaze, but I can't tear mine away.

Her laugh stands out from twenty others. It's distinctive. Proper. It makes you wish you were included, but it's just for Genni. And him.

Genni gestures at her drink, cups her hand to her mouth in a mime and Clara nods. Anthony nods too, but when Genni leaves he gives Clara his cup and whispers in her ear. She laughs and I twitch to intervene. But it's not wrong. Yet.

Anthony puts his lips on hers. She lets him. But she peers out of her corners. She meets my eye. She pulls back and shakes her head at the floor. He pulls her close again. She twists her face away.

I wait for them to move. I'll stop it, don't care what I have to do. Make a scene. Call the police. Burn the house down.

I watch. Wait. Blink. Drink. Blink.

They keep dancing.

I keep watching.

Someone screams. Then another.

I'm up and off the couch, running for my life out through the living room doors to the hall, double-back through the kitchen towards the source of the sound. It could be Worm, broken and bleeding and naked and drowning; could be Mia choking on too much wine. My legs don't move fast enough and my insides give a low, ominous rumble to remind me I'm running on empty.

In the kitchen it's pandemonium. People are shoving through the doors, screeching their heads off like a flock of terrified birds, no concern for others as they push inside. The outside lights are shimmering, the beams like golden glitter through the night. There's the thunder of footsteps on and on and on and I can't make sense of what I'm seeing, what I'm hearing or the fresh, strange air replacing the usual waft of smoke and vape-steam. I stand at the sink and stare at my own weak reflection gazing back. Refocus and catch the churning, bubbling surface of the pool.

It's not Worm. Not Mia. Not death and injury and pain.

It's raining. The drumming's not footsteps, it's water.

I push through the crowd. Screams turn to giggles. Mia gives me a nudge and a smile I can't return. I stand in the door and catch some water in my palm. Rain.

It doesn't rain. It never rains.

I turn and meet the angry eyes of Genni Grey. She brings me back to myself. Clara. Wonder gives way to breathless panic, but when I return she's exactly where I left her. And that's good. That's fine. That's exactly what I want. Except for one small concern.

Her hands rise and fall, eyes narrow, hair whipping around. She weaves her head and stumbles against Anthony and giggles as he puts his hands anywhere he wants.

Clara Hart is off her face. And that's not how I left her.

And as I watch, Anthony begins to unwind her. He pulls her tiny hands in his huge ones and coaxes her across the room.

'Why's it always her?' I bar the base of the stairs, wedging my body between wall and bannisters. Clara giggles from under half-closed eyes and Anthony looks like I just spat in his face.

'Spence, you're in the way, mate.'

'Yeah. Look, I can't let you go up there.'

'It's my house.' Anthony shifts Clara's weight to one arm. 'Look at the state of this. I'm putting her upstairs to sleep it off.'

My arms lose some of their rigidity. This sounds exactly like Anthony. How many times has he put me to bed in this way? I narrow my eyes, steel my muscles. 'Put her on a sofa then.'

'Spence.' He reaches out with his one free hand and grabs my wrist. Yanks hard enough to uproot my arm and send me grabbing for support that's not there, dragging my fingers over smooth wall. I crash against his shoulder.

'There. Be a good boy and bugger off. It's none of your business what I do with her or where.'

I grab hold of her elbow, reach up to touch her face. Her skin is so cold, so pale.

'Clara,' I say. 'You OK? You want to go home?'

Anthony puts her on the stairs and she stays there like a doll. He steps towards me and his extra inches feel like miles. I tilt my head to look at him.

'What the hell is your problem? You've been a little bitch all day. Do you have some issue with me?' He jabs me in the chest and I take a step back.

I see the face he's wearing and talk fast. 'Won't let you go up there with her. It all goes wrong, trust me. And look, she's wasted, Anthony. Too drunk.' I throw a hand in her direction and he doesn't turn. I want her to react, to remember he's a pig, that she doesn't want to go up there with him, but Clara doesn't seem to register I've said anything. 'It's not your fault,' I say desperately. 'It's this day. A minute ago she was sober and now look at her, she's bloody lost. That's not right.'

'She just needs to lie down.' He turns and I lunge for his shoulder and pull. Hard. Too hard. Hard enough. He stumbles, grabbing the bannister.

'I'm not letting you.' I force a grin to soften it. Like I'm doing him a favour. Which, of course, I am.

He laughs and it matches my smile, not an ounce of happiness or humour in it. Steps towards me again and says, 'Spence, let's be clear. She's coming upstairs with me. She was all over me just now – all over me – and she's not changed her mind even if she's a bit tipsy, has she?'

'She'll die.' I'm aware how pathetic I sound, the pleading note that's crept into my voice. I stick my hands in my pockets. Anthony gives another of those laughs.

'What are you talking about? Die? She'll probably hardly even remember. I will put you out if I need to.'

I shrug. He's bluffing. My heart jumps back and forth between this and the alternative.

'Going nowhere,' I say.

His left hand comes up, a swift open-palmed crack across my cheek. My hands reach my face a second too late, too slow to catch it. I'm frozen in shock. Still ice when his right fist ploughs my belly. My knees go. I buckle.

It hurts.

Immense arms haul me off the floor, pin my arms to my sides and drag me through the hall. I have no breath. We are in the kitchen before I can put up resistance and, when I begin to squirm, I'm no longer dragged, I'm upright, a fist to my face and my night dissolving in stars. I'm shoved. Flying. Falling.

6.5

I hit the water and don't stop falling. There's a hard crack to my tailbone. A shock of pain up my spine.

My breath fills my pipes with water and I surface spluttering, gasping. As soon as I'm breathing air again and the risk of death is passed, I'm cold. I'm dripping red. Thin threads of my insides snake the water. The tang of chlorine hits me; at least the water's clean.

I turn to the house. Breathing through my mouth, because my nose feels wrong. My eyes sting. A weight collides with my back and I'm under again, sucked deep. My toes stub on

133

the tiles and pain streaks my leg. When I find my feet again, a sheet of water hits me, blinding me. I'm hit again. Splash, splash, again and again. I stagger backwards and hang from the edge. Try to focus. People are joining me. Bombing in fully clothed. Mad bastards.

'It's freezing,' I shout at Ryan, whose face looks squat, his usual gelled three inches of hair dampened into submission. He grins.

'Ant reckons fifty in the pool last time. Amateur effort. Woo!' He pumps his fist.

'Where's Anthony?' I say. Ryan shrugs.

I dodge falling bodies. The rain peppers my skin, feeling hard enough to pierce. I pull myself out, too slow, everything hurting. My brain sinking. I slide over on the tiles. Back on my feet, I cup my throbbing elbow, go slower. I wind through the crowd.

My classmates tumble from one slick, wet surface into a tub of deep water. What the hell is wrong with them all? Surely no-one's enjoying themselves out here as they whoop and holler and scream like it's all a joke when it's about to end in tragedy.

Bee snags me in her arms and holds tight, hands moving to my cheeks. 'What happened to your face?' she gasps. I tell her and the urgency doesn't translate. 'Oh god, sorry, love.' She winces. 'Alcohol's a bitch sometimes, darling. That girl's an idiot.'

'What?'

'Sweets, honestly, she's nothing, she's so up herself and you're a hundred times –'

'Nah.' I shake her off.

134

I tear back up the stairs, half dragging Bee, who whines it's none of her business what Anthony gets up to any more. She doesn't want to encourage him. I whip to face her. The world turns faster and I grab for the bannister, smacking my head on the wall.

'If she goes with him, we're all screwed. Understand?'

'No!' Bee casts her arms out wide. Blank. A new baseline starts up, thudding through my chest. The stairs sink and swell and shift under my feet and I claw the wall.

'Do it myself.'

On the landing Bee catches up.

'He's really going to kill you in a minute,' she says, and this time she sounds scared.

I wrench Anthony's door open and we tumble in and there's nothing. Just mess and dark and our shadows in the shape of the doorway.

'Happy now?' Bee says.

I walk in, flip the light and turn, as though they might be hiding. I check the bathroom.

'Oh my god, you seriously need to stop this, or –'

But I haven't got time for Bee's warnings. They follow me out of the room and down the landing. Family bathroom is empty; guest room, empty; Eric's bedroom, locked.

It's locked. I pound it. Again. Again. Bee catches up. More warnings. Again, I knock.

The bedroom door opens and he spills out.

'Thank fuck, Spence.'

The panic on Anthony's face immobilises me. It unravels every theory I've ever had about this day in an instant and I know, somehow, I've made a horrible mistake. In some way

I can't yet imagine, Clara's the one who's done something terrible. I've had it wrong all this time. It's Anthony who needs rescuing. He's paper pale.

'She's not breathing,' he says, and I still don't understand. I move through the doorway into the room to where Clara's lying. Her legs are at odd angles over the edge of the bed, knees apart, arms limp and untidy. Clara's eyes are closed. Her dress is bunched at her waist. She's naked from the stomach down, naked from the stomach up.

I pitch across the room. My shins hit the side of the bed, the room spins.

'Clara?' I tap her face. Nothing. I move her knees together and smooth her dress down, pull the straps up, trying not to look anywhere she wouldn't want me to. I snap, 'What did you do?'

'Nothing.' Anthony's hands go up and spread out, as though I've a gun on him.

'Oh my god, Clara?' Bee's hand muffles her voice.

'Clara, can you hear me?' I run my thumb over her blue freckle. Lean in close. 'Bee! Phone!' She fumbles it out of her bag and throws it to my feet mumbling apologies.

'What are you doing?' Anthony says as I scoop it up.

'Nine, nine, nine, dickhead.'

'No, you can't.'

I hit the call button.

In the background Anthony is speaking to Bee, words jumping out of him in odd gulps. His noise mixes with the distant thump of music creating a background score, over which I try to hear Clara's breathing. In and out. Is it real? I'm too numb. My eyes focus on the glint of her nose stud.

'Think sh-she's breathing,' I tell the voice.

'You're doing great, James. Just stay with her, the ambulance will be with you soon, OK?'

I put the phone down next to me where I can still hear the voice reassuring me. Beside it on the carpet is a flimsy stretch of black lace. I kick it under the bed and smooth down Clara's dress again.

'Oh, Clara, Clara,' Bee whispers to herself. 'I'm so, so sorry, I'm sorry.' I want to ask her to shut up.

Time stretches out. I wait. Check Bee's phone again, but not even a minute's gone. It's strange to see Clara in the light like this. Usually it's headlights at harsh angles.

Anthony is wrapped around Bee. She's crying. 'What are my parents going to say?' he asks no-one in particular.

'Oh my god, what?' Bee snivels from his chest. Anthony seems surprised to see her there. 'Is that your concern? Your parents?'

He worries at the carpet with his foot, the rasping sound like a spider in my ear. There's a hole in his sock and his naked toe stares at me. I clap a hand over my mouth so I don't laugh and Bee sniffs in disgust. Can't blame her.

'You did this,' I tell Anthony when I'm under control again. 'If she dies –'

'She's not going to die,' Anthony says too loudly, running his hands over his forehead, the friction stretching out his skin for a moment. His voice lowers, 'No-one's dying. She needs a stomach pump or something.' His hands stay on his head. 'She's not going to die.'

'Stop it. Could both of you just stop?' Bee chokes.

And Clara stays sleeping. I wonder if she's already gone.

'What has she taken?' the paramedic in charge asks as soon as he sees her. Ripe green uniform, skinny-strong and a face that'll never laugh.

'Nothing.' I shake my head. 'Just drink.'

'We need to know.'

I shake my head.

'It's the difference between your friend living and your friend dying.'

Dying. The shock of failure shoots through my bones and I plaster my hands over my mouth, fingers so cold they don't feel part of me.

'Anyone?' the paramedic says.

'Shit!' Anthony steps forward. 'OK.'

The paramedic's eyes snap to him. Anthony stretches his hands above his head, rattles in a deep breath and spills his guts. Hesitant details, as if searching for unfamiliar words. If you didn't know Anthony maybe you'd believe it. The way he gulps before every word, the hand-wringing. Oh yeah, mate, oh yeah.

'How much?' the paramedic says. 'With alcohol?' They have a mask on her. Anthony lingers beside them, mouth twitching.

We trail the paramedics downstairs and out to the waiting ambulance, tagging along behind the stretcher. The gathered crowd parts to let us through, phone paparazzi snatching souvenirs and I don't have the energy to tell them no. It won't matter in a few hours.

I try to get in behind Clara, but a hand holds me back. I say, 'I want to go with her.'

'Sorry.' This guy's face is granite.

'Will she be OK?'

'She'll live.' The doors shut.

She'll live.

The engine starts.

She'll live.

'You spiked her,' I say.

'Of course I fucking didn't.' Anthony's soaked blue and shocked. The face is spot on, but he gets the tone all wrong, like a poor actor with clunky lines to work with. 'She was drinking from my cup – she must've known there was a bit of G in there. I didn't force her. I thought she could handle herself, didn't I? Didn't know she was drinking too.'

Too many words. That's how you know it's a lie. The G, fine, sometimes Anthony has a bit himself and skips the booze. But wasn't he drinking tonight? And he's not in the back of an ambulance. Either way, it'd be easy for him to slip it to someone else. I can see so clearly how he'd do it. Not every time, no. But this time. She was fine and then she was gone.

There's something else. All Anthony's jokes about chemsex. And, if I wrack my brain, a few jokes about spiking too. Not so funny now. My stomach flops over.

The siren whoops. People begin to go back inside, phones at their ears as they plan to flee the scene.

The rain hits my face and makes me flinch. I say, 'Why does it have to be her?'

'She was all over me.'

'Why did you take her upstairs? Why is it always her?'

'Hey, come on. She's going to be OK.' Anthony's already himself again, standing tall and slapping me on the back as he says, 'She was high and up for it. Will she be upset when she wakes up and realises we aren't going to be boyfriend and girlfriend for ever and run off into the sunset? Who knows? Not the best screw of my life – honestly, got ten seconds before wondering if I'd banged her into a coma – but if you wanted it to be you, I apologise.'

He puts one hand over his chest as though there's something underneath. For the first time I realise what a poor substitute 'I apologise' is for 'Sorry'.

'How's she "all over you" when she couldn't stand?' I say. 'Was she even awake?'

'Spence, what? I'm a good guy.' Anthony takes a step back. The rain slithers down his forehead. 'I hope you're sure what you're implying.'

But I'm not sure. Maybe I'm inventing things. A cause and effect that isn't there. Anthony looks so sure. So proud. Anthony didn't do anything wrong and it's all my mad fantasy. Why stop there? Maybe this whole night of horrors is my hallucination. Maybe I crashed my car Thursday and it's me who's in a coma having this vivid, corporeal nightmare. Maybe I'm eighty years old being fed by tubes, dreaming of being eighteen again. Or maybe I'm exactly where I believe I am, eternally recurring, not in an identical way, but with an identical result.

Maybe the question isn't what's true, it's what feels real. We never know what is coming for us, we never know the whole picture and I'll never know I'm dreaming as long as the gravel hurts my hand when I squeeze too tight. Philosophy is irrelevant. Speculate, theorise and question, sure, but if all we ever experience is our own reality, what's the difference?

So I'm here, in this mess. Unsure of everything except I'm the wrong man for this job. Cheers, Universe. I can't save her.

And then I realise. It comes to me all at once as if I already knew, an electric euphoria making me prickle. I hook Anthony's wrist and hold it tight. He tries to twist free, but I hang on. Stare through him, eyeballs drying in the night.

I did save her. She's alive.

I've won.

It doesn't matter how it happened. All that matters is she's alive. She's the key.

I lean into Anthony's face until he leans away. Take in where his eyes turn from brown to green. I let a sour smile creep over my lips and say, 'When she wakes up tomorrow you're fucked.'

THE SEVENTH TIME
7.1

The car.

'Holy crap. Spence, I'm so sorry.'

I close my eyes. Open them.

No.

There's a tap on my window and the girl I've watched fall, die and overdose peers in. She doesn't. She can't. Because she was alive. She was the key.

But here she is anyway, of course.

I'm back in my car. Clara's grimacing at me in mock horror. Mock, because she doesn't know about the real horror waiting for us tonight. And every night, because all nights are this night, the real Night of the Living Dead and Clara is another zombie.

Past the window the sky is darker. Even the sun is giving up.

Bloody dead girl. Bloody ghost. I put my hands on the wheel, but there's nowhere to drive. So what now? My imagination strides off into form room and I picture my fist smashing through Anthony's smug face. Satisfying, no doubt, until the day resets and he starts again thinking there's no issue between us.

I pull my blazer up to cover my head.

'Spence?'

Clara taps. Once, twice, a barrage of hollow knocks.

The passenger door opens. Should've locked that. I crack my eyes as Clara hangs in the door.

'I'm sorry, honestly so sorry, but I hit your –'

'No shit.'

She slumps down, letting rain spatter on the seat. The rain is new.

'I can give you my insurance –'

'Don't bother.'

'It's –'

'Said I don't care.'

'OK.' She nods. 'OK, well whatever, then, it's your car.' Her defences slide up and she swings out the door. And she's getting away again, annoyed at me again, ready to start the cycle again. It'll never end, this. It'll always be this shitty Friday with this girl and me and the ghost of Mum for a hundred years.

'Fuck,' I shout. I smack the steering wheel hard and the whole car judders. It feels good. I do it again. I punch the dash and my fist rebounds to throb in my lap. 'Shit, shit, SHIT.' The last word is a wrench. Almost a sob. My lip wobbles and I tuck it under my front teeth.

'Spence.' Clara reappears in the doorway. Anger gone, all concern. 'Are you …? You look like you might not be having the best start.'

143

I snort and shut my eyes.

Clara slides into my car and lands beside me. She pushes wet strands of dark hair from her forehead and smooths her blazer. 'I'm sorry, it really was my fault. I've had a bad morning and I was distracted. I can give you my insurance details for the car or I can pay. Depends how much it is really … I …' She trails off and I know she's looking at me in my day-old clothes with my crumpled spine and closed eyes. Hear the pause of her taking in the car interior, the rough notes stashed in corners and a tangle of cans. I'm a mess.

The rain smatters the soft top of the car, constant noise like an untuned radio. I can smell Clara's hair, the light, sweet scent of her cleanness, and I bet she smells me right back. I should tell her to go away. What business of hers is it that I'm having a tough one? But, of course, it's all her business – she's the beating heart of this bad day.

'Could you put the engine on, please?' she says, blowing on her hands.

I oblige and she fiddles with the dials until stale, cold air blasts from the vents.

Clara looks around. I want to stop her. I want to shove her out the door. I want to fall asleep for this day and the next and every day until it turns to Saturday.

'There's a big party later. I don't know if you've heard?' she says, quirking her mouth to underline the sarcasm like I need the hint.

'It's all I bloody hear about.'

'It might cheer you up.'

'Doubt it,' I grumble. 'Why you even going? Don't go to parties, do you?'

Her jokey expression fades. Clara jerks her head up and there's a flash of, I don't know, hurt? Retaliation? But she softens at the sight of my misery. 'I can't be a hermit for ever. It's not like I haven't wanted to come to stuff ...'

She twists her hands in her lap and looks out the window at the rain as if she's watching the end of her sentence play out. My lips crack and I'm about to ask her why.

'Spence, I know we don't know each other –'

I snigger, then sniff because it's not really funny. 'Sorry.'

'Um, well, do you want to talk about it?'

'Can I just sit?'

'OK.'

She has her mouth pressed into a chirpy smile that makes me hate her a little bit. That's not fair, though. She was good to me a few days back, making me cake and chatting. Now she's preparing to do it again, getting comfy against my car seat, keeping me company in silence.

Don't know why I can't talk. I'd go crying to Mum over the smallest thing as a kid – dead frog on the road, the neighbours with the friendly cat moving away. Don't know how anyone survives that way. Can't wear your heart on your sleeve. A heart's got no protection like that.

Sometimes mine still feels too exposed. Everything's painful. Not only this day, everything. It scares me. This misery coming back, strong almost as it was after Mum died. For a while I didn't know myself, couldn't find a way out of the vast black hole. For a few weeks all I could see was how I was going to lose everyone and how unbearable it would be each time. Over and over until it was my turn. What kind of warped world's set up that way?

I don't talk about it. It's a downer for whoever listens and a slippery slope. But today, what's the harm? It doesn't matter any more. Clara's sitting here with no memory of six times before. So if I tell her – if she knows – nothing matters, because it doesn't stick. I could confess to murder and Clara'd forget again in twenty-four hours.

And it'd feel so fucking good just to say it out loud.

So. 'My mum died.'

'Oh.' Instant horror.

'Yeah.'

Clara's eyes go wide and I'm viciously victorious for a second. Whatever Clara's problems are, dead mum trumps it. Then that bitter thrill subsides and I add, 'While ago.'

'Do you want to talk about it?'

'No.' The lie's out without thinking.

'OK. You don't have to.'

'So people say.'

Clara pushes strands of hair from her damp forehead, but they stick to her fingers and fall back over her face. 'I'm sorry.'

'Yeah, everyone's sorry.'

When I can look at her and I see the expression on her I know all the things she'll say. She's sorry. Again. Still. Always sorry. She can't imagine. No, she can *only* imagine. Time heals. She's lost people too. Go easy on yourself. She doesn't know what to say. There's nothing she can say. There are a hundred clichés to choose from.

Worse still, she'll asked a pointless question. There's so many of those. How did Mum die? When? How old was she? Mum's life's always measured in stats and facts when people first hear, as though the cause of death tells them all they need. Ask me what her favourite song was or my favourite memory, I fucking beg you.

Clara wraps her hair around her finger; her eyes flick back and forth.

Here it comes.

She says, 'Were you and her close when she died? Like, was everything good between you?'

I blink. Surprised.

'Sorry,' Clara says again. 'That's rude, isn't it? Or … I don't know, intrusive.'

'Yeah.'

'Crap.' She looks genuinely cut. Mouth wobbling with awkwardness and turned at the corners. And I am the worst.

'Don't worry about it,' I say. 'At least it wasn't just "Sorry."'

'Oh?'

'Most people don't know what to say.'

'They're probably scared of upsetting you even more.'

'Yeah, well.' I pause, then add, 'Me and Mum, we were all right.'

'All right?'

She waits again. Her hands are pinched between her knees and her thumbs are very white, but she doesn't wear that sad, pitying look I'm expecting, the face other people wear sometimes that says, *I'm sorry, but I'm also sorry I asked.* The face that begs me to be quiet before I've even started. I get why people wear the look – I'd have worn it too, before – but it doesn't make things easier. Instead, Clara watches and I feel every ounce of her focus. The quiet intensity, staring into my bones.

147

Her question's good. When it comes down to it, maybe it's the only question that matters. But it's not a question I'm ready for.

'Why're you having a bad morning?' I ask quietly.

Clara rolls her eyes and her dimple pops up. 'It's way, way too much to explain when we're already late and way, way too petty of a story when you just informed me that you have big real-life sadness of your own.'

'It's been a year,' I say. 'It's, you know ...' I shrug to indicate how over it I am.

'Only a year?' Clara's face crumples and I have a sudden, awful fear I might cry. I touch the door handle. 'Spence?'

My hands turn into fists against my knees.

Clara says, 'I think it's OK to let yourself feel things, you know? Do you ever give yourself that chance?'

I shake my head. Can't trust myself with words.

'Have you ever just gone back to the beginning on it all? Felt all the feelings from losing her.' I finally look up and Clara's expression is so serious, but her cheeks are pink, like she can't believe we're having this conversation. Who can? She says, 'Sometimes I feel like I've been sucked back into the past. Like all the progress I've made over ... like I've lost years. But getting over something so huge isn't a race and it doesn't go just one way. You shouldn't give yourself a hard time. It's OK to feel crap.'

I snort. 'Great.' And it sounds ungrateful, so I add, 'How did you get so wise?'

She smiles on one side, eyes full of something that's hard to see. 'A year isn't a long time, Spence. Why do you think it is?'

I don't answer. For a while we sit together in the kind of quiet that's nice. The distant school bell sounds and Clara doesn't flinch. She doesn't make a move to get away and make her excuses to Barnes. Her volunteering to be late so she can sit in silence with me is more than I can take. My throat lumps.

'Want to know something else tragic?' I say. I think about Anthony, Worm, Dad, Barnes, Bee, all the supporting actors of my life and how no-one's here for me now. How I don't want a single one of them. 'You'll just forget this tomorrow.'

'I won't forget.' She shakes her head. 'And you can talk to me any time, OK? If you want to.' She smiles politely, the teacher-smile of someone who's doing you a favour because it's the right thing to do. It breaks the spell. Clara doesn't know me.

She opens the door and, after failed attempts to persuade me from the car, says, 'Well, goodbye then. I hope you feel better, Spence. I'll see you later.'

As soon as she shuts the door, my brain pings and I jump out after her.

'Hart!'

She turns and her ankle goes, body jerking and righting itself, face deep pink.

I say, 'You like Anthony, right? I'll set you up at the party, yeah? Repay the favour.' I gesture back at the car.

'What? Oh. No.' Her face curdles. 'No.'

Her shock tells me everything. There's been something wrong with my interpretation. Something that's dawned on me slower than it should.

What I saw in her eyes when she noticed him on the stairs wasn't right. It didn't match the picture I'd made. Maybe with her inhibitions lowered from booze she'd dance with him, laugh with him, have fun. Maybe if she was feeling shit she'd let him take her upstairs to lie down. But that's it, I reckon.

Clara doesn't like Anthony; I've had that wrong since the beginning. She didn't call him a pig in some hard-to-get, lady-doth-protest over-reaction; she just reckons he *is* a pig. Full bloody stop.

She doesn't regret it *afterwards*; it's that she doesn't want him at all. And dancing, drinking, trusting Anthony enough to go upstairs – none of that deserves how her night ends again and again.

Anthony Mansbridge is a fucking pig.

I don't usually go any distance in my car, but today we go for a run together. The Midget's an uncomfortable drive, especially after I've spent a night crushed inside. It burns through more petrol than I can afford and is a noisy little jerk and all, rattling away as it chugs noxious fumes into the atmosphere. But I love being free on the road. And it sometimes feels like being with Mum again, as though, like her restored furniture and her garden, the car's a piece of her.

I don't know where we go when we die. No-one does. Well, except Clara, who dies and comes straight back. But everyone else, the people who stay gone, no-one knows where their tiny spark of soul ends up. Whether it snuffs out, goes to heaven or gets recycled into the next guinea pig born. Maybe it's tied to our physical bodies to rot – maybe there are levels of comatose consciousnesses decomposing beneath my feet.

Where our bones go is easier. The final resting place of all our skin and muscle, the hair that was just like Aunt Jess's and those eyes people called 'smiling'.

Mum was cremated. We scattered her down by the coast, where we'd once gone on holiday and she'd said she wanted to swim through this vast stone archway and see where it led, even though it was October and the air was pinching.

I'd thought ashes were dust. Imagined her flying through like a movie scene, delicate particles carried on the wind in some symbolic, uplifting swirl. Reckoned I'd feel better somehow, like her soul was flying.

Nah. Some of her flew, but the rest fell. There was grit in there. Fossilised chunks of what used to be Mum that tumbled to the ground, sticking in the scrubby cliff-top grass. Scattered, but also buried, or at least trodden in for feet to pound and dogs to shit on and birds to circle. I didn't expect that. Didn't expect the wind to whip bits of her back against us.

Dad and I wrote letters and burned them on the clifftop. We didn't read them aloud, course we didn't. All those words are gone now. Scribbled in a heave of grief and forgotten.

It takes two hours to get there, fifteen minutes to hike to our spot. The seagulls loop in the breeze smack-talking each other. The sea churns beyond the edge of the cliffs. The salt stings my skin.

I sink to my knees in the damp clifftop moss and scrunch it between my fingers. I imagine the beetles in the earth and flies overhead and shrimp in the sea, all those living things. I conjure Mum. Freckled nose, eyes sparkling tired, warmth leaking from her, a chin dropped on my shoulder. Every time my memories get fainter, broader, time stretching them thin.

'You'd not believe this day, Mum,' I say, and laugh and run my hands over my head. Fool talking aloud to himself.

I stay staring out to sea, listening to the gulls and the waves for I don't know how long. The sea is a good place to think.

Not that I believe she's here. She's gone, snatched away by the guy who hit her. Just crossing the road, then gone. But this place takes me closer to where we were together, like going back in time. The sadness slips away a bit with a lungful of salt and the wind chafing my cheeks. Mum would've told me to wear a coat.

I've spent so long wondering why this day hurts more than yesterday. But Clara's right. A year's only a year. Maybe it hurts exactly the way it's supposed to.

I stay out at the cliffs then wander into town for a chippy dinner on the beach. I try not to think about this version of today and what might be playing out.

I need more time for what I want to do.

Much later I drive back in the dark and pull over for a coffee at some bleak modern services with glittering windows and rancid toilets. My phone blinks a slow, regular rhythm.

Anthony: Something's happened. Call me

I sit in my car and make a plan. And I'm ready to start again.

THE EIGHTH TIME

8.1

'Are you sure?' Clara glances incredulously from me to the strange new shape of my bumper. 'I really whacked it.'

'Well ... yeah.'

The rain's started. The sky's smudged blue-grey to match the shadows under my eyes, the clouds sagging in sympathy. A bead of rain snakes the crumpled skin of my MG. It hurts to see it banged up, but this day needs fixing more than the car.

'It doesn't matter,' I say. 'Don't worry, honestly. Come to the caf? Reckon we're both in need of sugar and caffeine to calm us down.'

'Um.' Clara pinches her lip with her teeth. 'We're both pretty late for form room.'

The rain picks up. In the distance another straggler runs for the school building. Clara shields her face with her hand.

Gotta say, I didn't expect resistance, but at least she's considering the offer. If I'm not hostile and angry, Clara's not angry in return. She's got a sparky temper and suspects I'm

153

a pig, sure, but she's kind. Yesterday showed she's willing to believe I'm worth something, that she'll give me the benefit of the doubt if I let her.

Clara might've already forgotten our heart-to-heart, but I haven't. This is me taking her advice. I'm going back to the start.

I try one last time. 'Consider the circumstances, Hart. And look, Bounty and a vending machine hot chocolate – my treat.'

'Oh?' That gets her eyebrows up. 'Two pound fifty's worth of snacks is a pretty enticing offer.'

'Too right.'

We walk towards school side-by-side. When her ankle twists, Clara grabs my shoulder to pull herself straight again, apologising profusely. We break into a run just as drizzle turns to downpour.

Between the chocolate dispenser and the ancient coffee machine noisily grinding out a bitter latte, Clara apologises for the car until my guilt bubbles over and I say, 'Look, never mind, I'd already pranged it.'

She swipes at the damp strands of hair on her face. 'Is that so?'

'Earlier today.' My little in-joke there. 'Don't worry.'

She cradles the coffee cup. 'Do you … why are you being so nice?'

'Why not?'

The truth is impossible. I could ask Clara the same. Why's she willing to talk today? Why would she get in my car and be so nice last time? She wouldn't give me the time of day when I asked her out, wouldn't pause to listen in the first version of today.

Better to dodge the question. I ask about the party later. The eternal question. Why this party, Clara? Why tonight of all nights?

'It's an open invitation, isn't it?' Clara snaps off her coffee lid and blows away the steam.

'Right, yeah.' I bend down and grapple with my backpack zip. There's an old smudge of blackened gum on the caf floor by my shoe. It's fascinating, bloody fascinating. I clear my throat and ask it: 'Only, did you maybe want to do something else instead? Um. Together?'

Plan A: get her away from the party and Anthony.

I straighten up and fiddle another quid from my wallet to feed to the machine. I'm jittery, hopes in the gutter as I remember last time I asked this girl out. Her dismissal at the folly, the cold, *I don't think so.*

'I really would,' Clara says. 'But I promised Genni, and I don't think I can bail.'

'Ha, yeah.' I scratch my neck. Genni's Jay infatuation is a terrible excuse for rejecting me. 'You know Jay once ate a whole bulb of raw garlic 'cos Anthony offered him a tenner.'

'So?'

'Just saying. He smells like garlic.'

'Still?'

Whatever. It's not like Clara wants to lick his face. Genni's bad taste isn't her problem – turns out it's mine.

'Aren't you going to the party? I'll see you there.' She offers this poor compensation with a smile. 'Isn't that the same?'

'Not really.'

'Oh … well, thanks for this balanced breakfast.' She holds up the chocolate and coffee. 'And for being so great about the car.' I nod and she takes two steps back.

Plan B time.

'Look, I'll give you a lift later. Your car's wrecked.'

'So's yours.' She smooths her hair. 'What is this, Spence? Some kind of joke?'

'Nah. Just an offer.'

She searches my face and, for a moment, I'm sure she won't even give me this, but then she says, 'OK, sure. Thanks.'

And I'm all warm in a way that's nothing to do with the coffee.

After Clara's given me her number and gone, I wait for the boys. Sit and ponder the answer to my riddle. She dies and dies again, but then she lives and the day still repeats. Why? Because she still got hurt?

The other thing that's been nagging me is this: I never saw her at the hospital after the overdose. I was so sure, putting faith in that paramedic who told me she'd be fine. 'She'll live,' he said, but what if he was wrong? Perhaps Clara didn't make it after all. Maybe she OD'd and game-overed and that's why it's still Friday.

I imagine it played out the way Anthony said: Clara taking whatever he was offering, mixing it with the little booze already in her system. I try to sync it up with my knowledge of her. Try to imagine her being so reckless. Would she take it? Willingly? Does it matter? Wasted or not, she didn't want to go with him and maybe that's the key – keeping them apart. Keeping her safe not just from dying, but from Anthony too.

It's not only Clara I could keep from harm. Now I know every beat of this day, I really can do better. Save Jay's face, Worm's dignity and Mia's blood-alcohol levels. I can save

Anthony from himself and his terrible decisions. After all, he's not a monster, just a lad making shit, selfish choices and hurting people. He doesn't have to do that, though. He's not beyond reason.

Anthony and Worm filter in and collapse into their respective seats. Worm ditches his rucksack on the table, same biro-scrawled one he's had since year nine. My version of this bag, lyrics tattooed all over, retired to the south of my wardrobe a few years ago. Worm's is still going strong.

'Where've you been?' Anthony asks. 'You look like you've been wrestling hobos.'

'Yeah, you look like you've been …' I shrug. He looks bloody pristine.

'Abandoned in form room?' Anthony supplies. 'Now you mention it, some lazy twat never turned up.'

'Had a right morning. Leave me alone.'

'You 'kay?' Worm says. 'What's up?'

'Car got messed up.'

'How?'

'Accident.'

'Great story, Spence. It's all in the way you tell it,' Anthony says. 'Sucks about the car, but you need to get yourself something from this century. Being ancient doesn't make it classic, mate.'

My hands twitch into fists. The fleeting urge to smack him passes; there's no sense alienating Anthony, no sense beating the hell out of him.

'You're even chattier than usual,' Anthony says. 'Are you hanging from last night?'

'Wasn't drunk last night.'

'Really? From your messages I'm surprised you're even alive,' Anthony says. Worm laughs.

I check my phone. Check the group chat – the one for just the three of us. Thursday night's hard to remember. Cold, alone in my car, a bunch of essay notes and dreary self-indulgent songs on my phone. I look at the shit I wrote to Anthony and Worm, all, 'Tomorrow's going to be hard, boys,' and, 'Anyone about for a drink?' at gone midnight on a school night. The state. And these two reckon that's a normal one for Spence? Screw them and their bargain-bin friendship.

But then, they do reckon it's a normal day, because they don't remember. Not that the day's repeating and not the significance of the date. And that's something worth trying. Stop the party. Break the cycle. No more excuses. My heart steps up a beat.

I say, 'Not just my car, is it? It's this day.'

Two blank faces, one thin, confused and worried, one wide and more interested in his phone.

'Ah yeah?' Worm says. He scratches his nose, expression apologetic. Anthony glances up. I look between them. Why didn't I tell these two at the beginning? What kind of mates are they that I'd go to a party rather than talk? What kind of mates are they for forgetting?

'It's been a year. A year to the day. You know, since …' The words dry up. But then:

'Bugger,' Worm says.

'Shit. Your mum?' Anthony says and I nod, grateful, so bloody grateful they got there in the end.

Worm says, 'Sorry mate.' He shifts closer in his chair.

Anthony says, 'Obviously I knew it was around this time. Exam season.'

'Obviously,' Worm echoes.

'Obviously.' I wait for them to absorb the news. Watch my fingers fight. I say, 'Really not feeling like a party tonight.'

'Of course,' Anthony says quickly. 'Don't worry about that.' He smacks my shoulder.

Relief shudders out of me. Despite it all, I want to fix him, want him not to do this thing and be this guy. We'll hang out, the three of us; him, Worm, me. We'll talk about it all and turn it back to before he became the kind of guy who would do this thing. The kind of guy who would hurt people to get what he wants.

No Clara. No party.

'Thanks,' I say. 'We'll do it next week. Just the three of us tonight, yeah?'

Anthony puffs out his cheeks and slowly releases a breath. 'Just us?'

'Yeah, like, cancel the party?'

'Oh shit. I don't know about that. Why didn't you say something sooner? Literally everyone knows about tonight.'

'Thought you'd remember.'

'Clearly not. Even I'm not that much of an arse.'

Worm gives my shoulder a half-hearted rub. 'Sit it out.'

I rest my chin in my hands. Anthony takes his phone out. 'It won't be the same without you, mate.'

I tilt my head. 'You can't sack it off? For one night?'

'The wheels are in motion. The parents are in 'Nam. If I tried ditching it now, I'd probably end up with some sad sack from the year below on my doorstep with a mini-keg.'

159

'But –'

'What good will it do you if I cancel?'

'It's my *mum.*'

And that really is my last word. The only way I know how to reach Anthony and make him understand how important today is.

'Tomorrow you can come around for FIFA and pizza. How's that?' Anthony spreads his hands out like he's offering me a great opportunity. 'You'll want to be with your dad anyway. I'm sure you've got things on.'

'Yeah, right. You met my dad?'

'The party's all set.' Worm rubs my shoulder a bit harder and finishes off with a tentative pat.

I fidget with my bag. Take my phone out for no reason and flick through feeds full of photos I've already seen. All my ideas are too extreme: torch the house, tie Anthony up, plant his drugs on him and call the police. Too risky.

Anthony loses interest in my uncommunicativeness and takes the piss out of Worm about the trainers he wants. I prick my ears up. Usually I'm in the gym block showering or losing my mind in the car park when they have this conversation.

'Worm, mate, how are you going to afford them when you still owe me fifty quid from last month?'

'Need some.' Worm massages the table.

'Are you ever planning to pay me back?'

'Course I am.'

'Yeah? Selling a spare kidney, are you?' Worm cringes and Anthony says, 'If you want to call it even, my fresh fifty says you haven't got the stones to streak across the party and end up in the pool.'

'Don't be stupid,' I say. 'That's dangerous.'

'Dangerously funny.' Anthony nudges Worm, who still won't look up. 'Go on, Red Rocket.'

Worm rubs his nose. Another puzzle piece clunks into place. Anthony stands up, pockets his phone and stretches, then hops up to sit on the caf table looking pleased with himself. He puts his feet in the chair he's just vacated.

The caf doors swing open and Mia strides in, her walk faltering when she catches sight of us.

'Give us a smile, Mia,' Anthony shouts. Mia speeds up.

'Are you serious?' I say.

'She is – look at her.'

'She's a person, not a dog. Maybe she doesn't like you yelling.'

Worm smiles, rolls his eyes and, even though he's pointed my direction, I can't tell who he's sympathising with.

Mia begins her walk back from the vending machine. Anthony shouts, 'Party tonight. Bring your sister.'

'What did I say?' I whack him on the shoulder. 'Serious. You'd not shout shit like that to me or Worm.'

'You're way over-estimating how bangable you or Worm are.'

Worm sniggers as though Anthony didn't just blackmail him into getting naked later. Idiot.

Anthony says, 'Oh, cheer up, it's only Mia. She's maybe three stars – does the job, but –'

I say, 'Spoiler, she never brings her sister. Probably 'cos you're a twat.'

Anthony looks at Worm again and this time the eye roll's definitely mine. Anthony says, 'You're clearly having a shit morning with the accident and your mum, so I'm letting you off, but don't be a little bitch all day, OK?'

'Rather be a bitch than whatever you are.'

I throw my head back. Anthony calls me something cheap and Worm laughs and I tune out. I don't want to look at Anthony any more, nor Worm and his bobbing head. I wait for Clara. Stretch my arms on the table and prop my chin in the crook of my elbow. I watch the double doors of the caf and I wait. And wait.

Nearly second period, but she's not here. I trace her usual trajectory from the door to the vending machine. And then it dawns on me. The Bounty. Clara's already had her terrible chocolate choice, courtesy of yours truly. So there's no reason for her to come here. It's a change and it's simple, reassuring logic.

Guess I'm going to a party tonight. But everything's going to be different.

8.2

I wish I could forget. The feeling of Anthony's fist in my stomach, hands shoving me in the pool and how, even before we knew Clara was OK, he was only worried for himself. Wish I could rinse clean my memories and swill out the sight of her on his bed. Her dress pulled away while she was sleeping. But I shouldn't forget. There's too many other important memories I've chucked away. They're why I'm here.

It's easy to push aside when he's playing party host, buying you drinks and weed, letting you crash. But there were signs.

He's got a temper, sure. And he's a sore loser – he pinned Ryan to the changing room wall once for a poorly timed crack about skinny ankles after a bad game. Bit of an over-reaction. Then there's the stuff he stole from Eric over the years – money, a leather jacket, an iPad, his ID – mostly material stuff, easily replaced, and it seemed funny at the time to undermine Golden Boy and see him lose his rag. But why steal when you can afford it all? Then there's the way he talks about girls, but don't we all? Maybe the way he does it is worse.

But he's got his good points. Anthony's generous and he's loyal. There's no doubting the big expensive bottles on my birthday or the hours he's sat by my side after Mum. Then again there's this day, this party, that timing, and his refusal to give a shit even when presented with a golden opportunity. There's what Clara said over her art four or five tries ago: Anthony put up with me, but did he help? But I know I've never talked to him the way I talk to Clara. Anthony's never made me feel lighter. His company's been good for burying, but Clara helps excavate things. And maybe that's what I need.

I try to think when Anthony changed. Because he did. We all did. Can't put a date, day or age on when. Can't even put a face to it, as though he's always worn this same spoiled smirk.

Anthony was my best mate, but now all I can think of is avoiding him.

I kill time at the library and find a corner to pull my blazer over my head and nap. Fast forward to lunchtime and I sweep into the cafeteria, man on a mission. This day's been getting worse and one of the victims caught in the existential crossfire is Jay's nose.

As Jay leaves the lunch queue with his full tray, I swoop in on him and swipe the precarious cup and rolling apple. No skidding on the floor today, no table to the face, no broken nose. You're welcome, Jay. You're welcome, Genni.

'Be careful,' I say, as I steer Jay to safety and he glowers back as though I'm taking the piss.

At his table, he throws me a sarcastic, 'Thanks.'

Welcome, you wanker.

I blow off the rest of school. Pop into Bingo Booze, but I don't recognise the day shift. I put twenty quid on the counter, ask for a whole line of scratch cards, then scrub the silver windows with a twenty-pence coin, figuring this day's good for something. But I'm wrong. Shocker. My money's gone, my fingers covered in sticky silver lint. No loss; the cash'll be back in my pocket next time the sun's up.

I treat myself to a movie. Empty daytime screen and a deep fill of salty popcorn. Story about some swinging-dick finance guys who swindled people, lost it all and made a million off the movie rights. Modern heroes. Cinematography, script and acting are bang-on, but then the main guy slaps his girl and I lose my taste for popcorn.

There's only so long I can avoid home, even if it's easy. All the missed opportunities wear me down. So I go home today, only a little bit late. Late enough that Dad's already here and he appears out of the kitchen, rubbing a plate with a tea towel. There's the hum of the oven warming up and in the hall the smell of shoes and coats, earthy and damp.

'Oh hello,' Dad says. Like he didn't expect me. Like I don't even live here. And yeah, fair, maybe I haven't been around much, what with dodging Dad and my bad memories, but my annoyance notches up.

Dad rumples a hand through his hair. 'How was er … how was your day?'

He's got on the polite business face he wears for work. It's a watercooler expression for sipping tea and small talk about your weekend. This is the problem with Dad. The false-fine expression I can't bring myself to crack, because I'm too scared it might be real.

So I say, 'Fine.' And smack on a matching face.

'Did you want dinner? I'll make … something.'

'We've both got to eat.'

That makes him happy. Dad potters through to the kitchen. I follow, find him opening drawers, clashing pans and chopping – olives, mushrooms and bacon all lined up.

All the time he's labouring over the oak worktops, I sit at the table with my phone, but in my mind I play memories over this scene. Add Mum in so she's stacking dishes in the machine, turning on the radio and nattering over the DJs, telling me in tedious detail about her day. I miss it – her effortlessly filling in the blanks the way she did. Not like Dad, who doesn't know how to talk to me any more, instead stuttering through every interaction like life's a speech he doesn't know the words to.

I close my eyes and when I open them it's me and Dad alone again with the gaping blanks between us.

Dad finishes up, puts everything on the table and sits opposite me, nodding over a steaming great lump of carbs. He says, 'It's a bit of a relief this week's over to be honest.'

'Yeah?' I grab a spoon and go to work on the pasta, heaping a pile onto my plate. Always the same words grating. 'Good for you, Dad. Glad you feel better now it's done.'

'That's not what I meant.'

'Right.'

'How was Anthony's last night?'

'It's always shit,' I say, and it doesn't matter that Dad and I are talking about two different nights. It doesn't matter that I wasn't there for either of them. Any night at Anthony's is bloody shit. Judging by Dad's face he doesn't sympathise.

My fork stabs through some penne and screeches against my plate. 'Do you even know what day it is?'

'Of course.'

'Then say it.' I poke the fork towards Dad and a piece of pasta falls off onto the table.

Dad blinks at me. Three, four times, as though he's trying to turn himself off and on again. Or maybe it's me he's trying to reset.

'I … I didn't mean I want it to be over. I just …' He sucks in his lip. Whatever he was going to say goes with it. And I'm on edge now. About to slip off and rage at him like I've been dying to on every one of these endless fucking Fridays – go on, Dad, say something real. Dare to finish a whole bloody sentence.

His mouth opens and he jerks his hand forward like he's actually going to try. There's a skitter, a crash. Glass shards all over the floor and a splatter of red.

Dad's on the floor in a flash, plucking up glass with bare hands until he stops and sticks a finger in his mouth. He hunkers back on his heels and stares at the tiny crime scene.

'It's just been ... It's hard without her. And with you ... I don't know what you want and how I'm letting you down.'

Shit. The sound of his regret. It kicks the rage out of me and what it leaves behind is something like fear. That we might have to talk after all, or that we won't, I don't know.

I pick my way carefully across the glass-strewn kitchen to retrieve the dustpan and brush, hand them to him.

He swipes at the glass. He should stop and get a bandage on the cut.

'Your mum would despair of us. The two of you always got on so well. She always knew exactly what to say.'

'Yeah.'

We do this now. We lie about her.

Memories are derivative. Based on bad sources. Every time we remember we're recalling the last time we remembered, not the original event. So if we change things – subtle corrections here and there – our false memories become true, until the people we've lost are stories we've told ourselves. It makes memories a kind of time travel. A way to alter the past.

I don't want that. I want to remember the things the eulogy missed out. The annoying quirks, like how she'd narrate over films and always needed the last word.

Even the memories I wish I could change, I shouldn't. Every shouted word, every time I made her frown. I figured I had time to be better. Thought she'd live long enough for me to make her proud. It's worth remembering how I screwed up, but I haven't learned, because here I go making the same mistakes again.

I wash my hands, letting the hot water turn them red.

'I didn't think the anniversary would hit me quite so hard,' Dad says.

'It's been tough, yeah.'

'James. Do you want to watch a film later? Together? Maybe … I don't know, *Little Miss Sunshine*?'

I see what he's doing there. One of Mum's old favourites. It could be good.

'Or can I tempt you with a terrible monster flick? Cheap CGI and worse acting.'

'Sounds good, Dad, but I've got somewhere to be.'

'You're going out?'

'Party.'

'Oh? Oh … Sure. OK.'

He finishes folding the last of the broken glass inside today's broadsheet and turns away with it. He nods slowly, as though relieved. Or rejected. I say, 'Look, but tomorrow …' then let the thought slide.

He hovers over the open bin, his foot on the pedal. 'Tomorrow?'

'Midget needs some maintenance and a wax, if you're in? Got to keep her in good shape – she's an old girl.'

He nods again. Places the newspaper-wrapped glass carefully in the bin and straightens up. 'I'd love that,' he says.

And there. That's something.

8.3

7:28 p.m. and I'm outside the house GPS announces is Clara's. She lives in a regular street a bit like mine – red brick and small gardens, too many parked cars – but the houses are narrower. The drive over's a blank. That frightening sensation I've driven without my brain engaged. I check my mirrors, expecting traffic cones wedged in the wheel arch.

7:31 p.m. Clara's late, but I don't knock. Anything could lurk behind red door number ninety-three. Parents, siblings, all sorts of possibilities for embarrassing interactions. Instead I drop Clara a message. Three redrafts go into this gold-plated masterpiece:

Me: Here

Clara pops out the door and totters the ten metres to the car on her stilts.

'You need better shoes,' I say, as she gets in and I remember her bare feet scratched from the gravel.

'Do I look OK?' Clara gestures down at her outfit. It's the strappy thing. Red and black, clinging where it should, stopping halfway up her thighs. It's lovely and she's lovely, but I've watched her die too many times in that dress.

I sniff. 'It's fine.'

I put the car in reverse, check my mirrors and manoeuvre. It all goes smoothly until the end of Clara's road. Third gear appears while I'm searching for first and I stall. Some honk-happy suit in a blue Renault isn't pleased, but hey, me neither. I grind my gears, start-stopping as Clara holds her seat belt.

'Are you nervous with passengers?' she asks.

Don't know why I'm nervous, honestly. Perhaps because I'm delivering Clara gift-wrapped to the scene of her death. If I had some balls I'd lock the doors and drive her to deepest, darkest Wales. Or a basement. But even with an infinite number of Fridays racking up I'm not chancing kidnap. With my luck I'd keep the day she suffocates in my boot or I drive us both off a cliff.

But I have my plan.

The nearest I've been to success was the time I stuck to Clara all night. If Anthony hadn't chucked her in the hot tub, she'd have made it. Now I've a head start: Clara's here with me, we're mates. And the longer I can delay getting her to the party, the better.

I swing all the way round the next roundabout.

It's weird to see Clara browsing the shelves of Bingo Booze, like when your parents have to go into school and two worlds collide. Or when you take a new friend home for the first time and realise afresh that your dad is an unbearable try-hard.

Clara's feet fidget around a brown stain on the beige lino. I say, 'That's old,' but this clarification isn't as reassuring as it sounded in my head.

As I grab pop, Clara bobs her head in time with the faint buzz of background music. I nod back in rhythm and she dimples. The riff is familiar. Who knew Clara had decent music taste? But then the vocals come in and she's right in there.

Her voice is low and pitch perfect, but the words she's singing are not the words. My jaw clenches as I concentrate on the sound of her voice and not on:

'I'm a latte and a rhino, I'm a skater and a beetle.'

I hate to be this guy, but –

'You know that's wrong?'

She keeps nodding, her dimple a sassy middle finger to the proper lyrics. 'Oh? Close enough.'

'Nowhere near.' I dodge around her to reach the sweets.

'Wow, Spence. You feel strongly about this, don't you?' Clara's foot taps. Her eyebrow twitches. I try to look unbothered. She whispers, 'There you are now, instantaneous –'

'Know what you're doing,' I say as she continues hissing nonsense lyrics. I refuse to let a smile creep on. Can't let her win. As we round the corner of the shelving unit towards the counter I'm enunciating the actual lyrics at her, when Clara puts a hand on my arm and says, 'Oh wow, no way? You get everywhere.'

I figure she's experiencing some sort of mid-evening memory wipe until I see she's not looking at me, she's looking at Hannah-who-used-to-be-Jane. Hannah straightens up from the counter and flips her paperback shut.

Clara picks it up. 'Book four? My god, you're such a speedy reader.'

'Eh?' I say. Both girls look at me. 'How d'you know Hannah?'

'How do *you* know my name?' Hannah wears pure suspicion under her fringe.

'I listen.'

'An art project,' Clara says. 'That's how we know each other.'

I heave the fizzy pop and sweets onto the counter so now I'm standing between them – Clara, who looks like she wishes she hadn't said anything, and Hannah, who looks ready for a fight.

'Art?' I say.

'I made some cover art for Hannah's band friends,' Clara admits after a second. She won't make eye contact.

'That's awesome.'

'Is it?' Clara's cheeks get pink. 'I thought you'd think it was … I don't know, silly.'

'Awesome,' I repeat. 'Wait, Hannah, you're in a band?'

'No, I directed the music video for them – Violet's Revenge. There's no way they'd be your thing,' Hannah says. My awkwardness must radiate through the entire store, because after a beat she takes pity on me and adds, 'Part of my part-time degree. Film and digital art.'

'What?' My voice goes all high and excited. 'Fucking legendary. Since when?'

Hannah smiles then, all toothy and a bit shy, and gives Clara a look like she can't believe I'm not taking the piss. And Hannah tells me about her project, making this video for some artsy music students. I love filmmaking, I tell her, and Hannah's all shock and Clara's all, 'Ooh, hidden depths'. I try not to look too happy. There's a gig coming up soon, Hannah says I'd be welcome. And Clara tucks her hair behind her ear and bobs her head forward and says, 'Oh wow, yeah, you should.'

Hannah puts my change in my hand, fingers brushing my fingers, then passes over a flyer from a stack stashed behind the till. Tickets are a fiver, proceeds to some women's charity. I swallow as my eyes snag on the word *violence*.

'I designed the flyer,' Clara says quietly. The art's in black and white with bold lines. Different from her paintings, but detailed. Interesting. Around the band name and timings she's drawn a crowd of girls partying. Long hair, short hair, headscarves, no hair, even armpit hair, this whole eclectic mix.

'It's bloody great. All of this is ... awesome.' Like I've no other words.

But it *is* awesome to know Hannah's got a life outside Bingo Booze. Of course she does, but I never considered. And Clara – I figured if she only had Genni at school, she only had Genni in the whole world. I never knew she and Hannah were mates. Never knew they did this stuff together or that things like this even happened in this town.

Fuck me, I've been oblivious.

The bell rattles over the door and I chuck a wave at Hannah, who's a thousand times more interesting than I ever gave her credit for. Clara tears open a pack of strawberry laces with her teeth.

'You're shocked, I know,' Clara says once we're out of earshot of the store. 'How does a loser like me have a life outside school?'

'That's not ... nah.'

'I do all sorts of interesting things, Spence.'

'OK.' Clara wears a hint of smug. My skin prickles.

The MG is right where we left her outside Bingo Booze. From this angle I can't see the crunched bumper. It looks immaculate again. Reset.

We get in. I hand Clara my phone and tell her to pick the music.

'So ... party?' Clara says.

Isn't that the question?

8.4

We swing back to mine to pick up my guitar. I make Clara promise to read the words off her phone for any duets later. She reckons she'd rather die than sing to a crowd, but I promise to drown her out with my singing and drown any critics in the pool. I expound on my theory that taste equals personality and she claims I don't have hidden depths after all and I'm 'shallow as a summer puddle'. Then she playfully flicks me and tells a looping story with no point. And I don't mind.

By the time I've manoeuvred the car into the last inch of vacant driveway at Anthony's, we're determinedly late for this party and my teeth are tacky from too much smiling.

As we walk to the door, Clara says, 'Yikes. This answers a few questions about Anthony's popularity.'

Clara's awe snuffs out my happiness. I want to say something petty, point out the house is a characterless tribute, a flat-pack Georgian wannabe. Could point out it'd cost two million more in a better area, that being minted is all relative. Instead I say, 'They've got a pool.'

'Wow. That's ...'

'A bloody waste of cash so they can dip in two weeks a year when it's sunny enough? Ultimate wankery.'

Clara's mouth twitches. Our feet crunch the gravel. Inside someone gives an animalistic howl that reminds me I'm throwing Clara to the pack.

The door's unlocked. Clara's head swings round to take it all in, but she doesn't mention the space and all its expensive, glossy surfaces. She creeps arms around herself and glances to the corners, probably wondering how to get rid of me so she can find

Genni and start giggling. To test a theory and give her the excuse she needs, I say, 'Probably going to find Worm for a smoke.'

'Oh.' She pulls five expressions at once, all judgemental. 'I didn't know you did that.'

'What's that face?' I laugh. 'Only sometimes. Only a bit of weed.'

She says, 'I just don't know why anyone wants to be so out of it. I like my own brain.'

'If you're offended by people getting stupid, you'll not like what happens next.'

I try to laugh off that I've just shrunk her estimation of me and point to the lounge where the crowd's already too loud. And really, it's a bit judgemental. Not like I haven't seen this girl blitzed on a gallon of schnapps.

'People can do whatever they want, I just sometimes think they have their priorities wrong.'

'Make sure you tell them,' I say. 'People like that.'

'Of course. That's why I have to beat away crowds of potential friends with a stick.' Her eyes reach the floor. 'Thanks for the lift,' she says, taking a step.

'Still owe me a song.' I shuffle back.

'I made no promises.' She steps.

'Can't keep hiding your gifts from the world, Hart.' I half turn.

'I don't think the world particularly wants me.' She blushes. 'Or my gifts.'

The moment we turn away feels like ripping off skin.

I plan to find Worm, but first there's something else. Clara's over-reaction to a harmless smoke tells me everything I need. It's painful to drop Clara's opinion of me simply to uncover information, but it was worth it to be sure and now I am: Anthony lied.

I go to his room. White walls, dark furniture, a floor I've slept on too many times to count, though it's practically invisible under heaps of Anthony's junk.

In the middle of it all, his bed. The navy sheet's rumpled, thrown back on one side so it gapes, blank-faced, unaware of its crimes. Smug-bastard bed. It only takes a second to rip the duvet off and chuck it to the floor, pillows sent after into the opposite corners of the room. My attention turns to his drawers next – spilling their guts out so clean clothes mix with dirty on the floor. Standing in the middle of the destruction, I catch my breath. I topple his desk chair with a well-aimed kick. There. It's a different sort of mess now. Not the sort of place a girl would stay five seconds. This room looks like a warning. And I feel pretty bloody satisfied.

I go into the bathroom, taking the contents of his bedside table with me. I empty pills and powder into the toilet and they scum on the surface, swirling beneath a rim speckled with congealed droplets of Anthony's piss.

I flush it all. The water churns away and comes back clean.

Let's see how lucky he gets now.

The garden's chilled. No-one's yet angry, naked or stupid. Out past the pool there's benches, lights and a wide strip of lawn before the trees. After the trees there's even more grass where Anthony got rid of a trampoline five years back. He'd be too heavy these days, probably mangle the rusty springs on his way through the rubber. The image of Anthony thudding to the ground puts a smile on me.

I spy a stickman wedged under a fir. Walk towards it on a hunch, rewarded when it fattens out to Worm slumped under the trees.

'Here on your own?' I say and sink down beside him onto the damp grass.

''S nice,' he says, pointing.

Worm's not wrong about the view. The house is glamorous from a distance, golden and white, the pool a perfect oblong of turquoise, patio pale and slick. The sky bears down, heavy, blue, while all the tiny people party. It's all Gatsby from here.

'Thought you weren't coming,' Worm says.

'Yeah, changed my mind.'

Worm thumbs his lighter. 'We were worried. Bailing out of school like that. Not a Spence move, is it?'

'Who was worried?'

'Everyone.' Worm shuffles a tobacco pouch from his pocket then takes out a joint and holds it close to his nose, expression serious as a sommelier inhaling something fine and old.

'Not Anthony. He only worries about himself.'

Worm looks at the sky. He clamps his spliff between his teeth and flicks his lighter. Mini-fireworks spark. No flame. He says, 'All them stars, yeah? They're probably already dead.'

'Who cares?'

'Exactly.'

'When's the last time Anthony asked you about anything real?'

Worm slumps back against the tree and re-focuses on the air above my head. 'When did you?'

And ouch. Fair point. Worm's lighter sparks and flames, and he holds it in front of his face, then extinguishes it in a puff of smoke.

Through clenched teeth he says, 'Ever think about how people always give a damn about the big animals? Tigers, rhinos, them. No-one ever cares some toad went extinct last week.'

'Right, yeah. I guess.'

'Toads don't get the breaks.'

It's true, toads do not get the press they deserve. But toads are not what I'm here to discuss. 'Anthony's not just a bad friend, you know? He's shit to girls, Worm.'

'Doesn't stop 'em.'

'But it's not right.'

'Lots of stuff isn't right.' He takes a deep drag.

'You ever been with a girl, Worm? Like, *really*?' Because I spy his bullshit machinery turning.

'Too busy.' He puffs out three smoke rings. 'Ah, screw it. Who'd want me? I'm a toad.' His face crumples for a moment, before it disappears in another thick puff of smoke. From behind it he adds, 'Or a worm.'

I reach out and rub his shoulder. Worm. Gross and unfunny, though sometimes funny – I guess law of averages – and somewhere in time, in a version of this day, Worm made a bad call. One he didn't repeat. Since the first time Worm didn't go in that room, but Anthony did again and again. There's a difference, I think.

Worm's not rotten to his marrow. He's a follower, that's his problem.

'You even like that nickname?' I say.

'Would you?'

My neck heats up. Guess now I think about it, I never asked. 'Worm' stuck so easily and quickly. And for nothing – just one time Mr Taylor called 'Wormley' instead of 'Worley' on the register and Anthony never let it die. Wormley became Worm and there was nothing he could do. His real name's Gary, poor bastard; Worm seemed almost an improvement at the time.

'Don't streak for fifty quid. It's messed up. I'll pay you not to, OK?' I say. 'You don't even have to repay me.'

Worm shifts on the grass, squints suspiciously and I shrug like, yeah, who's Mr Moneybags now? Fifty quid's an eye-watering hit on my personal finances, sure. But it's worth it.

Of course, there's always the chance my generosity will get wiped out by another loop of this day.

'I'll damn well pay you,' Worm says.

'Done.' I fist-bump his shoulder.

He offers me the joint, puffs a smoke ring. I breathe in the warm, dank scent of Worm's seconds.

'You'll stay safe, yeah?' I say before I go.

Worm shuts one eye and shoots his fingers at me.

Fifteen minutes later I'm scuttling through the house, head down. People are jammed together, prone to stepping back onto my toes and I'm jabbed in the face by multiple elbows. But Clara's exactly where I expect her, crammed in a corner with Genni, giggling till her face goes red.

'Spence, look at you, all chic.' Genni looks through me; guess Jay's around. I rumple my hair and glance down at my T-shirt. Stripes. Chic as a block of cheese.

'Decided what tune you'll be cranking out later?' I ask Clara.

She smooths her hair back even though it's perfect. 'You seem to have misplaced your guitar.'

'Stashed it, don't fret.'

Genni says, 'Mon dieu, I'd pay money to see the great Clara Hart sing in public.'

'Sadly there's not enough money in the world,' Clara says.

'Doesn't know the words,' I add.

Genni says, 'Oh, you're one of those! Clara isn't confined by your narrow bourgeois concepts such as "correct" lyrics. Free your mind, you robot.'

'Sing the nonsense,' Clara agrees. The girls link arms. I'm wondering how to extricate Clara from Genni's evil clutches when it happens for me. They must communicate something without words – just the widening of eyes, the smallest nod – because Genni says, 'Ohmygod, this drink is too dry,' while dramatically sloshing her half-full cup. She unwinds herself from Clara and the conversation and disappears into the crowd before I know what's happening.

As I watch her go, I clock him. Anthony, standing in the doorway, scanning the scene. I duck out of sight as his spotlight turns my way.

Clara laughs. 'Are you actually hiding?'

'Get down here.' I motion and she drops to my level.

I've flushed Anthony's stash, but I'm not sure that'll keep Clara safe. Those first few times he hurt her, she wasn't spiked, I reckon. Alone at the party after Genni and Jay hooked up, Clara had a bad case of the party-nerves and tried to drown them – I do the same. Frequently. The time he chucked her in

180

the hot tub she was sober too. I don't like to think about the way she shivered on the stairs and stared into nothing or the stupid things I said to her and how she could barely talk. Shit. I didn't understand then, but I get it now.

It's not drugs, it's opportunities – that's what Anthony uses. Clara'll never be safe. Not with him around. Not when he can twist events a million different ways to get her alone. I need to keep her with me and, crucially, away from him. If not out of the party, at least out of sight and mind.

Sometimes the simplest solutions are the best. I say, 'Need to get out of here.'

'Oh, we do? Why's that?'

'Um. Reasons. Look, come here.' I take her hand, just for ease. She lets me and I stash that fact in my brain for later. 'We're going treasure hunting.'

The crowd creates cover. We stay low, weaving our way towards the hall. Clara's breath shudders with laughter, her hand is hot in mine. I shove her ahead of me as we thunder up the stairs. We arrive panting on the landing.

'This is illegal,' she whispers.

'No going back.'

Not for her, not for me. Here we go.

8.5

The first rule of the Mansbridge House Treasure Hunt is: there are no rules. When posh folk jaunt off leaving their house in the hands of their unreliable son, they're practically begging to be ransacked. Their personality-free décor makes it extra-tempting, an invitation to dig for buried weirdness.

Upstairs there are cupboards, drawers and dark spaces galore. Upstairs is also safe from Anthony's devious eyes, so it's my chance to make him forget Clara exists. Although it's tactical, it's also fun. Who wouldn't enjoy delving into the random shit rich people pack their homes with? This isn't my first rodeo, but Clara's better company than my usual partner in crime. Give Worm his credit, mind, he has a fine eye for a hiding spot.

Mr Mansbridge's den's all dark wood with framed movie posters on the walls. *Shutter Island*, *A Clockwork Orange*, *Rope*. He's a man after my own heart until I see the other wall lined with Bond: *Dr No*, *Goldfinger*, *Casino Royale*, yeah, classics. But *Moonraker*? Have a word.

Clara runs a miniature Aston Martin along a bookshelf. She lets a low 'Neooow' noise out from her lips and ploughs the car into a film-case. She flips it, a silent scream on her mouth until the car lands in slow-mo upside down. Hands to the side of her face in faux-shock she says, 'There were no survivors.'

I grimace and push on our scavenger hunt. As we search, we natter and it's nice. We find some cracking stuff. Old photos of nerdy-kid Anthony; a dodgy tiger-print kimono Worm'd love; a box full of teaspoons which cracks us up for a full five minutes; and Anthony's parents' sex toys, which turn the laughter awkward. We even walk in on a couple of rulebreakers sneakily getting it on in the family bathroom, but we shut the door and retreat without saying a word. What we don't find is any trace of Anthony's childhood Lego obsession, so I guess Mr Mansbridge's famous year-nine purge was successful. Lego's for kids apparently, but miniature spy cars? Check the double standards on that.

Anthony's brother Eric's room houses plenty of travel tat. A brightly painted didgeridoo, bongos and a Spanish guitar I guarantee Eric can't play. It's out of tune; still, I strum some wonky chords and Clara smacks a beat on the drums, but refuses to sing.

'You'll only complain about my lyrical freestyling,' Clara says and giggles.

'Dunno about that. Coming round to the idea. This day doesn't have any rules after all.'

Clara's forehead crinkles. She puts the drums aside and strokes the quilt.

'Is Anthony's brother nice?'

'Better than Anthony.' I pick up a snow globe with a tiny Empire State inside. 'But who's worse than Anthony?'

'Why are boys always so casually rude about their friends?'

'You're the one said he was a pig.'

'Did I?' Her face twists again. Ah, yeah, wrong day.

'You should've. You're too nice.'

Her face splits in exaggerated outrage. Full of good expressions, this girl.

'What? Hardly an insult,' I say as I steer her from the room and into the one across the landing.

'No? "Nice" is definitely code for "intensely boring".'

'Nah.' The next door takes us to some guest room. Cloying smell of citrus and spice, basket of mini-toiletries in the middle of the bed like it's a hotel. Fancy. 'You're not boring, Hart. You're different, you know? Properly unlike other girls.'

'No girls are like the other girls. Just admit you don't really know any.'

'Fuck. All right. Look, nice's good, OK?'

'It's for old people, biscuits and bubble bath.'

'Better than shitty and disappointing like most people.' I'm still holding the snow globe from Eric's room. Glitter chunks rain down, bigger than the faceless figures staring from the tower. I catch my reflection in the dark glass of the window. Tired black eyes.

'You're such a pessimist,' Clara says.

There's an explosion of laughter downstairs, then a lull. Someone probably fell down or vommed. Or maybe Worm streaked after all. Maybe he's floating belly-up. But outside I can't see any bodies, only the patio and Bee sitting on the grass where I'd usually be with my guitar. She's chatting away, Mia beside her looking glum again. Bee nudges Mia and points to the sky. She waves her hands wide and her mouth forms words I can't hear. Can she see Mercury in retrograde? Is that how it works?

I don't feel anything for Bee. Not even while she squirms on the grass. No twinge of regret, no sense of betrayal and only the faintest attraction. She's beautiful, yeah, but I can't seem to remember why it was such a wrench when she went out with Anthony, not me. It's a relief. That resentment's been lingering too long.

'Do you reckon people change?' I ask. 'For good or bad. Do you think they really can?'

'Yes,' Clara says. Quiet now. 'Definitely. I hope this isn't who we end up being eventually. How boring would that be?'

'What if we're all getting worse?'

'Why would that be true?'

Even though Clara's safe up here, I begin stewing some pre-emptive misery at the inevitability of losing her again. As though by talking about Anthony we've summoned him here to wreck our night. All my optimism about this version of today drains away. I was sure before, but now I look at my hands, clenching too hard around the snow globe, my knuckles quivering. My hands don't look sure.

The room's dim. Clara's features stand out, cheeks bright and round. A dimple, a pinprick blue freckle. Repeating shapes within shapes. Sweeping curve, comma, dot. I could run my thumb over the semi-circle at the top of her lip, but no. Get a grip, Spence. It's not OK to have weird thoughts about this girl.

'You're a good guy, Spence.' Clara steps towards me, eyes sparkling with humour as she adds, 'Not like the other guys.' Her chin tips down, but she looks at me. She's close. I wish I'd had a drink after all. My mouth cracks open. My foot shuffles forward an inch.

'Nah.'

She's still looking.

'I thought, maybe –' I start. 'Do you remember …?' Then stop. It's stupid, that thought I almost had. The folly. The time I asked her out and she shot me down. She wouldn't remember and it's not smart to remind her.

'Remember what?' she says.

I look outside again. 'We could get out of here.'

'The window? It's a long drop.' Clara looks too. 'But yeah, I probably should find Genni and –'

'Nah. Not down there. Can't we leave? Drive?'

'Where would we go?'

I shake my head. We could go anywhere, do anything. We could sit in my car in a Tesco car park and have a better time. Desperation scrubs my mind clean and I can't think of anywhere. Nowhere exists except this party.

'You really like her, don't you?' Clara says. I blink and refocus on where my fuzzy vision drifted. Bee whispering in Mia's ear. Of course Clara knows I used to like Bee. It must be such a joke in our year, everyone knowing how I pined over my best mate's girl.

'Nah. Way over that.'

'Oh? Oh right, OK,' Clara doesn't sound OK. Out the window Anthony approaches the girls. He locks his arms around Bee from behind and lifts her, arms pinned at her sides, legs wiggling, mouth screaming with angry laughter. I step into the window to watch Bee squirm free and punch his arm. Nervous, shivery energy jolts through me, an urge to leg it downstairs and jab Anthony in the throat. My fists clench.

Clara's watched the events outside too. She's watched me. Her expression's gone blank. She fixes her gaze out the window and says, 'We should head back downstairs. You've probably got more important people to hang out with.'

'I don't.'

'Well …' She gives her head a quick, dismissive wobble. The heat rises again and sweat springs up in awkward places. I don't know what I've done. Don't know why she's gone cold. Outside down below us Anthony is still talking to Bee.

I say, 'I'm not jealous.'

'It's none of my business,' Clara says. 'But actually I need to –'

'Nah, don't be like that.'

I step forward. My face twitches and fails to smile as I put my hands on Clara's shoulders, holding her still. Exactly where she needs to stay.

Her eyes widen. 'Umm, Spence?' She puts a hand up and twists free, because she wants to go downstairs. Down there where he is. Panic rushes through me, strong and fierce; I grab her wrist.

'You can't,' I say.

Clara stares like I've lost my mind. And all of this happened way too fast, accelerating from philosophical wonderings to rejection in five seconds flat. But now time slows down to compensate and my watering eyes fix on the freckle on her cheek and the glossy black of her hair and my hand on her skin and I breathe to stay calm. Because I can fix this.

Clara's eyebrows furrow and her mouth opens and this is the moment.

I put my mouth on hers. Too quick. My teeth hard behind my lips.

Clara wrenches away. Grunts. She pushes me, but she's the one who stumbles backwards. Her elbow hits the window with a loud thunk. 'What the hell, Spence? Ouch.' She touches her mouth. 'Why would you do that?'

My mouth feels bruised. My chest heaves. What a stupid question! What am I meant to say – that I like her? Nothing's so pathetic as those three words said out loud.

'Thought you wanted me to,' I say instead. I glance through the window to where Anthony and Bee are standing.

Anthony's looking up. Right at me. And I hope he doesn't see, can't see through the window. But a broad grin splits his face and he lifts his fist in the air and swings it around, his mouth round in silent whoops as though Clara and I are a spectator sport and I'm winning.

I never win.

Worse, Clara's watching. Her hand now gripping her elbow where she fell. 'Are you messing with me?'

'What?'

'Is that what all this is today?'

I shake my head. Baffled by this line of questioning.

'What was the plan, Spence? Where were you going to take me?'

'Woah. Nowhere.' I hold up my hands, cloudy from the kiss. Adrenaline mixed with a sick slick of regret that this is how I chose to make my move. Making a hash of things in the Mansbridge house. 'You're the one who hit my car.'

'And that's why you're messing –'

'No!'

'Then why were you so desperate to leave?'

I can't tell her that.

'Whatever,' she says. 'I'm going downstairs.'

'No.' I reach and she dodges. 'Clara, come on.'

'You were right. People are disappointing,' she says. 'And I guess they don't change.'

Her expression closes down. She steps towards the door. Away from me. Towards the party. Towards him. And she's setting in motion a chain of events I know like my favourite movie; scene after scene, I know how it goes. There's no twist ending here.

I won't let it happen. And if she won't stay here with me, she needs to go. Time to change the script.

'Yeah, that's right.' I force a harsh laugh and Clara's walk falters.

'Go on, then,' I jeer, sounding nothing like me. 'Go running back to your mate. Your only mate. God knows no-one else is bothered. Why're you even here tonight, Hart?'

Her head turns to the side, eyes shiny as glass.

'You were a bet,' I say. 'But I couldn't even stomach that. Who'd ever want to get with someone like you?'

My face locks in a sneer. I'm heavy. All my feelings sink down, down, down to my feet where they can't be felt and can't betray me. It needs to be done. Get Clara out of this house, whatever the cost.

'No-one bloody likes you down there,' I say. 'Not one.'

I watch it land. She flinches. I think she'll run, but she doesn't.

She turns and says, in the smallest voice I've ever heard, 'Thanks.'

She walks away. All calm. All dignified. I go into Anthony's room so I can watch the front drive, waiting for her to leave. Hands in my pockets to stop them shaking.

8.6

She's gone.

Exactly what I wanted, right? That's what I tell myself. Gone. Exited the party. Grabbed her mate and left, the two of them squealing away in Genni's car. Anyone would think I'd be bopping my way through the party, swigging a celebratory beer. The night's been a rip-roaring success. Far as I know, Worm's clothes stayed on, Clara's out and safe. So why do I feel like all my lights have been switched off?

Anyway, I'm not done yet. One last order of business.

It takes me an age. A tedious twenty minutes or more breathing the warm, sour stink of too many people. Everyone in this place gets too close. In my face, on my feet. Their pointy elbows in my ribs and obnoxious laughter battering my ears. The weight of the night and the heat of the house press down on me and my head starts to throb.

I should be done here, only I'm not. I'm searching again.

Mia. She turns up in the last place I look, when I barge to the front of the loo queue and the girl behind me says, 'Umm, good luck. Mia Turner's in there HAVING A BREAKDOWN.' She punctuates this with a fist to the door. 'But I'm next.'

Bingo. I try the handle.

'Did I already try that, or am I an idiot?' says the girl, hopping from foot to foot. I ignore her full-bladdered anger and fiddle with the outside of the lock. Wide and round, it has a long slot right down the centre like an oversized screw.

I know this trick. We rescued a passed-out Worm once before. He was pretty grateful until we used the same trick a week later to barge in on him having a shit.

'Give me a minute,' I tell no-one in particular and head for the kitchen. After a rifle around the kitchen drawers, I bring back a thin, blunt knife, which slots perfectly into the external bolt. With a careful twist and a click of the lock, the bathroom door swings open. Inside on the black and white tiles, Mia's slumped around the base of the toilet in a haze of soft, dark hair.

'Is every single post-puberty boy a closet pervert?' Bee says as she comes out of nowhere to wrap her arms around my waist. 'You can't illegally break into an occupied toilet.'

I tug her inside and shut the door on the rest of the crowd. And then it's a towel, the sink, a damp cloth to wipe Mia's face, and paper to wipe down the rim. Meanwhile, Bee sits Mia up, gets her purse and phone. She uses Mia's finger to unlock the screen and dials Mrs Turner to arrange a pick-up.

'Should've done this seven turns ago,' I tell Mia as Bee gives directions.

'I shouldn't have come.' Mia's mouth turns down. She sniffs and runs her thumb under her nose. She rattles off this string of words without air, all, 'What's wrong with me?' and 'Why do I do this?' and then drops her wet face to her knees and moans, 'I want to feel better.'

I say, 'You can't keep doing this, Mia. Been there myself and all I did was rack up regrets.' Like letting a friend die over and over again. Letting a friend get harassed and drugged.

I bodge Mia's shoulder with mine. No longer sniffling, she shakes her head. Fair enough, I'm being a patronising wanker.

'See you soon,' Bee tells the phone and then to Mia: 'Twenty minutes to stop puking and look parent-ready. Let's get you presentable.'

Bee sticks her arms under Mia's pits and hauls her up without fuss. They stumble over to the sink so Bee can do a better job of helping Mia get washed.

'So what happened tonight?' I ask Mia, a memory sticking with me from a few times ago. She fell out with someone, I reckon, but not Bee apparently.

'God, Spence, I don't think she's in the mood to chat,' Bee says. 'Could you be helpful, or leave?'

I choose the latter.

I head home and slam the door shut. What a night! Taking the facts at face value, it was successful and all. No-one was hurt, no-one died, Clara and Mia both went home safely. Mission accomplished and only seven versions of this day overdue. I should be celebrating, but the victory's pretty hollow.

Dad calls out from the kitchen. 'Making a coffee if you want one?'

I go through and he is indeed making coffee. No clue how he sleeps. It's pretty late, though don't know how late because the clock above the door's still fixed at 1.15.

'Decaf,' I say.

I rattle through drawers, rummage behind bin bags and tinfoil, under tea towels, and find what I need. I stick a chair in the doorway, climb up and fish down the clock. The old batteries shake free. I replace them with two shiny new ones and adjust the clock to the correct time. The second hand stutters to life. Now all we need is new batteries in the day.

'Good time?' Dad hands me a coffee.

'Nah.'

'No?'

'Wasn't in a party mood.'

'Hmm, yes. Maybe it wasn't the best day for a party,' Dad says, with his eyes on his coffee and his glasses steamed up. I let the dig slide with gritted teeth.

After a while, Dad says, 'Was there anything in particular?'

'Nothing, really.'

'Just … the day?'

He looks at me, all tired and a bit red round the edges. There's a patch of too-long stubble at the back of his jaw where he missed a bit this morning. Wonder what he's been doing all night without me, whether he watched that film and cried or read a book or watched the news to be distracted by other people's disasters.

I say, 'I upset someone. That's what happened.'

'Oh.' Dad's whole body relaxes. He asks me to elaborate and, to my own surprise, I do. Tell him all about her storming away from me, a bit of how I messed up. I leave out the kiss, because I don't need Dad blushing over my PG content. He does his bit. Grips his mug, watches me and says, 'Hmm.' It's a solid portrayal of a parent. Ten out of ten. The critics are calling it 'Stellar' and 'The performance of his life'.

He rubs at the side of his nostril. 'Clara sounds like a nice girl.'

'Should I go over? Or message her or …?' I trail off as I get a mental picture of myself, sitting here, asking this bespectacled oldie for advice about girls. 'Just want to know she's OK, really.'

Dad pushes his glasses up. 'I think you probably should let her cool off.'

'Right. Or?'

'Once you've apologised, it's with her.' His tone goes firm. 'You have to let her have some space.'

'Uh huh.' One problem there. My eyebrows head up as my lips head down for another sip of coffee.

'You did apologise?' Dad says. How typical that this is the moment he chooses to be perceptive.

'She was angry. When did I have a chance?'

'Oh.'

I grunt. Feel a bit judged. Maybe I'd have apologised if she'd waited two minutes.

'Well, you'll have another opportunity at school on Monday,' Dad says. 'Best make it a good one to compensate for the delay.'

The judgement keeps coming. Dad knows just how to mash my buttons.

I'm on the verge of moving away and turning in when Dad slurps and coughs. Even though it's just liquid down the wrong pipe, his eyes water. He looks sad and sorry and too old. Choking in his saggy PJs, holey slippers and grey T-shirt.

I say, 'Sorry to you too, I guess.' Which, yeah, it's a crap apology.

Dad's silent for a second. 'What for?'

'Going out tonight.' I grip my mug. 'Should've stayed in and watched your movie.'

Here it all comes. Told me so. Bad son. I'm braced for it when he says, 'It was your loss. The film was an utter masterpiece. Extreme weather and apex predators? Together? It was just …' Dad brings his fingers to his lips in a chef's kiss of appreciation.

'Yeah, right. My good taste in films wasn't hereditary, eh?'

I crawl upstairs and get under my covers. I stare at the ceiling and wonder if I might wake up to the same sight tomorrow. Somehow I don't believe it. Every morning it's the car park, every morning the same cricked neck, same stinking pits.

Even though tonight left everyone alive, I made a royal balls-up of a lot of things. I think of the worst: Clara's lips on mine – so quick before she wrenched away – and wonder how it might have gone if I hadn't panicked and jumped in. If only I'd slowed down and explained.

On my phone I stare at Clara's name. There's a hundred different messages to type, but Dad's right – can't force it. Clara's home safe. Not drunk or drugged or passed out. Not shredded on the road. Clara's alive. Me and Dad are talking. Mia went home. Worm kept his dignity. These are things worth hanging onto.

Maybe it'll end it, maybe it won't. Who knows? Maybe I succeeded, but I feel defeated.

A message comes through:

Anthony: easy meat

Photo of him licking some girl. I swipe it. Weird to think of the party raging on. Weird Anthony's playing party clown without a shred of gratitude for the mistake I've stopped him making.

It's before midnight, but I'm beat. I force my spine to relax. When I rewind the day and play it over it wasn't so bad, but I could take another crack. After all, it's a shame to leave Clara hating me.

THE NINTH TIME
9.1

This time I'm not sneaking after Clara on my way to the art room. I'm walking with her side-by-side across the quad, not knowing what to think or feel. As much as I was counting on another chance, I've got nothing. The key hypothesis is thoroughly shattered. Clara lived. She went to sleep in her own bed in one Clara-shaped piece.

So what's my play?

An hour ago I woke up in my car with Clara hitting me. I bought her coffee and a coconut snack, slicking over a few of the awkward moments from yesterday like this day's a well-thumbed tune on my guitar. Now I'm here. Walking. Determined not to muck it up with Clara, who's telling me how she's going to study art after high school and describing the terror of taking her portfolio for judgement by university suits.

'It's like putting your soul out on show,' she says and then blushes. 'No pressure to be complimentary about my work or anything.' She looks so nervous I itch to tell her I already know it's amazing, but I can't, so I wave her words away.

She leads me to the pokey secret room with the paint-spattered benches and one tall window. I examine her work again as she chews her lip. Closer up I can see there's texture underneath the ugly colours. A pattern running through the purple and green, so the closer you get the prettier it is again. Layers upon layers.

I tell her I like it. Point out the layers, worrying that I sound thick, but Clara nods enthusiastically and says, 'I like this whole idea of, you know, what's pretty, who decides and why do we let them? But I also like the idea that your perspective changes depending on how far away you are. You don't know what's buried or what history there is.'

She throws a hand limply at her portraits, then goes back to fiddling with a paintbrush. 'It's silly.'

'I get it.'

'Yeah?' She looks up. Smiles.

'All the splodged bits – they make it more interesting.' I rub my ear. 'No good at art interpretation, obviously.'

'No, exactly. Our bruises stay with us.' She runs her thumb over one flat paper cheek.

I get it. It sounds like the way I feel, bruises on top of bruises. Clara knows things the same way I do. How fragile life is. How all that ever protects us is glass. Every trauma a sudden crack in the windscreen. Chipping away at our illusion of security.

'What knocks earned these?' I say running my fingers down the edge of another drawing.

Clara picks up a wooden board with a work in progress attached to it. She tilts her head around to check her portrait from a few angles.

She says, 'Sometimes all I can think is how it's never the perfect version of what I see in my mind.' She squeezes out colours onto a palette and mixes the paints together. 'Anyway, that's what I love about art, you can't be right or wrong. It's all interpretation and experimentation and learning, you know? No-one can say someone else's art is bad.'

Clara didn't answer my question, I notice. She arranges herself in front of the board with the half-finished painting, paper stretched out. Another portrait, half-done. There are white blanks on the skin, the hair is only an outline. She reaches out, brush loaded with deep purple, and stabs it to the flat, empty cheek of her paper twin.

I consider pushing it, trying to uncover what's underneath. But she didn't do that to me. And Clara's smart, she knows talking helps. She just doesn't know me.

'Wish I could be good at something like this,' I say.

'You used to be good in year nine.' Clara stops painting. 'You were great at lino printing and carving the blocks. Mine always came out wrong.'

'Yeah?' I laugh. 'Was I? Who remembers?'

Clara concentrates on her painting again. Turns a bit pink. 'The accident wasn't that bad, Spence. I don't need supervising.'

The dark splotch on the portrait she's working on grows under her brush and takes over the blank spaces. I'm mesmerised as she slashes and jabs, hands moving fast to add damage.

A day isn't long enough to find out about the knocks that have shaped Clara Hart.

I remember how I saw her cry in this room on an identical day and how, because she's not crying now, I missed my chance to be there for her, to be useful. But, when I think about it, that day wasn't identical: I'd given her shit about the cars, been too harsh probably, and then Anthony'd shouted at her in the caf. I feel a twinge of good. Maybe I didn't miss my chance. I was better this time, here for Clara. That's not nothing.

I get to philosophy early, go in and check the room for an audience, but it's just Barnes and me and row after row of ugly orange desks. On the board 'Nietzsche and the affirmation of life' is already glaring back. He's bent over, bald head mooning until I let the door slam and he notices me. One feral hand runs over his dome as he says hello.

I dive in, outlining my predicament, not even bothering to say it's hypothetical, because who'd assume otherwise?

When I'm done Barnes says, 'Well, James, from a Nietzschean point of view, you'd have to be able to imagine yourself being forced to live that day over and over again. Imagine living it infinite times and still being happy with the choices you've made. That's the ultimate goal. *Amor fati*, the love of one's fate, wanting nothing to be different. When Nietzsche defined the affirmation of life as the ability to welcome its eternal return, he knew this was a demanding ideal –'

'OK, sure,' I interrupt, because we're wading into irrelevant territory here. 'But what if you try to fix the day and other people mess it up?'

'James, you're missing the point.'

'Clearly.'

A pause. I've gone too far, but then he says, 'It's about you – or not *you*, but the personal. Living as if eternal recurrence were true would put a greater weight of significance on choices. Your actions, your decisions, your life. In your scenario it wouldn't be about fixing everything, but instead being at peace with your own conscience.'

A fuse fixes in my brain and a light pings. Somewhere after Barnes says *my actions, my decisions, my life*, I've stopped listening. He's nailed it. My life. It's not about what anyone else is doing tonight. It's me living day after day. I'm the only one with the memories, the only guy with any real skin in the game.

And it's my actions that have been messing up the repetitions so far. I tried to stop Clara drinking, I tried to control where she went, got so obsessed with keeping her safe, I didn't give a shit how she wanted to go about her night. Even Mia just drank faster when I tried to intervene and ended up worse off. I'm the guy who's been ruining everything with my asshole interventions. So what if I don't? What if I let Jay and Mia and Worm all go about their night and focus on the only person who really matters to me?

The door cracks. Ryan and Jay filter in. Barnes stutters out something else, but I'm already gone. Walking off, sitting in my seat, Anthony landing beside me. 'Where the hell have you been?' And I shake my head.

The room fills, and Barnes launches into his usual. The eternal repetition of eternal recurrence.

'What if some day or night a demon said to you, this life you're living is what you'll have to live over and over again. There'll be nothing new, just eternal repetition, everything exactly the same. Even this moment now.'

'What would you say? Would the proposition fill you with happiness or horror? That is the question of Nietzsche's eternal recurrence.'

I'm listening, but I'm not. Sprawled in my chair, legs forward, hands clasped behind my head. I beam at the crinkled corner of one white ceiling tile.

Clara smiled and apologised after she hit my car this morning, because she forgot I was ever a dickhead. She doesn't know that I messed up before. She doesn't know I once yelled at her for denting my car. She doesn't know I left her to get hurt because I was so wrapped up in my own shit. Every past error's been scribbled out in sleep so I'm a brand-new Spence, one day better than the last version.

Barnes gets a quote up on the board and obligingly translates the typically obscure rambling: 'Nietzsche argued for an approach to morality that encouraged personal responsibility and ...'

He keeps going, but Barnes is a blur. All I can focus on is one thought, staring back at me with brilliant, sparkling clarity: it's about me. Not a curse, but a blessing. The universe noticing I royally fucked up the first time and handing me an opportunity to do this day *well*. Again and again until it's right and until I'm right. The right kind of person who even Clara Hart might not find unthinkable.

I'm the bloody key.

9.2

Most people don't like new. They like old and comfortable sameness, not taking chances. You see it at the movies, the sprawling universes churning out six monthly films full of characters you know will save the day, the only respite from remakes and live-action versions of your childhood cartoons made word for word. Most people love the familiar. They like their lives on repeat.

Usually I buck the trend. I like different. Genre bending and twist endings. This day ought to be unbearable as I try to replicate every move, but it's weirdly OK. Because I finally know why I'm here in this recycled day. Time, the universe, some faceless, unknowable entity threw us together, Clara and me, and I'm here to not only fix what went wrong the first time, but to live well. A good day.

So I do it all again, with one difference. I don't intervene in the caf as Jay goes down. As his face smashes the table, my fingers are crossed. I leave with a smile as his nostrils start to spurt. Unlucky, Jay, guess it's not your perfect day.

I breeze through school, hitting every one of my marks. And at the end of the day I return to the far corner of the car park and lean against a battered red Micra to wait.

She's one of the first out. Can tell her from a distance with those stompy shoes and gleaming ponytail. As she walks closer she watches the ground until she's within shouting range. 'Did you change your mind about compensation?'

'Nah, you're OK. Can barely see where you hit me.' I jerk my chin at the crumpled mess of my car. 'Hear about Jay's broken nose?'

'I was in the splash-zone, actually. It was the most blood I've seen spilled in the cafeteria for a good week. I hope he's OK.'

She's right, it was a good one. A dramatic fall, a broken nose, bad as the time he missed the party. 'Guess he's not going to Anthony's, though.'

'I suppose.' Clara pops her boot. I move out of the way as she chucks her bag inside.

'Guess he was the main reason you were going, though. Him and Genni?' I say and Clara frowns. 'So, like, there's no reason to bother now?'

Clara folds her arms. 'You're going, aren't you?'

My whole day, all these days, have been building to this. Waiting for me to say the right thing in exactly this moment. My guts churn. I clear my throat, dangerously close to bottling it.

'Nah. If you're not going, I won't go,' I say. Clara receives this news with a blank face that gives nothing away. 'Because then we could do something together. Go somewhere?'

For good measure, I hold out my hand. And I hate the feeling of it hanging there. Palm empty, waiting for her to take it. Or not.

Clara twists a strand of hair around her finger. 'Is this a joke?'

'It's really not. Been meaning to ask for a while.'

'Why, though?'

'I don't know, Hart. Why not?' My hand quivers, so I flex my fingers and drop it.

Clara smiles and her forehead creases and she says, '"Somewhere"?'

'Yeah.' My face spreads out in a grin. 'Somewhere back in time.'

She smooths her hair behind one glittering ear and dimples and my heart leaps. I know she'll come with me. And it'll work, because Nietzsche promised. Even though it feels like pinning my hopes on Bee's kind of woo-woo – horoscopes, retrograde planets, all that snake oil – it's all I've got.

9.3

My evening at home isn't restful without Clara. I'm busy wondering whether she's safe or if the universe will discover a new and imaginative way to kill her off outside the party. It's ridiculous, though. She always makes it to the party, so she'll make it to our – what? Our evening together.

I'm chopping a courgette when Dad says his usual.

'It's a bit of a relief this week's over to be honest.'

Dad doesn't know how truly stuck we are, but if there's one person in this endless Friday who wants it to be over as much as I do, it's him.

I tighten my grip on the knife. 'Yeah, I'm done with this week. Done with this day.'

We eat and, for once, we feel OK together. Still a family even with our missing piece. It's a genuine wrench to turn down his tentative offer of a movie night, but I have somewhere to be. A girl to meet. A day to solve.

Even though this solution feels like the simplest one of all, my hands are clammy as I get in my car.

I'm still freaking when I pick her up. But my driving is smooth and sure. Clara natters away in the passenger seat and it's relaxing to have her chat to me and demand nothing. It's soothing. As I turn off the road onto the gravel track, she drops the hand that's been fiddling with her hair all the way and says, '"Somewhere back in time" indeed.'

'Where else?'

The car wheels grind on the grit as I pull under a tree and kill the engine.

Here we are. The sky over town's an orange haze, but out here there's a spatter of stars faint on the grey. Out of the car and I take her hand, step into a space that's quiet, empty and simple, the flip of every other noisy, cluttered version of tonight. I pull Clara behind the trees, into the black.

'God, I haven't been here in years.' She giggles as we break out over the grass into the moonlight towards crumbling, ivy-clad ruins. Technically Clara and I outgrew the folly a good year ago, but it's nostalgic, isn't it? And where else was I going to take her – home to watch a movie with Dad? No, thanks. We duck under the stone arch and startle a bunch of lower-years with their bottle of cheap cider.

Clara turns to me with her mouth pulled faux-serious and startled and we speed up a little. We nip behind the wall on the other side and find an uninhabited space away from the riff-raff. Away from everyone. Just me and Clara. The safest place she could be.

I shrug off my hoodie, lay it on the damp grass and invite her to sit. A brolly beside us just in case. My phone, propped against a stray brick, turns our faces weak black and white. Past a line of dark treetops there's a view of the motorway, the faint rumble of cars and pinpricks of yellow and red.

'Is this weird?' I ask. 'Wish you were at the party?'

'Oh nope.' She eyes my bag. 'Did you bring cheap beer? Because no folly experience is complete without ...'

She does a drumroll as I unzip my backpack and bring out a bottle of pop and some fizzy sweets. 'I'm driving,' I say. 'Besides, trying to cut down on booze.'

'Well, then it's perfect.' She draws her knees up to her chest and rests her chin on them, turning her head to face me. I fiddle with the sweet bag. Clara tells me a story about a time she came here with Genni and they convinced some college boys she was a French exchange student. I tell her about a time Worm got his bum out and wish I had more wholesome stories to choose from.

After a while all the sound behind us, the kids laughing on the other side of the wall, gets quieter and I wonder if they're clearing out and leaving us alone. And it strikes me that I've brought a girl to an isolated field at night. What's more, I'm left alone in a dark place with Clara all night. No background noise or party-goers to fill the gaps. And my little-boy-crush I harboured back in the day, before I'd ever properly kissed a girl, suddenly isn't something I outgrew. Seems maybe it's been growing back bit by bit over the last few versions of today. Now it's my heart starting to pound and the words in my head all muddling up with the feel of her body against my arm.

'Ever wish you could do a day over?' I say. 'Something people wish, isn't it?'

Clara quirks an eyebrow. 'It's not going that badly, Spence.'

I laugh and run a hand over my hair. 'Nah, OK. But really, ever think about what you'd do if you got stuck in a day? Today. Over and over?'

'Like, not hit James Spencer's car in the morning? That sort of thing?'

'For starters.'

Clara gives a self-deprecating roll of her eyes. 'Apart from the car-based mishap I think I did OK, actually.'

'What if you had a hundred goes and made a huge mistake?' I shift in the grass, a bit closer. The temperature's diving and I hope she's not cold. 'Or what if you just wanted to do something batshit? No consequences.' This all sounds intense all of a sudden, so I add, 'Kiss someone? Kill someone?'

'What a question to ask out in the dark, cold night. Is this why you brought me here? To kill me?'

Interesting tick of the multiple choice there.

Clara says, 'Hmm, I think I'll pass on the free-kill. Even if you don't get to keep the day, you'd still remember, so there'd always be consequences.'

'True.'

She's right. Even with my days in a tangle, they all hang off me like threads. Eight Claras on my conscience. Aborted timelines with different versions of Spence living them. My fuck-up leading to her paying the price. Eight versions of today when my failure ended with Clara's life snatched away, a call to her parents, her family all trying to remember their last words to her. My consequences are the echoes of those days haunting me.

But right now, today isn't the day I need another go at. I'm thinking of a different day, different light, same setting, but summer temperatures and a pretty girl walking by.

'This place is …' I start. 'Do you remember …?' And then stop. It's so stupid.

'Remember what?'

'Kind of …' I rub the back of my neck, feeling it flame. 'Asked you out here once.' My laugh sounds so fake and so shite I half-wish the day would reset here and now and save me the bother of killing us both with awkwardness. 'Turned me down flat. Brutal, Hart, absolutely brutal.'

Clara looks confused. 'That didn't happen.'

'Ha. Mm, OK.'

'Nope. I'd definitely remember that, Spence.'

'It was ages ago. Shit, wish I hadn't –'

'You did take the piss out of me here once,' she volunteers. 'I was with Genni and you were with your friends and you kind of … yelled.'

My vision thins as I rack my brain. She turned me down here. I was embarrassed. Did I yell? Not the way I remember. All I remember is her walking with Genni, the sun on her hair and her face crinkled in disgust. 'I don't think so.' And then the merciless teasing from Anthony and Worm.

'Wow, that's what you're talking about isn't it? You were like, "Hart, come here."' Clara drops into an impression of me for this last and it's not good. It's gruff and Neanderthal. Cue more nervous-laughter.

'Yeah, well. Didn't come over, did you?'

'I thought you wanted to mess with me.'

'Nah.'

'I didn't know.'

God, I wish the ground would gulp me down. 'Figured you thought you were too good for me.'

Her forehead crunches. 'I don't think that. Why would I think that?'

A silence settles.

That time repeats again, a song I don't know the words to. Clara seems so sure and her version of events sells itself well. Of course I mucked it up without even realising. Nice one, Spence, always getting the moment wrong. I should've gone up and asked her properly. Would it've changed the outcome? Made her take me seriously? But asking outright would've taken guts, so course I didn't.

'So why did you bring me here?' Clara says quietly. 'If not to walk me to the ideal site for a shallow grave.'

'Ah yeah, brilliant spot for a bit of crime. Because there's never witnesses in the bushes at the folly.' I jerk my head towards where the grass gives way to woodland. 'There's probably twenty kids getting pregnant back there.'

Clara's lips fold together and she dimples. *Ah, shit.*

'Not that that's the reason we're here either,' I add hastily. 'Just … you don't ever talk at school. Kind of keep to yourself. Figured it'd be good to … chat.'

'You make me sound cool and aloof.'

'Aren't you?'

She smiles at her hands. I nudge her. She nudges back. In the moonlight her pale arms half-glow and all the skin there is puckered with cold.

She lifts her head again. 'I don't think I'm that interesting.' Her lips press together and her smile gets smaller.

I glitch under the pressure. The way her eyes look up at mine and away. And again. Her mouth trembling slightly. I'm scared – bloody terrified – I'll shrug or laugh and fritter away this moment like I always do. Wasting any opportunity for realness. Keeping my whole life bobbing on the surface, too scared to shove my head under. I take a deep breath.

I say, 'That's not true.'

'No?'

'Nah. You're … there's a lot to you.'

'People don't like me, though, do they? At school.' Her mouth quirks and she looks at her knees and I'm glad the question's rhetorical, because the truth hurts. Clara says, 'I don't know why. I don't think I'm worse than anyone else.' She looks at the sky, eyes shiny.

She's lovely. She's so much better than anyone else. And I wish I could've known Clara all this endless year. Can only imagine the things we might've talked about with more than one day between us.

'Don't know about everyone else,' I say. 'But I like you.' My voice sounds rough.

'You don't know me.' She doesn't make anything easy, this girl.

'What I do know, I like.'

'OK.'

She nudges me again and it turns into a lean. My arm creeps around her. She looks at me. Her breath goes silent.

'Good. That's settled then,' I murmur and look away.

We lean together in the dark and talk. We meander back and forth between serious and throwaway and Clara makes it all seem the same. Every word comes out of me with a five-beers-down ease, though I'm dead sober. We talk about inexhaustible cultural filler – music, films, TV. We talk about school – teachers, friends, aspirations. We cover old ground.

Never knew talking to someone could be this easy. Whether it's the darkness around us that makes it feel like throwing words into a void, or knowing she might not remember tomorrow, or just Clara. But when I talk I don't second guess what I'm about to say. I totally lose my grip and everything and nothing spills out. I talk too much. And nothing I say ever makes her laugh the wrong way.

We keep going till we have to stop. It's a matter of survival. The chill sets in and we finally surrender when Clara says, 'I don't have any feet. Just ice blocks where they used to be.'

We walk back through the ruins where the cider-drinking kids are long gone. It's near midnight and my phone is at thirteen per cent, defeated in the fight for light and signal. At the car it jumps to life, reinvigorated by a patch of reception and a volley of notifications. They queue on my screen and I swipe them all away.

I pop the boot and talk Clara through my inventory. One high-vis jacket, a first aid kit, a torch that would've been useful if I'd remembered it existed and, of course, blankets. Mum equipped the car for breakdowns in murder-town, biblical flooding, snow-pocalypse and other equally unlikely natural disasters. Doubt Mum reckoned it'd be so handy for keeping girls out all night.

I throw the blanket round Clara's shoulders and my hands hang around as if they're waiting for permission. One of hers tugs the blanket closed and her fingers skim my knuckle.

My hands go back in my pockets. We get in the car. When the engine turns on, the radio pipes up playing some chirpy pop song that's way off the mood I'm looking for. And when I open up my phone to search for music, Clara says, 'We don't necessarily have to go home, you know? We could stay –'

But I'm lost. Those notifications on my phone.

I flick through the messages, back up and down as though hoping the order will change. Wishing the last few sentences would drop away.

Clara's voice is drowned out by the rushing in my ears.

I stare at her. Take her in. Her eyes slightly too far apart, her small pointy nose, silky hair that won't stay behind her studded ears. She's so pretty. So normal. So nice, even when she's tearing me up. And if I turn time back to nine days ago I would've said she's nothing special on the surface, back when the surface was all I knew. Why did Anthony choose her?

There's no reason. And if there's no reason, it could've been anyone.

I look at the latest message one last time:

Anthony: Something's happened. Call me.

9.4

The speed limit's a crawl, the roads twice as long as before. The night pushes against the beams of the headlights. My face is stretched with anxiety.

Clara sits beside me. So pretty. So normal. She's corn-flakes and milk, the best thing since sliced bread. And if I forget everything I know about her, every wrong song lyric and sarcastic retort, self-deprecation and sincerity, I'm back where I started, wondering why this day revolved around her.

Anthony doesn't know Clara. She was just a girl. Any girl. She was unlucky, because it could've been anyone. And that's what I forgot when I took her out of this party.

On the last stretch we pass two taxis. A third's on Anthony's driveway.

The party's wrong. The music's off, people are shuffling in tight scrums in front of the house. No-one says hey. No more loose limbs, only tight lips. Someone, maybe Lana, is crying against the wall with Shaun. All these familiar faces look strange.

Just inside, among the abandoned cups, a shoe, a coat, Mia is hunkered against the wall, arms folded neatly over her knees. I'm relieved to see her, confusingly so. Somehow, in my bones, I thought it was her I'd let down. But Mia looks more together than I've seen her for a while. Tear-streaked but solid. She tips up red-rimmed eyes.

'What a night,' she says dejectedly.

'What happened?' Clara says. 'Spence said someone got hurt …?'

Over in the lounge, I spy Worm sitting on the coffee table enveloped in a fuggy cloud of smoke. He jams his joint in the side of his mouth and lifts one lanky arm. I can't find the energy to wave and, as I watch, he leans back until he's lying flat against the glass, his head lolling over the edge of the table. He shouldn't be smoking indoors. The smell mingles with body spray, booze, feet.

'Who was it?' I ask Mia.

'Bee,' she says with a sniff.

Clara murmurs her shock behind a hand clapped to her mouth. I shouldn't be surprised by anything any more, but this news is a fist to the throat. The world tilts.

'She …' I take a breath. 'She was hit by a car?'

'What?' Mia's face screws up in confusion. 'She fell down the stairs. She's gone to the hospital. Anthony too.'

The stairs, right. The stairs, the car, the hot tub, the bedroom, the drugs, the boy, the girl. Clara or Bee or anyone else.

'How did she fall?'

Mia lifts her shoulder and it doesn't matter, because I know, don't I? Clara out of the equation, Anthony bored. No Spence kicking about causing disruption. Beer pong and falling out. Maybe he dunked her in the hot tub or maybe he asked for a word. Maybe she was drunk or maybe not. Maybe Anthony didn't even mean to or maybe he did.

If it hadn't been Bee maybe it would've been another girl. If I left it all to chance again maybe there's still the possibility Anthony wouldn't do it again.

I don't know where I stand in the universe any more. Maybe there was no key, just some demon sent to unscrew my mind till the pins fall out. No solution and no way to stop it. An eternal punishment for the poor decisions that landed me here. Only it's Bee and Clara who keep paying for my mistakes.

Clara asks a question. Mia shakes her head. 'Her arm looked pretty wrecked and she hit her head, but she was talking. I can't …' Mia puts her head in her hand and the last words are muffled.

'Can we give you a lift home?' Clara offers. And despite everything, that's neat, because – ah yeah? – it's 'we' now?

Clara sits silently beside me, Mia alone in the back. Somewhere between Anthony's home and hers, Mia starts crying. In the rear-view mirror I see her head sunk between her knees. Clara reaches through the gap and mumbles assurances and rubs Mia's knee. I have a flash of another version of Spence riding in a taxi, deep in denial and self-loathing in the second version of this day, remembering a memory he tried to run from.

This fucking day.

At Mia's house she flops from the car with a 'Thanks'.

I roll my window down and say, 'You going to be OK?'

Under the streetlight her eyes seem accusatory. 'I just hate these parties,' she says. 'They always end badly.'

And she slopes off towards the house, raising one hand in a final backwards wave.

I stop the car outside Clara's and turn the engine off. Feels like a thousand years since I came by to pick her up. Her hands are in her lap, fingers twiddling.

'Do you think Mia's OK?' Clara says. 'That might've been shock or something.'

'Hopefully her parents are in. Or her sister.'

Clara nods slowly. 'Thanks for bringing me home,' she says. As if there was a chance I wouldn't.

'Thanks for coming.' My fists clench around the steering wheel. 'Can't believe this night.'

'Returning to your question, if I could live this day again, I think there are things I would change now.' Clara twirls a length of dark hair around her finger. 'Poor Bee.'

'Mmm,' I say. 'Not sure I'd want to change anything.'

Clara frowns. 'We could do all this again, though.'

'Never the same.' My voice sounds too bitter. Clara's frown deepens. It's true, though. It'd never be the same. It's different every time I start again, in subtle ways that change everything.

And every single day leaves me with a new set of secrets to keep from Clara. It's not fair.

'Do you ... Do you actually like me?' Clara says. 'You're not just ... pretending? Or messing with me?'

There are a few beats of silence. My words sound like they are squeezing from a constricted throat when I say, 'I like you. Course I do. Ever since you bumped my car.'

'That's not very long.'

'It is.' I can't look at her face. It's her turn now. I want her to say something. Anything. I want her to like me back. I want her to think I'm worth something and make this whole endless day worthwhile.

Clara takes a small breath. 'I've always liked you. I guess you know that.'

'How would I know?'

'Well, you ... haven't always been the nicest.'

'Yeah. Sorry.'

I look at her and she's looking back, eyes shining. Something needs to happen. I stretch out my arms towards her and she leans in. My arms wrap around her shoulders and she feels smaller than I thought she would. Soft and warm and shivery in my draughty car. The handbrake sticks into my hip and my nose buries in her hair and she smells fresh and clean. Of nothing in particular. Girl-smell. Clara.

She pulls back and her hair slips through my fingers and she waits an inch from me. Nose to nose. Breath to breath. Her eyes flicker down.

I kiss her. I have to.

My lips meet hers, just quickly. Soft. And when I pull back she closes the gap and for a one second it's new and weird and too long since this last happened. But she's kissing me. My eyes crack and her face is there. Long, dark eyelashes and perfect skin.

'Is this OK?' I mumble and she nods.

And then my eyes shut and my fingers curl in her hair. Our mouths find their way and it's easy. I lose time with her lips on mine and her hands holding tight. I lose everything. Just her body, my body. Pressed so close. We dissolve in the dark.

I let go. I run my thumb over her freckle and where the dimple hides. Her face turns up, the dimple caves in. I want to kiss her all night. Tell her everything.

I say, 'Please stay with me.'

9.5

The bricks of the folly are cold and damp. They seem to prod straight through my flesh to my bones, and that's fine. The discomfort's what I need. It's early morning, but the night's still here. This isn't when it changes. I know what I have to do. Stay awake. Wait for the sun. Don't let the day turn over. So I let the bricks dig into me and hope it's enough.

Clara's not going on my list of losses. Those people I've lost for various reasons in various ways – Mum, Anthony, Bee – all those hurts tumble together and I hold onto them, the ghosts keeping me awake. This is how life goes, this is the real eternal recurrence: trying to find the heart to keeping loving people as they leave you, one by one, over and over.

Not Clara.

I tuck the blanket around Clara and pull her over onto my lap. I smooth her hair and thumb the skin of her ear between silver studs and rings and she murmurs, 'If I drool on you in the night, you have to promise to think it's cute, not disgusting.'

A smile twitches over my mouth. I want to keep Clara awake and tell her all the things she's missed every time this day gets erased. I want to tell her about Mum and Dad and Anthony and have her understand me again. I'll tell her tomorrow, though. When the new day comes. As soon as I've watched the sun start to rise, I'll wake her up to watch and we'll talk. She'll remember. She'll understand. We're the same, her and me. We know. And I'm keeping this day. Bee's alive. Hurt, but alive.

'You're adorable,' I promise. And I think this is the last thing she hears before she falls asleep, her breathing turning long and slow.

Now it's me against the night. Fighting my tiredness and holding on.

And I want so badly to keep tonight. The best night. And I'm hopeful because the rain never came, not tonight. It was better.

I want to keep Clara.

My eyes twitch awake.

It's selfish, but

Stay awake

Spence

Wake

THE TENTH TIME
10.1

Up.

Wake up!

I jolt out of sleep, just enough brain to slam hand against horn. It screams into the day, the noise filling the whole car, the whole car park. My spare hand flips the mirror to see a red car stopped behind. I let go of the horn and it takes a moment for my ears to register the silence.

Friday. School. Of course.

Clara's car pulls up. I press the heels of my hands into my eyes and smother a scream. She's gone. She's back. But at least she didn't hit me.

I open the door and slump out to wait. Disappointed and euphoric. Another bloody Friday, yeah, but another day with Clara and no crash. Perhaps this day will be the best of all.

'I could see you, you know? I'm not blind,' Clara says, hands trembling on her door as she closes it. I scared her. Shocked her by hitting the horn.

'You were about to hit me.'

'At two miles per hour doing a manoeuvre I've done a hundred times before?'

'It happened yesterday,' I say, which clearly isn't right, so I gesture at her car and its many bruises.

'Excuse me?' She holds up two fingers and folds the first one down. 'Firstly, I wasn't going to hit you! Secondly, not everyone has a minted mummy and daddy to buy their cars.'

'Look, I didn't want you to –'

But she whips her other hand up to stop me. 'Don't worry. No harm done.'

'No, but you were –'

'You know you're late for form room?' She opens her car door and leans in to grab her stuff.

I follow. 'But I –'

'Spence, some advice? You might want to check out a mirror before class.'

'Harsh,' I say with feeling, and she stops.

Clara gives another short, sharp sigh. She presses her hand to her heart like it's beating fast as mine. 'Sorry. But you actually could've caused an accident, you know? And you – look … unwell.'

I nod. Worried if I open my mouth again I'll scream and never stop. Right in the face of this angry stranger.

'We're so late.' The smile she gives me doesn't touch her dimple. She slams her door and her knee bounces as if desperate to be done with me. Her gaze slipping off towards school.

It's all wrong. She's not gushing apologies because she didn't smash my car. Here I am, back to being a piss-taker and a pig with no evidence to the contrary, nothing to forgive. I try to remember how it went last time, prepare to take up the slack.

'Didn't mean to be rude. But look, about the party later –'

'I'll be there. It's an open invitation, isn't it?' She shoots me one last apologetic look and starts walking without an answer.

As I crawl over to gym block preparing to tackle this day, I have to put Clara to the back of my mind. There's a suspicion grinding away inside. Detail in this day I've been overlooking, or at least haven't been thinking about hard enough. And that negligence cost me my perfect day with Clara.

Clara, who I've been so preoccupied with. Clara, who isn't the key.

I plonk down in the caf next to the boys, dropping my bag on the floor. Anthony and Worm make their jokes and I grunt and nod and half-laugh in the pauses. I tell them it's Mum's anniversary. I beg Anthony again not to throw a bloody party and he tells me no, the night's fixed on its course.

'It's my *mum*. Do you know what that means?'

Worm looks at his toes and Anthony says, 'Tomorrow you can come around for FIFA and pizza. How's that? You'll want to be with your dad tonight anyway. I'm sure you've got things on.'

And I am sick with how inadequate the offer is and how powerless I am to stop him now. It's all arranged, he says. The wheels are in motion.

'Give us a smile, Mia,' Anthony shouts.

I turn and watch.

I've never paid much attention to Mia before. Never thought about how her feet move a tiny bit faster after he

221

shouts or how she checks over her shoulder. She doesn't give us a smile. Mia punches numbers into the vending machine, then grips the corner. She glances over her shoulder again and our eyes lock.

These parties always end badly.

And I think about Clara telling me that Mia wasn't right last night. In shock.

And about Mia in the bathroom. And Mia getting too drunk. And Mia once being so bubbly and now, not.

Mia.

'She's not fucking three stars,' I tell Anthony. 'No-one is.'

'What would you give her, then? But bear in mind my opinion's worth more, because I have insider knowledge.'

'Do you?'

He smirks. 'Ancient history, OK?'

But then his pupils flick back and forth as if remembering something. A quirk of his mouth as though recalling a tiny mistake. Perhaps the reason he never told me about Mia the first time. Perhaps wondering if he should've ever let slip. *Nah, Anthony, nah.*

Something inside me ticks around full circle and clicks into place.

I stand. Swing my bag on.

'Where are you going now?' Anthony shouts after me.

I leave the cafeteria and wait. The foyer is empty, but for one bored receptionist. He takes off his glasses, yawns. Above him a dark blue clock obnoxiously announces every passing second.

From behind me I hear: 'Party tonight. Bring your sister.'

Mia comes out, walks past me, feet slapping grey tiles, hands shoving a Snickers into the bowels of a canvas bag, appetite obviously lost.

'Hey,' I say. 'Can we chat?'

'I was just going …' She points down the empty corridor. Her eyes are wide. Her bottom lip bunches. 'Why, what do you want?'

'Can we go outside?'

Behind his desk, the receptionist presses a button on the photocopier and it flashes to life. The clock ticks around halfway.

10.2

We walk out of school, out of the gates and into the roads lined with brick houses. I ask about her subjects at school, like I'm some out-of-touch relative, and she murmurs responses she clearly doesn't want to give. Some woman with a baby strolls past and eyes us, wondering what kind of delinquents are out of school before it's even started. We walk to the patch of grass with the small duck pond where Mia can perch on the low wall and I can stand, hands in pockets, wondering how the hell I'm supposed to ask this question. It shouldn't be me asking, I know this much. I barely know Mia in any version of this day.

'Bit concerned,' I tell her.

'About me?' The words are hard to catch, they're so quiet.

'About Anthony. Or, how he, you know, treats girls.' I rub my eyebrow with my finger, feeling sweat starting up in my pits, the creep of heat up my back. My lungs feel tight. The

223

air coming in and out of me no help under pressure. 'He's said some stuff, sent messages… there's just a lot of stuff going on with him that's made me … yeah, worried.'

'What's it you're asking, Spence?' Her lips disappear.

'Just … what happened with him? And you?'

Mia hesitates, the tips of her curly hair quivering in the breeze.

'That's none of your business.' And she gets up. She starts walking away from me.

I should let her go, I know. She doesn't owe me anything. It's none of my business. And I've grasped a fraction of how hard it will be to tell me what I'm asking for.

I raise my voice and tell her retreating back, 'No. Just wanted to say … you know, it wasn't your fault –'

Mia makes a gurgling noise, could be a laugh, but there's no humour in it. She stops, hands by her sides. Her head shakes slowly.

'Found out sometimes he takes things a bit far with girls.' I wait. Mia doesn't move. 'Thought maybe –'

'What would you know?'

'Mia, I –'

'Do you think I want to talk about this?' Mia says fast, turning around again. 'Because I don't. I'm fine.'

'But –'

'I'm *fine*,' she says to the floor. 'Really.'

Yeah. I know all about 'fine'.

I want to say she shouldn't have to pretend. I want to say I know what he did and he did it on purpose. Want to tell her he'll do it again tonight. But how can I put that on her? It's not her fault; it's not up to her to stop him or help me.

I say, 'OK, yeah. Sorry.'

Her body slumps. We walk the way we came. Mia a few steps ahead, keeping the pace faster than I want it. I control the panic. If I scare her, I'll lose her.

When we're nearly back at the school gates I say, 'Just want you to know, I'd back you up if you ever change your mind. It's what I should've done.' Mia gives me a questioning look and I shake my head. 'Need to make something right.'

'Maybe you can't fix it? God, who do you think you are – some kind of white knight in a shitty school uniform?' She stares at me. 'I'm not the one who did anything wrong, Spence.'

'Yeah, I know.'

'I shouldn't have to tell anyone.'

'Yeah, I know.' And I really do. Why the fuck should she?

We walk in silence for a few more steps. I say, 'But don't be on your own, yeah? It doesn't do any good. Even if you just want to, I dunno, sit or whatever. I'm … well … here.'

She nods. I spread my hand against my forehead, tightening the skin and letting go.

And we'll be back at the school soon and then apart and then Mia will be back in her life with this thing that's happened to her and out of my reach. I'm losing her and losing this moment and my chance to say something real. In the end, only one thing properly matters. Maybe I'll have to say it every day for the rest of my life if this day goes round and round and I bloody will. I let it out in a rush hoping it doesn't mangle on the way out.

'The thing is, Mia, I believe you. OK? That's all.'

Mia's mouth curves down and she struggles to pull it straight. Her eyes glisten. 'I don't need you to tell me that.' But she slows down again. She slows and she stops.

We talk for a long time after that. Let first period turn to second. It takes some false starts. Some small talk before the big talk. But then Mia starts.

'It was almost a year ago. It was the next morning when I woke up – it was a Saturday.' Mia says. 'I wasn't sure it was Anthony at first.' She tucks her bottom lip under her teeth and closes her eyes.

'Did he spike you?' I say.

'No. I just drank too much. I think.'

'It doesn't matter. People do that all the time. Should be safe with … like, anyone.'

'When I went to school on Monday he was there, making jokes to my face. Talking about what I could barely remember and I felt so sick I could hardly even stand up, him acting like it was some hilarious story. As if he didn't realise I'd been nearly unconscious.

'I left school. Went home and sat in the shower. But the next day I had to come back and he was still here.'

Mia tells me how hard she tried to move on and forget about it. Not to make a fuss.

We sit on the brick wall and she hugs her arms around her tight and I ask if she wants a hug. She doesn't. Course she fucking doesn't. We sit like this for ages. Mia's story comes out in drips.

'I wanted to feel OK again, so I acted like I was. I went to a few parties, then a few more and then I thought, no-one will believe me now. Not when they've seen me at parties – even his parties, god, because I was going to go tonight, Spence. I don't know why. And everyone will say I lied. So I kept pretending, I kept drinking. And I thought if I pretended hard enough …

'I felt sick all the time. Anxious all the time, but I had to pretend. If I didn't …'

I nod. Yeah, Mia came back from summer all scrawny, I remember. Anthony bumped her rating down.

'I couldn't even tell Bee when she started dating him. Such a bad friend.'

'No.' Her eyes flicker to me as if checking for doubt. Or judgement. She won't see that there, but I hope she can't read my guilt.

'They'll say it was my fault. That I was too drunk.'

'No.' But we both know it's a lie. It's what people say. Ignorant fucks.

All the time I'm listening to Mia there's a thought digging away like gravel in my shoe, impossible to ignore: would I have been one of those people? I want to think that nine Fridays ago I could've believed Mia. I'd have seen the truth in her eyes and turned on my oldest friend. But nah, I reckon that's giving old Spence too much credit. He didn't look properly. He couldn't be bothered to. Maybe he'd have thought it wasn't really rape if she was drunk, or if she went with him. He'd have said Anthony couldn't tell, that he made a mistake. But you can tell.

I listened to Anthony shout at her every morning. *Give us a smile, Mia.* Jesus. Did he get some sort of kick out of that?

She says, 'I wanted to tell someone. I've thought about reporting him. I've written it down and thrown it away.'

Mia's dark eyes are bloodshot, puffy, but there's steel in there too. And the hairs on my arms stand up, because I know what she's going to say next.

There's nothing I can do to fix today – I started trying too late. This day was broken before it began. Anthony broke it back when he attacked Mia.

At least I can do what I should've done for Clara that first time. Tell the truth and believe her. It's so easy compared to what Mia will do.

10.3

It's 5.30 and I'm exhausted. Knife-edge nerves. Waiting.

The coffee table at Anthony's is packed with snacks and there's a spare controller waiting for Worm. Anthony is kicking my ass up and down a pixel playing field, but I don't care. I'm not really in the game. I'm waiting.

My anxiety is hangover-sharp. That day-after feeling of recalling every minor embarrassment from the night before, cringing with the power of sober retrospect as your chemicals go haywire. You wake up and remember: I danced, how shameful; I puked and forgot to clear up after myself, oops; I made a stupid comment to that girl, Jesus. Except the feeling's caught up quicker today. No time to sleep on it and process the actions that got me here.

I screwed over my oldest friend, whoops.

My hands slip against the controller, my body stinks and I'm sure he must see right through me. Must know what a state I'm in and wonder why. A muscle jumps at the corner of my eye.

Anthony says, 'You're more than welcome to stay. Have a few drinks, play some games. Maybe a party would help you to forget a bit.'

'Forget Mum's dead?'

'No.' He side-eyes me. 'That's not what I meant.'

'Yeah, well, rather not.'

I shuffle further away on the sofa. My trousers feel too tight. How much longer do I have here?

'Bets on what time Worm'll join us?' Anthony says.

'Tomorrow.'

Anthony laughs. He's not changed for the party yet. His shirt buttons are open at the neck, tie discarded. He holds out a beer and I take it, the can cool against my hot palms. I take a sip, as relaxed as I can pretend.

Time's ticking on and Anthony's setting up another match and my opportunity's nearly lost. If I don't ask, I'll always wonder.

So I say, 'When you said about Mia earlier …'

'Yeah?'

'Did you guys ever … you know?'

'What do you think?' He leans back and frowns. 'Oh, come on, don't look like that. Any port in a storm, mate. She's not bad looking.'

'Don't say that. She's nice.'

'Yeah? I think you could get in there at the party later –'

'Nah. She's a friend, not like that.'

'What's up then?'

I pinch the neck of my beer bottle and thumb the brown ridge above the label. 'Did she want it?'

'What?'

'You heard me.' But my voice gets smaller. 'Was she definitely into it? Sometimes it's … hard to tell, if you don't listen. If you don't … give her space. If you just assume.'

229

'As if you know about that.' Anthony puts his elbow on the sofa arm.

'Did you talk to her?'

He looks me in the eye. 'Are you sure you want to be suggesting what you're suggesting?'

I nod. 'Look, if you made a mistake you could tell me. Everyone makes mistakes, Anthony. Everyone.'

He takes a sip of his drink, mouth still twisted. Silently, I press my lips together and stare at my friend. I will him with everything I have in me. *Please. The truth. Please.*

Anthony shakes his head. He laughs and when he turns back the smile on his face is sure and clear.

'Spence, I'm going to let you off because it's a shitty day for you.' He slaps me around the face with a brightly coloured postcard and says, 'Now shut the fuck up about Mia and check out this pair of jokers.'

I look at the postcard in my hands. *Wish you were here.*

It's not much later when the bell goes.

'As if Worm's early for once,' Anthony says and leaps up for the door. I'm bleary with anxiety. Paralysed, because it's not Worm. It's happening.

It plays out like this: two of them coming in, both in blue. Telling him what's what. They've got some questions for him. The ringing in my ears drowns them out.

It feels like a joke; one of them is going to cue the music and start stripping.

It feels nothing like a joke; this can't possibly be real.

Anthony's face hangs open. Eyeing me like he wants something. Even after what I said, even though the truth will

230

come out, I know I look innocent. And even though I knew it was coming – Mia messaged me, after all – I didn't expect it. That's how life is. Can't imagine the shocks until they hit you.

Didn't expect him to look so fragile.

'Spence,' he says. I nod, agreeing to an unspoken something I'll never make good on.

'You'll be OK.' It doesn't sound like a lie.

'You'll wait for Worm?'

'Yeah.'

Just some questions, that's all it is, but they take him. The door closes and I'm in the house on my own. The light outside turning dirty.

I can't move for the longest time. When I do, I get my phone out and weigh it in my hands. I send it to everyone I've a number for, ask them to spread the word. I settle on this:

Me: Party cancelled.

I want to sleep for a thousand years, but I only have one day at a time. Before I can rest there's someone else to see.

10.4

I go straight from Anthony's to her house. Knock at the door and wait, jittery as if I've downed a hundred coffees. Clara opens the door, arms already folded. She's wearing jeans and a jumper, no party gear now. Her hair's loose over one eye and she glares suspiciously from under it as I spin her a bunch of lies about how I came to be in the area and then on her doorstep. There's noise from a TV show on in the house and

I wonder who's there – a parent, her brother – and if they're listening out wondering who this fool on the front step is. The paving slab wobbles underneath my shoes, keeping me off balance.

'So Worm told you where I live,' she says, 'but how does he know?'

'Uh ... Worm gets everywhere, you know? He used to do a paper round.' Not my finest lie, but this day's rinsed my brain. 'Anyway and you said you'd see me at the party –'

'I did?'

'And the party's cancelled.'

'I heard.'

'Right. Thought you might not've heard.'

'And instead of messaging like a normal person you came all the way here. Why? To accuse me of dangerous driving again?'

'Nah. Sorry about that earlier.'

She lifts her shoulder. No smile. No dimple.

This girl said she liked me. She cared enough to get in my car. But even if I know she doesn't despise me as much as she's making out, this reception's giving me frostbite. I feel like a bloody prick in my school blazer too. Wish I'd found time to change.

'Do you want to do something instead of the party?' I say. 'With me.'

'I don't think –'

'Look, what else do you have on?'

'Pardon?' Her eyebrows furrow. 'Why do you even want to?'

The truth is impossible. Truth is, we've had three great days together and she can't remember a single one. Truth is, I like her more every day. And I know she likes me too, at least a bit, and it'd be OK if she'd let her guard down. Can't tell her a different Clara fell asleep in my arms, because this one's waiting.

'Want to hang out with you, Hart. Is it that weird?'

She rolls her eyes, but a smile twitches across her lips. 'Yes.'

'Come for a walk?'

'It's cold. And I think it's going to rain.'

'Come for a walk to my car? It's a pretty nice car. That is … no-one's ever hit it in the school car park. If you hate me you can come right back,' I say and point at where the Midget's parked a couple of houses down.

She grabs her bottom lip with her teeth and I shuffle back like I'm going to leave, which I will. Course I will. But Clara steps out to look up at the ominous sky, then yells a goodbye into the house. She slams the door and says, 'This is very strange behaviour, James Spencer.'

Clara gets in with me and I turn the key for the engine to get the heat going. It feels better in the car than standing awkwardly in her driveway, but still something's off. I can't put my finger on it. Can't get a sense of what's missing. She chats and I chat and I feel just like yesterday. Today. But the air between us doesn't carry the same electricity, because I'm the only one sparking. She doesn't make jokes or natter away. Her hands twist in her lap and she fiddles with her phone. Probably messaging Genni. Probably getting terrible advice.

'Want to choose some music?' I say, unzipping my phone and handing it over.

She scrolls, slowly drifting past my music collection. I want her to pick the song from Bingo Booze and serenade me with terrible lyrics, so I suggest the band, trying not to smile when she says, 'Sure.'

But the wrong song fills the car. The tense, pessimistic sound of 'Heart-Shaped Box'. Nothing you'd sing along to, not the tone I'm after.

I say, 'Isn't this a bit slow?'

'It's your music. Sorry if you don't like it –'

'I do. It's just …'

Clara looks at her hands.

I'm desperate for her to sing, talk, laugh at me. Desperate for her to fill the silence like she used to on the days when she hit my car and we chatted in the art room. I've missed all of that today. And I can't remember what I'm supposed to know and not know. Every subject seems too deep or too shallow. There's either a risk of giving away how much I know, or it's embarrassingly basic.

'What is this, Spence?' she says. 'Is this a joke?'

'Nah. Been meaning to talk to you for a while.'

'Why, though?'

'I don't know, Hart. Why not?'

'There must be a reason?'

'Yeah, but god, don't make me say.' I screw up my face and Clara dimples. Relief makes me laugh. 'We don't chat much at school.'

'I didn't know you were capable of chat.'

Clara checks my phone, still held in her hand. Her dimple deepens. She skips the song and the next starts.

'You're not a skipper, are you?'

'What can I say? I don't want to be locked into one song for a whole four minutes.'

'Good job we didn't make the cinema – a two-hour movie would blow your mind.'

'I'm a sucker for subtitles …' Her voice trails away and she frowns at her lap.

'Are you –?'

'What happened tonight?' She's suddenly tense, pressed to the door.

'Huh? What do you –?'

'What the actual fuck is this?' She holds up my phone.

I squint to read the words.

Ryan: No? As if anyone would rape Mia

Ryan: She wishes

Matt: That's why it's cancelled? Girls. Ruining everything

Worm: Ruin them right back. Lol

Oh god. The rugby group chat. Anthony's gone on the offensive and the boys have got his back.

Scars scatter my vision, blinking white and pink and mould green. My heart collides with my chest over and over.

'Just chat,' I strangle out.

'*Chat?* Is that actually what happened? Mia? Was it Anthony?'

I don't move.

'All of this is sick,' she whispers, scrolling, and I want to snatch my phone away. Want to push her out. Want to pinch her eyes and hold them shut. I clench my hands on the wheel.

She turns the screen to me. It's another group chat. From yesterday, only yesterday. The real yesterday for Clara, but more than a week ago for me.

Worm: Fuck, snog, kill, Lana, Sophie, Genni: GO

Anthony: Fuck Lana, snog Genni, kill Sophie (then fuck her too)

Worm: lol. Not f then k?

Anthony: less resistance my way

Me: more humane to just paper bag her, isn't it?

Worm: snog lana, kill Sophie, fuck Genni but gag her first

Anthony: with your dick?

Anthony: whats French for bitch suck harder?

And behind the chat Clara's face wrenched with disgust.

'Shit.' I wish I could dissolve into my seat. 'It was a joke.'

'You're disgusting.'

'Didn't mean it.'

'You said it.'

'Them. They did. I wasn't the worst.'

'Are you serious?' I close my eyes so I don't have to see her expression. 'That's so weak.'

She's still scrolling. I reach out and she jerks away. I press my body tight to my seat. My head spins and I wonder if I'm sick maybe that'll do it; if I vomit in my hands and show her the chunks, whether she'll take pity on me and stop.

'Were you trying to be funny when you said that you'd give Lana "four stars, haven't used yet, but the mate who recommended her said she rides like a charm".'

'Yes,' I gurgle. Nothing sounds funny in Clara's voice. It's not funny. It was never funny.

'What about, "Mia's so ugly she'd be grateful for any dick in the dark?"'

'Not me.' I'm sure that wasn't me. *Please not me.*

236

'You said, "Good one." Is it a good one?'

'No.'

'Who are you?' she says.

'I don't know. I don't know who that was.'

She's scrolling.

'Please stop.'

She scrolls.

I fold my hands into each other and hold them out. My voice goes low. 'Please, Clara, please stop. Like, I will get down on my knees and beg you. Seriously, anything. I'm not that guy now.' I'm another word from crying. She doesn't stop.

And then she does. And she looks at me with an expression I want to scrub away.

'I'm going to search my name. If there's anything you want to tell me before I do that, you should say it now.'

Her name?

I tighten my grip on the steering wheel. I can't tell her, because I can't remember. I don't know any more. I know I'm better now than I was in that phone, a better version of myself. And I don't trust who I used to be. That version of Spence could have said anything at all.

Clara drops her gaze to begin typing and I shoot out my hand. My fingers close around the phone and her fingers and I wrench the two apart. My fingernails scrape her skin.

As I slump back against my door with the phone cradled in my hands, the relief's so powerful I actually smile. Breathe. And then I look at Clara whose eyes are huge and wet. She cradles one hand.

'I guess that's my answer,' she says.

'No, look –'

She gets out and slams the door. She walks away down the road, crosses to the opposite side. She holds herself tight. She walks into her house. She never looks back.

Alone, I search 'Clara' and there's nothing found. Nothing. I never mentioned her before tonight. But I ruined it anyway. I drop the phone, slide my hands behind my head and grip the headrest, pulling like I want to rip it off and my head along with it.

I wait here, listening to my music shuffle, watching the light disappear. I watch her house, but she never looks out.

What was it Clara said at the folly? Consequences. We have to live with ourselves no matter what. Crack after crack at this day, but I'm always me at the end. That's the tragedy.

I'm so tired I feel drunk. Barely able to keep my eyelids up, yet as soon as my body hits my own mattress it feels like a trick, because I'm wide awake.

The day went wrong at the start: the first collision that wasn't. My hand on the horn stopping her from hitting me: that's what did it. Follow the thread: no accident meant no guilt and sympathy from Clara, no chance. We were wrong-footed, but tomorrow I'll nail it. She'll hit my car and be sorry and it'll be fine. Maybe we'll talk to Mia together, make it right together.

I'll keep my phone locked. I'll make sure she never looks at me that way ever again.

I turn onto my side. If I squint I can find her in the shadows. If I hold onto my duvet, I can imagine her in my lap.

'What would you do if you got to live this day over again?' I whisper.

NOW

1

I jolt up.

I flick away my duvet and shoot to my feet. Out of bed, onto soft carpet in my bedroom, not my car. My body's rested, PJs on and the light through the window's gold, not grey. I rub a hand over the starchy, slept-in skin of my face and check my phone, even though I know.

It's Saturday. Tomorrow. Today.

Why now? After all those Fridays of sweating, grafting, puzzling, what did it come to in the end? Mia's hurt. Anthony's messed up. Clara hates me. I didn't fix shit and this is the Saturday I keep? Cheers, Universe, but really, you shouldn't have.

I shower, hot water needling against my numbness. I climb out, pull on joggers and a clean, old T-shirt. There's this empty-eyed idiot in the fogged mirror. I throw a towel over and rub my face in the dark until my skin hurts to try to feel something. Anything. But I end up red and blotchy and just as hollow. In my room, I retrieve my school bag and go back to the bathroom. I carefully unscrew the small vodka bottle and hold it, smell it, want it, then ditch it down the sink.

The house comes back to me. The police. The look on Anthony's face when I asked him about Mia. His face when the police took him. Don't want to think about him, but old habits are hard to shake. Did he know it was coming, deep down? Or did he not know what he'd done – is that possible? Will he tell the truth? This not knowing screws with my mind.

I sit on the closed toilet lid and put my face in my hands. Mia talking, that's stuck now. The police questioning Anthony, that's stuck too. And even though he deserved it, it hurts. He was my friend. Maybe not always the best friend. But still, seven years.

Downstairs the house is empty. I put the kettle on and peer out the window. The shed door squeaks. Cars, right. My suggestion. I make two coffees and carry them out. Dad emerges, arms full, banging his head on the low doorframe.

'Shhh-ugar,' he says. 'That hurt a lot less before all my hair fell out.'

'Don't say that.' I offer a mug and Dad puts his bucket on the ground to take it. He smiles like he's taking a compliment, so I clarify. 'Have your genes, don't I?'

'I hate to break it to you –'

'Nah, I'm keeping my hair till eighty.'

'What happens then?'

'Oblivion.'

'Cheery thought.'

We drink our coffees, fill our buckets and go through the garage to the front drive where the Midget's parked. Dad starts with the hose and the pre-rinse, so I step under the garage door to avoid the spray.

On the bare brick wall inside there's photos recording from when Mum first picked up the Midget to when we finished the work. There's me, a touch narrower, shorter, scruffy in my work gear; and Mum with one grubby cheek, half a head shorter, throwing an arm up around my shoulder. She's beaming and I look awkward, like I didn't want the hug. Sure I did, though.

'Your mum loved a no-hoper,' Dad says.

And for a moment, with my eyes on the photo and my mind on how disappointed she'd be, I think he means me. Everything crashes down at once. How Clara looked as she left the car; the ugly things I wrote; the uglier things I did; all the times before this that I got it wrong. How Clara will never speak to me ever again and I deserve that, because Mia. God, Mia.

'Good job,' Dad says and, even though he's talking about his own bloody rinsing, I break. My mouth opens, but nothing comes out. Dad hesitates. Walks over. He puts an arm round my shoulders and I sniff and leak, like I've forgotten how to cry properly, tears getting in my mouth and tasting salty.

I press my fingers to my eyes.

'Ruined everything, Dad. Ruined it and I can't undo it.'

'OK,' Dad says.

I shake my head.

'Tell me,' he says.

And I do. I chuff it out in shaky breaths, hiding in my own hands and heaving against the weight of Dad's arm like I'm a kid. Mia, Anthony, Clara, the group chat. Dad listens and it all comes out. A surprisingly short story and at the end I have to suffer through Dad's awkward questioning about what I've got up to with girls and I'm bloody grateful that's a short story too. Ashamed as soon as the tears dry up, I pull away and walk into the kitchen to blow my nose. Pat cold tap water against my swollen lids and catch my wonky reflection in the gleaming chrome. Red-eyed miserable prick. Loser.

But even though my eyes itch and my mouth's gone dry, I'm better for it.

'You did the right thing,' Dad says from the doorway and then adds with a wry smile, 'eventually. And a few wrong things, obviously.'

'Messed everything up.'

'It's not your fault.'

'Isn't it? Who else was meant to stop him?'

'You can't think that, you can't ...' Dad steps in and flicks the switch on the kettle. Settles back against the counter.

'Can't what?'

Dad doesn't seem to notice the harshness in my voice. 'We're all responding on the fly to what life throws up. Of course we make mistakes. We don't always know how things are going to pan out.'

'Got every-bloody-thing wrong.'

'You missed chances that you didn't even know were chances at the time. You trusted someone too much. You behaved badly.' He takes two mugs and puts milk in one. 'Feel guilty about it, but be kind to yourself, because you had no way of knowing about Anthony. You weren't there in the room with him. How could you know? You couldn't have stopped him.'

My heart squeezes at the trust on Dad's face. He doesn't know. I was there. Not for Mia, but I was there for Clara. Right in the room and I did nothing.

What if the first time had stuck? What if I never got a second chance or a third or tenth? Clara would be dead. Mia would be alone with her secret and I'd be carrying Clara's. Would I have ever spoken up?

'Should've known,' I say. 'Should've said something.'

'Yes, but ...' Dad shakes his head and pauses between spooning coffee into one mug and reaching for the other. 'I've been there, James. I've thought if only ...'

'Mum?'

Dad's face sticks in position. 'If things had been better between us. I would've never ...'

'Were you breaking up?'

'No. No.' He blinks. The kettle rumbles in its cradle. 'Do you blame me? Is that why you ...?'

'Why I'm a shit son?'

'No. You're a brilliant son – look at me – the best.'

I nod. I appreciate the lie, but the intensity is awkward.

He pushes a mug across the counter towards me. I retrieve his abandoned teaspoon from the edge of the sink and put it in the dishwasher.

'Do you wonder ...? Sometimes I ...' He cups the mug hard between his hands and sips. His glasses fog and clear. When he lowers it he doesn't finish the sentence. Instead he says, 'Yesterday was so much harder than I thought it would be.'

'Yeah.' Dad is truly the master of understatement.

The quiet settles and it's less uncomfortable. It's progress. Even if our silences are longer than our sentences.

'Are you OK?' Dad says.

'Yeah.'

'Yeah?'

I add a couple more crocks to the dishwasher and start it off. It rumbles and churns. The kitchen's tidy again, ready for Dad to make a new mess later. And I think, why not? What am I trying to prove?

'Look, I'm a liar,' I say. 'I'm not OK. I've not been OK in ages.' There's a loose thread at the hem of my T-shirt, a damp patch on the cuff of my jeans, and I can feel Dad's eyes on me. God, I wish I was just OK and didn't have to tell anyone anything ever again. Wish people would see through me into all my messy insides and just tell me what I need to know so I don't have to ask shit like:

'Will I be OK?' When I say it out loud Dad's face softens and it's all so pathetic I could kick myself.

Dad's index finger prods underneath his eyes, slowly rubbing each lid in turn. And I think, here we go again. The soundbites, the platitudes.

'You'll never be the same,' he says, taking his glasses off to polish them with his T-shirt. 'Neither of us will. But you'll be OK and I'll do better.'

I nod. Not the reassuring, empty thing I expected and I appreciate it. But my throat shrinks and I want him to stop now. Enough heart-to-heart.

'She'd be livid to see how we've let the garden go,' he says, watching the window. And I can cope with that.

Dad and I finish our coffees and go back to the car, both our stiff upper lips back in place, just a little bit softer than before. Dad finishes hosing; I get the soapy bucket and hand over fresh water so he can go behind me. Team effort.

'Dreamed I smashed the car. Can you imagine?' I hiccough a dry laugh, then say, 'Don't know what I'm going to do today. Or tomorrow.' Because one day over and over suddenly seems a lot easier than the unknown future stretching out ahead of me and all the ways I could muck it up.

Dad smiles a weird non-smile as he adjusts a wing mirror. He says, 'We can't undo what's already happened, James. Not mistakes. Not bad choices. Not hard times. But we can find ways to live with them. We can find ways to move forward and we ... we can help each other. We'll try.'

He wipes the back of his wrist over his forehead and leaves a smudge of dirt behind. Squints my way. He nods, and I nod, and I feel like I'm watching us from far away, outside my body, looking at this pair of idiots wondering what the hell they're going to do now. Better, I guess.

2

I'm two weeks from the Friday that wouldn't end. Sunday arrived exactly twenty-four hours after Saturday and all days have been delivered punctually since. Impeccable service.

Instead of waking up to Clara morning after morning, I wake up without her. Two weeks now. I'm still carrying her with me like a bruise. Always aware she's out in the world thinking low of me. Always aware I could pick up my phone and type a message. I write and rewrite messages endlessly, but there are no right words, so the wrong ones stay in my drafts.

But a weird thing's happened. I've learned a lot about Mia Turner lately. Amazing how quickly you can get to know a person when they talk and you talk back. Amazing that Mia is interesting and funny. So we've been hanging out.

Sometimes I feel guilty, course I do. Mia's done what people do after trauma, gravitating to whatever bystander was on the scene when it kicked off. She's mistaken me for a witness, not an accomplice.

I'm a scummer, truly, for accepting her company. But here's the thing about Mia: she's great. She's easy to listen to, easy to chat with, a thoughtful sort. She's like Clara in that way even though she's nothing like Clara. And it's so nice, I've been fooling myself Mia needs a friend too, like I'm doing her a favour when really I'm doing myself one.

She's sprawled on my bedroom carpet, surrounded by paper, my laptop in front of her and Dad's big printer hooked up via a tangle of wires. Mia's shoes are off and the pink soles of her feet are folded in the air. She says, 'Even now it feels like it was me. Something I did. My sister said it's normal to feel that way and I think, why would she say that? Because she knows it's my fault?' Mia shakes her hair out and gathers it back up.

'Nah, look. That's bullshit.' I look Mia dead in the eye. The sides of her mouth turn down, but she keeps looking. 'That night could've gone the same no matter what. It wasn't anything you did.'

Mia lays her chin on the carpet. Beside her the printer rumbles on.

'I bet people think I'm attention-seeking.'

'People are disappointing.'

An A3 sheet finally, painfully, spits out onto the carpet and Mia smooths it out and puts it in a pile with the others. I swivel my screen and Mia squints at it. Nods.

It sucks that Mia's truth is still in question. Sucks that Anthony's still kicking about town scot-free. That thing the police did with Anthony? Turns out it's not an arrest. Questions, that's all. Still, he's not come back to school. Suspended. Which means fuck all when we're out for revision soon anyway. He's back for exams, because god forbid he should miss out on his quals. Anthony gets to be innocent till proven guilty, which I guess means Mia's – what? Living the worst of her days over and over to try and bring some kind of justice? It's bullshit. Who'd stand up and put themselves through it if it wasn't true?

I say, 'People love a lie when it's easier than the truth.'

Mia's mouth gets small. The problem is the person lying is Anthony and one of the idiots believing him is Bee. And even though Bee's behaviour must be an act of self-preservation – no-one wants to be the girl who dated the rapist – it doesn't make it easier on her former friend.

Mia says, 'Do you know I got my purple kickboxing belt last week?'

'Want to kick Bee's butt? Or mine, just for laughs?' I suggest. 'Reckon I'd crumple like paper.'

'Definitely. One swift whack in your soft underbelly.' She punches up her fist and shows off the world's smallest bicep bump. 'Lucky for you I'm a pacifist.'

Another piece of paper hits the floor. Mia grabs it and twists it my way. It's a poster. Simple, clean. A cascade of message boxes. One screenshot per sheet. The names are blacked out, profile photos smudged, but I left the initials for those who care to speculate. It's not a difficult puzzle. With the swear words also blacked out to minimise the risk of teacher backlash, the poster's like a game of dark Hangman.

Worm: F**k, snog, kill, ~~Lana~~, ~~Sophie~~, ~~Conni~~: GO

Anthony: F**k ~~Lana~~, snog ~~Conni~~, kill ~~Sophie~~ (then f**k her too)

Worm: lol. Not f then k?

Anthony: less resistance my way

Spence: more humane to just paper bag her, isn't it?

Worm: snog ~~Lana~~, kill ~~Sophie~~, f**k ~~Conni~~ but gag her first

Anthony: with your d**k?

Anthony: whats French for b***h suck harder?

There's different sets of messages on each poster, different rugby boys chipping in at different times, but the theme's the same. At the bottom in big black letters I've captioned each one #ShameOnUs.

It was Worm – sorry, Gary, but always Worm in my head – who gave me the idea. After the longest assembly of our lives – all of us called back into school to listen to Ms Hargrove explaining 'consent' as we squirmed – Worm and I chatted. We barely know how to fill the silence these days. Nothing left to say.

I went in hard. After all, Worm was there with Anthony the first time. But Worm said he never did and I believed him. Clara was the first time. The last time, hopefully. His track record wiped clean. He's the luckiest guy alive and he doesn't even know. He's the only thing in this day I fixed alone, because he knows now. You don't get away with shit like that, not even once, not ever.

And Worm fixed me right back with a few sassy retorts. Because who was I to lecture him? Wasn't I in the group chat with everyone else? Or as Worm put it, who made me the patron saint of vaginas?

He'd a point. After all Mia's courage, where the hell's mine? When was I planning to stick my neck out? And me and all these rugby boys, why do we get to pretend we didn't know who Anthony was? The evidence is right there to scroll. We knew – we all knew – even before Mia said it out loud. He told us who he was and we figured it was a joke.

So we fucking laughed.

Mia sits up and crosses her legs. She holds another poster, twin of the first.

'Are you sure you want to do this?' she asks.

I nod. 'As long as you're happy? Maybe it'll give people something else to talk about for a while.'

'Yeah, I guess. Thanks, Spence.'

As usual, I squirm. I mumble, 'Don't thank me. You're the one who …' I trail off, because she knows what she did.

She smooths the paper. 'There's this catch-22, you know? I said what he did and now people know and he has to live with that, which is what I want. But it means people know about me too. Is that fair?'

I stare at the carpet where one of Mia's long hairs is caught spiralling.

'Do you regret it?' I say. And I wonder if that's my fault too.

Mia flaps a hand. 'They're asking me what I want to happen. For him to be charged, for the case to go to court? I'm not sure I do. It's a lot, Spence. It's such a lot and it drags it out for ever.'

'Yeah. Get that.'

'What do you think I should do?'

'Your decision, I guess. Whatever's right for you and makes you ...' I search for the word. Not 'happy', but the word for coming to terms with something that'll never be OK again, the word for knowing the world cracked under you and it'll never be the kind of place you wish it was. Not safe any more, somewhere pain seems inevitable. Unstoppable. On loop.

If I could, I'd take the decision off Mia in a beat. I'd dive back five years or more, fix it all. I'd do it ten times over till I'm fifty years old on the inside like Benjamin-bloody-Button, time-sick and world weary. But none of Mia's options are that easy.

All I can do is make people see Anthony clearly. And face up to my part.

'I might ... not,' Mia says. 'I don't know. I'm tired of thinking about it.'

'Yeah. Bet I'm helping.' I straighten up and my back clicks. Don't want to throw a James Spencer pity party.

'You have. You and my sister, you're the people I can talk to. You make it ... I don't know ...' Mia scrunches up her nose.

And I know that, really, I'll never understand how this is for her, no matter how I try. And part of that's because Mia tries to be OK around me. I'm not the one she takes her tears and deepest fears to, even if we chat. I get that. She's got real support coming, some charity, some counsellor-type, someone who knows what they're doing.

'Of course, you're also my favourite human sacrifice,' Mia says with a thin smile as she strokes the paper between her fingers.

Right. That's me. Dread catches in my throat. Hard to swallow.

My phone flashes. Mia's sent me the photo. I post it from the account I've created before I've got time to think myself out of it.

@ToxicBoys: Coming soon to St Peter's High. #ShameOnUs #ToxicBoys

Someone's liked it: **@MiaNoFear.**

'They're going to shit,' I say.

'They'll take them down.'

'But they'll see them.'

Mia sighs. 'I'm glad I don't have to go back. Not really, at least, just for exams. And then I'm out of here.'

'If you ever need someone to go in with you. Moral support or whatever ...' I leave it hanging there. Mia nods.

Worm was right. This heaviness I've been heaving round like rocks in my belly, there's a reason it's still stuck there weeks later. It's not some self-pity, regret or the horror of Clara catching me out. Nah, it's guilt. I'm guilty.

Anthony raped Mia. He was there on his own, but was I there in his mind? Was I egging him on? Did he think him and me were the same sort of person? Of course he did, because I never told him different.

Worm didn't understand or didn't want to believe that what we said and did mattered. We all made jokes and chatted shit and only one of us hurt someone. Guess he figured the rest of us are off the hook. But it all mattered. And that's the thought that's been hammering on my skull, the worry that wouldn't lie down.

The posters make it shut up.

When people see what Anthony's said, maybe it'll be less of a leap to believe what he's done. When the rest of the boys see their words splashed all over school and all over people's phones, maybe it'll finally click what we did too.

As for my own share of the backlash I hope is coming? Truth is I'm bricking it. Shit-scared of the attention I can't control and what people will think, what they'll say when they look at these messages and then back at me. It'd be easy to hunker down and wait for people to forget I was ever mates with Anthony Mansbridge without them ever knowing the worst of it, sure. But here's what I figure: you can only make right a wrong you own.

So yeah, what doesn't kill you makes you stronger, I guess. Nietzsche said that, the clever old bastard.

3

The posters sort of take off. Not in some viral way, nothing like that. Imagine it somehow blowing up, encouraging lads up and down the country to start opening up and challenging behaviour – nah, that doesn't happen. I'm not the guy it happens to. And in my selfish places I'm relieved too. I don't need the whole world knowing my mistakes.

But people see them. Students, teachers. It's a start. More people have stories about Anthony. Not as bad as Mia's, but bad. Stuff I didn't know about and stuff that rang a bell. I'm ashamed every time remembering what a dick I've been, what I've overlooked, what I've laughed at, the damage I've done. But it's good not to forget. Good it stays sharp.

The only lad who comes out well is Jay. When Mia and I went back over the group chat, Jay stuck out as the good guy. A lone voice pointing out lines had been crossed. That was a punch in the nuts, imagining how it might have been if anyone else had stuck up for Jay then. But even if Jay's a nice guy, I don't have to like him. He got his happy ending anyway: him and Genni are inseparable these days.

I've been thinking of that Friday more than's good for me. In the end, dunno if I found Barnes's key or lucked out. I'm not happy with the choices I made, but maybe they were the best I could do with the day I was given. I'm living with them anyway.

The other thing to live with is never knowing. That Friday: was it Clara all along, or Anthony, or Mia? Was it Mum? Maybe I'm wrong about death and souls and God and everything. Maybe Mum was looking down from wherever she ended up, keeping an eye and realising how desperately I'd mucked it all up. Maybe that Friday was her hand on my shoulder. That's what I'd like to believe. But I saw her pieces fly and crash and dissolve and I reckon she's gone. I wouldn't set it in stone, though.

Maybe my whole ordeal was a random burp in the universe. The further away it gets, the less real it seems. My memories crack and blister and smooth skin grows over, erasing the bits that don't make sense. Reckon I'll forget altogether in another few months. Chalk any residual trauma up to cheese and a scary movie I once watched. Days don't repeat, Spence, you fool.

There's been goodbyes. Anthony, Clara, Bee, Worm. Some I saw coming and others whipped the rug from under me.

They hurt. Even the ones that go slow, like bloody Worm, that strange, enigmatic little prick. Bet I'll wake up six months gone with a twinge of regret that we fell out of touch. I'll think about messaging him to find out where he ended up or to tell him that thing about dying stars is a bit of a myth.

As I pull into the school car park on another Friday morning, my eyes are drawn to a dim corner. A tatty red Micra lurks under the trees, bound to be bathed in tree bits and bird shit by the day's end.

I'm out of my door and coming round the back just as, over the way, Lana jumps out of this tiny lilac car.

'You passed your test?' I say. 'Nice one. Scraping through before uni.'

She slams her door and shoots me daggers. Stalks off without a word. So yeah, OK. Some people have feelings about those posters. Fair.

Clara probably does too, though I've heard nothing from her. I get it. Clara and me, we were never meant to be. Not when I needed a week's worth of Fridays just to talk to her without messing up.

I walk in the direction of her Micra anyway, because I'm desperate to – what? Stroke her bumper's undulating red craters? Decipher secret messages in her plates? Lucky for me, I catch sight of her before I've decided what kind of weirdo I want to be. She's half in the back seat, one leg behind on the tarmac.

'Oi, did you hit this car?' I say, squinting at the black Clio beside hers, studying the immaculate surface, fingers to my chin. Clara squirms out.

'I never actually hit yours.' Her arms fold over her chest. 'Felt it move.'

'Did you now?' she says primly. I nod. 'You know, if I was you I could probably find some awful joke to go with that set-up.'

'Earth moving? God, I'm funny,' I say. 'If you were me, you wouldn't have smacked my car, mind. 'Cos I can park.'

'Well, if I was you, I'd have made the joke in about ten minutes so I had time to think of it ...' As she trails off her lips pull up on one side, dimple appearing next to her blue freckle. She ducks in the car again, emerging with a box tucked under one arm, the sides of it groaning against art supplies.

I wish I could have kept Clara. Not like that, not really. She'll be moving out of town soon enough for art school and I'll be elsewhere. But we could've stayed mates. Talked once in a while. Gone to that gig with Hannah. I wish I'd got to play my guitar and listen to Clara accompany me with words pulled from her imagination and sung with absolute conviction.

'You know,' Clara says, 'the car was like this when I bought it. Super cheap.'

'Looks like it's seen some shit.'

'Haven't we all? It runs OK, though.'

'It's fine anyway, Hart, don't mind that you can't park.'

'That's very gracious.' Clara's brow dents as, in an attempt at chivalry, I take hold of the cardboard box she's wrestling. 'I didn't ask for your help, thank you very much.' With a final tug she pulls the box free and brings one knee up to take the weight, while she repositions its heft. She stares over the top, paintbrushes tickling her chin.

'Sure I can park, but I've got some flaws,' I say, to even the score.

'Oh, really?'

'Yeah, like, dunno. Poor judge of character? Lack of backbone? General arsehole? There's a lot to choose from.'

'Aren't we a martyr?' She takes a step away and turns back. 'I suppose a tiny amount of spine was required to share those screenshots.'

'You heard.' It's not a question, but she nods anyway. 'Dunno how people knew.'

'Mia told me. Some kind of effort to rehabilitate your image? She's nice like that. And forgiving, apparently.' Clara shrugs and I'm dead chuffed she's on Mia's side. 'It doesn't make you any kind of hero, you realise? I think you're probably back to acceptable-human-being status.'

I'll bloody take it.

'Jay came out of it OK,' I say.

Clara snorts. 'I think there's a real risk that no girls here are ever going to believe that any guys are OK again. The shit we put up with, god, you have no idea.'

I press my lips together hard. There's something I want to say, but I'm unsure of how to make her believe I mean this bit: 'It wasn't brave, you know? Mia's the brave one, even if she'd skin me for saying so. And the posters, the account, those messages: it'd be better if none of it existed.' I keep my voice matter-of-fact. 'And I'm so bloody sorry.'

Clara looks me over. For a moment, she might be about to call me out again for self-pity or trying too hard or any other way my behaviour could be interpreted. And I hate the idea of it, but I'll leave it here, all of it.

Clara nods and shifts the box and walks away. I watch her go and I fight the urge to call after her or catch up. This, after all, is the very end for us.

Clara stops a few metres away and twists around, awkward because of the bulk she's carrying. My heart leaps. She says, 'Are you just going to stand there? Don't you have an exam or something?'

I catch up, fall into step beside her, say, 'Are you still talking to me?' And realise a moment too late that it's all wrong. It's usually her getting all insecure. I'm on her lines today.

Her ankle turns and she stumbles, I catch her and she clings to her box of supplies.

She says, 'You seem like you could use a chat? After the exam, maybe?'

We pause. She looks at me, sees me and all my flaws and fuck-ups and some of the worst mistakes I've made. And the temptation's there, at the back of my throat, a thick glob of pride making me want to tell her I'm OK, I'm fine, never been better, right?

But I swallow all my comebacks and let my voice crack as I say, 'Yeah, actually. Yeah, go on.'

ACKNOWLEDGEMENTS

Many thanks first of all to my brilliant agent, Becky Bagnell, who made everything possible. I am so grateful for your incisive edits, your dedication to getting this book into the right hands and all the support in between and ever since.

Thank you to Siobhán Parkinson, Matthew Parkinson-Bennett, Elizabeth Goldrick and the whole team at Little Island for the care, attention and expertise you've lavished on this book. It's truly been a dream come true working with you all.

For lending valuable additional insight, many thanks also to Christine Sandquist and Frances Shearer.

For the bright and bold cover design, thanks to Holly Pereira.

I knew this would be a tough book to write before I put down a single word. I might never have started but for the encouragement of Lisa O'Donnell at Curtis Brown Creative. I certainly never would have got anywhere without the inspiring advice of Debi Alper, Jenny Bromham, Carolyn Ward and Emma Finlayson-Palmer.

I'm grateful for the competitions that provided vital encouragement along the way. Thanks to all the readers and judges of the 2020 WriteMentor Children's Novel Award, Wells Literary Festival and Times/Chicken House. That you saw something in those early drafts gave me such a boost. Thanks to Stuart White for creating such a kind and encouraging community with WriteMentor.

Thanks Kylie Jones, Davina Patel, Lorenzo Favata, Lauren Horncastle, Ella Gardiner and Noelle Strader for telling me to keep going, and Rebecca Shaw for taking this novel more seriously than my rock paintings.

The best part of writing has always been the community. I'm so lucky to have met so many brilliant writers, including the CBC class of 2018, the YA mentees of 2020, my fellow 2022 débuts and my SCBWI gang. I started to list you all by name, but the list was very long and the terror of missing out a single person was very real. I appreciate every one of you.

For swooping in at the last moment with some extra Nietzsche reading, many thanks to Jamie Buckland.

There are four women who have held me together over the last few years: Melanie Garrett, Becci Fearnley, Daisy Jervis and Georgia Gant – I truly don't think I would have made it without you all. Thank you for the wisdom, laughter, sympathy and stories.

Thanks to all my wonderful family and friends, who never stopped checking in on me and the progress of this book. Your support has meant the world. Particularly huge hugs to Faith Williamson for insisting I write the first draft in time for Christmas.

Mum, thank you for imbuing me with a lifelong love of reading and writing.

Last, but never least, Dan. Thank you for believing in me from the very first word.

We hope you have enjoyed reading *The Eternal Return of Clara Hart*. On the following pages you will find out about some other Little Island books you might like to read.

THINGS I KNOW
By Helena Close

Things I know. I'm a bad person.
I miss Finn. I could easily be a murderer.

Saoirse can't wait to leave school – but just before the Leaving Cert her ex-boyfriend dies by suicide. Everyone blames Saoirse, and her rumbling anxieties spiral out of control.

Saoirse feels herself flailing in swirling waters that threaten to suck her into the depths. No-one can save her – not her lovely nan; not the gorgeous boy who tries hard to love her; not her fabulous best friend; and certainly not her cheap-wisdom counsellor.

Can Saoirse, against all odds, rescue the self she used to know?

'Read it – and buy a second copy to thrust into the hands of the next platitude-utterer you encounter.'
The Irish Times

'An accurate portrayal of a young person's challenges, this book is also full of hope, love and laughter.'
The Sunday Independent

THE GONE BOOK
By Helena Close

Winner: White Raven Award 2021

Shortlisted: Dept 51 @ Eason Teen and Young Adult Book of the Year, Irish Book Awards 2020

Nominated: The 2021 Carnegie Medal

I know you'll hate me. But I can't help it.
I'm going to find you.

Matt's mam left home when he was 10. He writes letters to her but doesn't send them. He keeps them in his Gone Book, which he hides in his room. Five years of letters about his life. Five years of hurt.

Matt's dad won't talk about her. His older brother is mixed up with drugs. His friends, Mikey and Anna, are the best thing in his life, but Matt keeps pushing them away.

All Matt wants to do is skate, surf, and forget. But now his mam is back in town and Matt knows he needs to find her, to finally deliver the truth.

> *'This is as real as writing gets. Every line rings perfectly true.'*
> Donal Ryan

> *'A skillful and truthful novel from a wonderful storyteller.'*
> Joseph O'Connor

> *'Achingly sad but hugely funny. A gritty story full of heart.'*
> Sheena Wilkinson

NEEDLEWORK
By Deirdre Sullivan

Winner: Honour Award for Fiction,
Children's Books Ireland Awards 2017

Ces longs to be a tattoo artist and embroider skin with beautiful images. But for now she's just trying to reach adulthood without falling apart.

Powerful, poetic and disturbing, *Needlework* is a girl's meditation on her efforts to maintain her bodily and spiritual integrity in the face of abuse, violation and neglect.

'Reading Needlework is similar to getting your first tattoo – it's searing, often painful, but it is an experience you'll never forget.'
Louise O'Neill

'Needlework is a powerful novel that deserves to be read.'
Sarah Crossan

'A novel that is just as sharp and precise as its title suggests.'
Doireann Ní Ghríofa

ABOUT LOUISE FINCH

Louise grew up in a small town in the Midlands. After studying History of Art she worked for over a decade in the charity sector across women's and LGBT+ rights, and youth arts.

She now lives in the South East of England with her photographer husband, their two small dogs and too many house plants, surrounded by books, craft supplies and vintage furniture.

The Eternal Return of Clara Hart is Louise's first novel.

ABOUT LITTLE ISLAND

Little Island is an independent Irish publisher that looks for the best writing for young readers, in Ireland and internationally. Founded in 2010 by Ireland's inaugural Laureate na nÓg (Children's Laureate), Little Island has published over 100 books, many of which have won awards and been published in translation around the world.

RECENT AWARDS FOR LITTLE ISLAND BOOKS

Book of the Year, KPMG Children's Books Ireland Awards 2021
Savage Her Reply by Deirdre Sullivan

YA Book of the Year, Literacy Association of Ireland Awards 2021
Savage Her Reply by Deirdre Sullivan

YA Book of the Year, An Post Irish Book Awards 2020
Savage Her Reply by Deirdre Sullivan

White Raven Award 2021
The Gone Book by Helena Close

Judges' Special Prize, KPMG Children's Books Ireland Awards 2020
The Deepest Breath by Meg Grehan

Shortlisted: The Waterstones Children's Book Prize 2020
The Deepest Breath by Meg Grehan

IBBY Honours List 2020
Mucking About by John Chambers